ILLUSIONS

WANDA B. CAMPBELL

www.urbanchristianonline.net

Urban Books
1199 Straight Path
West Babylon, NY 11704

ISBN- 13: 978-1-60162-943-2
ISBN- 10: 1-60162-943-5

First Printing February 2009
Printed in the United States of America

10 9 8 7 6 5 4 3 2 1

Distributed by Kensington Corp.
Submit Wholesale Orders to:
Kensington Publishing Corp.
C/O Penguin Group (USA) Inc.
Attention: Order Processing
405 Murray Hill Parkway
East Rutherford, NJ 07073-2316
Phone: 1-800-526-0275
Fax: 1-800-227-9604

Dedication

To all my brothers and sisters of the Kingdom who have struggled with this addiction and have overcome; to those currently struggling and searching for help, and especially to the individuals who love and care for the addicted, this work of ministry is dedicated to you.

Acknowledgments

First and foremost I thank my **Heavenly Father** and His son **Jesus Christ** for empowering me to minister to His people. On my best day, I count myself unworthy of the grace and mercy He extends to me. Thank you, Father, for loving me when I didn't love myself!

To my husband, best friend and life partner, **Craig**: Our nineteen-year journey hasn't always been easy, but every twist, turn, crash, turbulence, and storm we experienced together would have been meaningless without you. Thank you for your unwavering support and trust. I love you way too much.

To my overprotective sons, **Jonathan** and **Craig, Jr:** Thank you for your support and for lugging boxes everywhere. One day you'll thank me for that six-pack.

My daughter, **Chantel**: Thanks for the long days and sore back from typing.

To my younger siblings: **Chris,** thanks for the talks and support. **Jessica,** thanks for reading and being a true drill sergeant. **JaNea,** words cannot express my appreciation for all your help. You will always be my first baby.

To my little big brother **Darryl:** You have only been in my life two years, but it feels like longer. Your presence is a blessing. Thanks for the encouraging words and inspiration. I love you and hope to see you soon.

Now to my family. My definition of family is not limited to human blood lines, but extends to those who have loved and nurtured me through the lowest valleys. **Deborah, Sabria**, and **Brandon**: Thanks for the love and for catching that major error. **Nicole, Libby, Amy, Mary, Latisha,**

Alaina, and **Mommy Harris**: Thanks for your prayers and the words of encouragement.

My pastor, **Servant Brian K. Woodson, Sr.**: Thank you for chastising me with the gentle, yet strong love of a father. I have learned so much about myself from you. God knew exactly what He was doing when he joined us together.

To my church family, **Bay Area Christian Connection**: Thanks for teaching me about community.

To the honorable **Dr. J. Alfred Smith, Rev. Brenda Guess, Minister Adumasa Adeyemi**, and all the wonderful instructors and students at the **Leadership Institute at Allen Temple**: You've made a mark on my life that will never be erased. Your knowledge and wisdom have drawn me closer to our Father and I am a better Christian because of you.

To **Bishop Anthony L. Willis, Lady Yvonne Willis** and the **Lily of the Valley Christian Center**: I shall never forget the foundation and the training.

To all my co-workers at Alameda County Medical Center and my free PR team: **Pat, Linda C., May**, and **Donna.** Thanks so much for "blowing me up".

To **Kendra Norman-Bellamy**: I owe you so much. I can't find the words to express my gratitude for everything you have taught me. Thank you for being obedient to the vision God has given you. No matter how far this journey takes me, you will always be my American Idol.

To **Terrance**: I shall never forget the day we met. I was too shy to speak, but you told me you wanted to see my name in print. Little did I know you would become not only my publicist, but also my friend. Thank you for your support and for allowing me to vent.

To **The Writer's Hut** and **BWChristianLit** members: Thanks so much for the knowledge and support.

To fellow authors, **Linda R. Herman, Lacricia A. Peters,**

Maurice M. Gray Jr., and Linda Beed: Your friendship means more than you know.

To **Joylynn** and the **Urban Christian Family**: I am humbled to be received into the family of such talented and anointed authors. It's my desire to uphold the standard that has been set.

To **Tavares** and **The Culture Clique Book Club**: Thanks for taking in a novice and teaching me the ropes.

To **Sisters in Harmony/Sisters in Conversation** and the **TLB Book Clubs**: Thanks for supporting the new kid on the block.

To **Israel & New Breed**: Thanks for taking me to a deeper level. May God continue to bless you in your ministry.

To **B.J.**: You have been gone for twenty years, but I have not forgotten your friendship.

To **everyone who reads this book**: Thanks for supporting me and know that every word was written with you in mind. Be blessed!

ILLUSIONS

Prologue

Bryce, having been married for a little over three years, stared appreciatively at the bare woman before him. By all accounts, she was everything he physically desired in a woman; ample and curvaceous from top to bottom. Her honey colored legs seemed to go on forever. He could look at her perpetually and never get tired of the view she provided. Bryce had an arsenal of beautiful women at his disposal, but she was his favorite. He could drink the sweetness of her lips through eternity and still thirst for more.

Bryce often wondered how he ended up with such a beautiful and voluptuous woman, considering he was just an average looking man, and relatively short at that. Bryce stood at a height of only five-feet-nine-inches. He didn't house the physique of a body builder, but he did wear his 200 pounds well. Thanks to his love for Ben & Jerry's Cherry Garcia, Bryce didn't have a six-pack, but a slightly budding pot belly. None of that mattered to the woman before him, though. To her, he was perfect. He was strong and secure. He was her king. Bryce was, by far, the best lover she'd ever had, and each time that they came together was always better than the time before.

Bryce blocked everything from his mind except her. He moaned deeply as his mind focused on the soft kisses she planted all over him and as her hands massaged him in places only known to her. He leaned back, allowing her full access to all parts of him. Bryce was hers and she could do whatever she wanted to do with the semi-sweet chocolate brother and she knew it.

Bryce was so engrossed in his woman, he lost track of time. The knock on his office door brought him back to reality.

"Are you ready, sir?" the voice on the other side of the door asked.

"I'll be right out," Bryce responded after steadying his breath.

He quickly closed the magazine and discreetly tucked it away in its hiding place between the wall and the tank of the toilet. After fastening his pants and belt, he washed his hands without looking in the mirror. He could never look himself in the face after an encounter with the woman he'd nicknamed, Daija.

Back at his desk, Bryce hurriedly put on his suit jacket and tucked his Bible and notebook under his arm then headed for the sanctuary. It was time for Pastor Bryce Hightower to preach the Word of God.

Chapter 1

Out of habit, Pastor Hightower greeted the elders and ministers seated on the platform with his customary handshake and brotherly hug. He continued the ritual by kneeling before his reserved leather chair and praying. The elders and ministers extended opened hands in Pastor Hightower's direction, symbolic of touching and agreeing for the Lord to anoint their pastor to preach a powerful Sunday sermon. Pastor Hightower was too busy repenting for the defiled behavior he'd just participated in to be concerned about his sermon.

Being certain his cries for forgiveness reached heaven, Pastor Hightower rose to his full height, raised his hands with closed eyes and joined the congregation singing *Total Praise* along with the Praise & Worship ministry. Once seated, Pastor Hightower's gaze drifted to the end seat on the front row. The overgrown smile that covered his face gave the appearance of being manufactured, but was genuine. That's just the way Pastor Hightower smiled. Every facial muscle appeared strained whenever he displayed his perfectly straight white teeth. Pastor Hightower added a wave with the smile he afforded his wife. When Denise smiled back, the pastor mouthed the words, "I love you," causing Denise to blush and cover her face. Satisfied that he still carried the ability to make his wife excited, Pastor Hightower directed his attention to his sermon. He grunted at the scripture text, then quickly closed his black leather organizer.

How can I stand before these people and talk about Samson's lust and weakness with Delilah? Bryce's heart asked the question, but his distorted mind blocked an honest answer from coming forth.

Pastor Hightower squeezed his eyes closed in an attempt to shut out his conscience like he always did before mounting the podium and preaching another message he was incapable of living. Today, his evasion tactic worked too well. In no time, Pastor Hightower's reality merged with fantasy, and in place of Samson, it was Pastor Hightower with the beautiful Delilah in the Valley of Sorek. It was his head lying in Delilah's lap, enjoying the feel of her soft expert fingers as they explored, sending a soft moan from his lips.

"Honey, are you all right?"

Pastor Hightower's head jerked forward at the sound of his wife's voice. His imagination had drawn him so deep into the illusion that he hadn't heard Minister Jackson call him to the podium. He hadn't noticed the entire congregation standing, waiting to hear the words the Lord had given him. When he didn't respond after the third call, Denise rushed to his side and was now shaking him.

"Are you all right?" Denise questioned again.

Bryce mentally and frantically searched for an answer. He couldn't tell his wife that the images he'd just experienced left him feeling better than all right. He also couldn't lie in the sanctuary.

"Just meditating," Pastor Hightower finally answered, then moved his head from side to side to demonstrate how "deep" he was.

Denise's doubts dissipated once her husband rose to his feet and began speaking in tongues then started dancing the length of the platform.

Once he settled down, Pastor Hightower said, "Let's pray," and opened his Bible to the story of Daniel and the three Hebrew boys.

"Son, you know you preached today!" Lucinda stepped into Pastor Hightower's office without knocking or being invited.

Bryce didn't address the mother's forwardness. Lucinda had been doing that since the day her daughter married Pastor Hightower. In Lucinda's eyes, being the pastor's mother-in-law had its privileges, and having free reign of the church offices was one.

"Thank you, Mother. I could feel you out there interceding for me."

"That's why you made me president over the Intercessory Prayer Ministry. You know I can get a prayer through. I can dismantle any attack of the devil once I start praying in the Spirit."

Bryce studied his mother-in-law's round face, searching her eyes for any indication that she was aware of how the devil not only attacked him, but triumphed over his will.

"Keep praying for me, Mother." Bryce placed his Bible into his briefcase the same time Denise knocked and waited for permission to enter.

"Hello, First Lady." Bryce leaned in to kiss Denise, but she didn't reciprocate.

In the midst of the congregation was one thing, but behind closed doors, perpetrating wasn't necessary. Before Bryce's flirtation from the pulpit, he hadn't spoken three words to her in as many days.

"Hello, Bryce," Denise responded emotionless, almost cold.

"How dare you speak to your husband like that?" Lucinda scolded. "He's a man of God. He deserves respect."

"So do I, Mother!" Denise shot back. She glared at her husband. "And not just from the pulpit." Denise continued holding his gaze.

Holding on to her anger was useless. Bryce knew with every squeeze, Denise's anger was evaporating. By the time his lips reached her neck, she couldn't remember why she was mad in the first place.

"Stop." She playfully hit him then returned his kiss.

"You know you like that."

Her mother cleared her throat. "It's time for y'all to go home." Before exiting, Lucinda addressed her daughter. "Let this be the last time I see or hear you disrespect my pastor. I don't care if he is your husband."

"If I didn't know any better, I'd think she endured twenty-six hours of labor with you and not me." Denise smirked.

Bryce didn't respond to the statement, but asked Denise what she'd cooked for dinner.

"Me," she answered flirtatiously and waited for his usual hungry response.

Bryce did respond, but neither fire nor desire radiated from him. His actions more closely resembled that of a convicted man being led off to prison, than that of a man needing to be alone with his wife. Bryce's shoulders slumped and he inhaled deeply. With his third labored breath, he still hadn't conjured up a tactful way to tell Denise he wasn't interested in sex, at least, not today, and not with her.

Bryce held the office door open for his wife. "Let's get something to eat first and then see what happens."

Nothing happened. After dinner Bryce hibernated in his study until bedtime.

Denise studied her husband's stiff torso and wondered what had happened to her once stress-free life. When she married Pastor Bryce Hightower three years ago, everything was perfect. She was both honored and delighted to be the wife of an anointed man of God. In the pulpit, Bryce preached powerful life-changing messages. It was one of those "hot" messages that burned Denise's soul and steered her down the aisle to her heavenly Father that hot Sunday afternoon in August. Having grown up in the church, the daughter of a deacon, Denise was familiar with God, but had resisted making Him her personal Savior. That is, until she heard Pastor Hightower's preaching. Bryce's teaching gift afforded him the ability to philosophically preach the Word of God on a scholarly level, but what mesmerized Denise was listening to him break down the same Word to the understanding of a two-year-old.

That second Sunday in August was Denise's first time in six years attending services at the church in which she'd grown up. She'd left the Bay Area to attend college. After graduating from Fresno State, Denise decided to give California's central valley a chance at residency. Unfortunately for Denise, the valley's thermostat reached an all-time high at the same time California was forced to rely on rolling blackouts as a way to conserve energy. When Denise's air conditioner broke down, she packed her belongings into her Honda and headed for cooler climate.

After confessing before God and the congregation of Word of Life that Jesus was the Son of God, died and resurrected to save her from sin, Denise rejoined the church to the delight of her mother and the newly appointed pastor. Denise didn't have to wait long before discovering Pastor Hightower was interested in more than the well-being of her soul. Along with the standard new member's welcome letter that she received, Pastor Hightower included a handwritten note with a dinner invitation. A brief consultation with her mother was all the confirmation Denise needed to accept. The lavish wedding eight months later was still a conversation piece after three years.

At home, Bryce couldn't keep his hands off Denise. As a

twenty-six-year-old virgin bride, that made her feel special, because she was apprehensive of her ability to meet her husband's needs. Bryce had more experience and his choice of available women in his church, but he loved every inch of her voluptuous size sixteen. In the beginning, Denise thought his sexual appetite was a bit excessive, but what did she have for comparison? He certainly gave her unlimited pleasure. The least she could do was to return the favor and give her husband all the loving he wanted, which is what she did. The problem was, lately, Bryce didn't want any loving from her.

Admiring his sleeping body, Denise couldn't figure out what had changed. As if someone had blown out a candle, the fire in their bedroom was instantly gone. Bryce barely touched her anymore, and when he did, it wasn't the same. Denise didn't feel that her husband cherished making love to her anymore, but felt more like he was simply obliging her. Bryce used to be slow and caring with her, making sure she was completely satisfied. Now, he seemed so engrossed in his own world, Bryce hadn't even noticed Denise counting sheep during their last encounter.

Denise turned over on her side and gave her body a thorough examination. She was the same size she was the day she married Bryce. She kept her hands manicured and her feet always looked like they'd been freshly dipped in hot wax. Denise had a standing appointment with Kadijah at the Hair Haven salon every week, insuring she was always presentable. She also made sure she dressed in clothes that accented her fuller figure and kept her makeup flawless. So why had Bryce lost interest?

Denise's job as Budget Director at the local medical conglomerate didn't prevent her from cleaning the house and cooking balanced meals every night. In the bedroom, she used powders and potpourri to scent their bed and candles to freshen the air on a regular basis. Denise never wore flannel pajamas or hair rollers to bed, instead, opting for sexy lingerie and sometimes nothing at all, depending on Bryce's mood. That's what she'd done tonight. She climbed into bed wearing nothing but a smile, hoping to get Bryce's attention. It worked. She held his attention the entire five seconds it took for him to say goodnight, and then turn his back to her.

At church and public appearances, things were the same as they always had been. Not a Sunday went by that Pastor Hightower didn't acknowledge his beautiful and devoted wife. "She's the beat of my heart," is what he'd say, or "the wind in my sail." Denise was trained by the older mothers in the church so the young wife knew all the "insert smile here," moments. Denise could put on the manufactured smile and nod in agreement faster than she could write her name. Every time Bryce preached, the devoted supporter provided him with his personal "amen corner." Tonight though, Denise was tired of the façade. If she couldn't sleep, then neither would the perpetrating Pastor Bryce Hightower.

"Bryce, wake up." She shook him until he groaned. "We need to talk."

"Can't it wait until tomorrow?" he grumbled.

"No, it can't," Denise determined. "I've held this in long enough."

Bryce sighed heavily, more out of irritation than fatigue. He turned over and sleepily looked at his wife. "What is it?"

His tone and demeanor told her this late night pillow talk would be fruitless. She pressed on anyway. "Honey, what's happening to us?"

"You're pushing for a conversation that I don't want to have. Aside from that, we're fine."

Denise's heart sank because she knew Bryce really didn't see anything wrong with their life. And why should he? He got every thing, including all the support and love from her that he needed.

"Bryce, we're not fine. You haven't touched me in over a month." Denise pulled the sheet tightly around her. She hadn't felt the need to conceal her body since their wedding night.

"Is that what this is about?" Bryce propped his body, using his elbow as support. "You woke me up because you want sex?"

Denise fought back the urge to cry. The expression on the face of her beloved husband was distorted and filled with disdain. "It's not just the lack of sex, Bryce. You hardly ever touch me at all anymore, and when we do have sex, it's quick and routine. The only conversations we have are casual. You don't even comment on how I look anymore." Denise was able to say all that without losing her voice, but a tear had managed to escape and burned a trail down her cheek. Bryce noticed the tear and softened a little.

"Baby, come here." He pulled her close to him and held her. She felt good to him and Bryce had to admit he missed her warm body against his. "I'm sorry."

Denise tried to accept the comfort he offered her, but couldn't just yet. It didn't feel genuine. She held her head so she could gaze directly in his eyes. "Bryce, are you having an affair?"

The direct question seemed to have caught him off guard, causing Bryce to hesitate before answering. "No, I'm not having an affair. I've just been preoccupied with other things. Being a young pastor is a hard job."

"Why can't you share what's on your mind with me? I'm your wife; I'm designed to help you."

"I know." Bryce kissed her forehead. "But some things I have to handle on my own."

Denise placed her head against his chest. She didn't say anything, just lay there listening to his heartbeat, wondering when it became out of sync with hers.

Bryce didn't say anything either. He was fighting a war

with his conscience and his spirit. He hadn't actually lied to Denise . . . or had he? He didn't view his time with Daija as an affair. How could he have an affair with his imagination? True, the things he did with her, he should have been doing with his wife. The time he spent with his imaginary friend, could have been spent with his real-life wife. But when he finished with Daija, he was fulfilled and too tired to be with Denise. Bryce enjoyed being with Denise, but couldn't let go of his fantasy. With Daija, Bryce was uninhibited and free, never having to worry about his desires being considered improper or berated. Yes; that's what it was. Daija allowed him to be free. What was so wrong with that? Everyone is entitled to a little fantasy. As long as he's not having sex with anyone else, what was the harm?

If it's right, why can't you tell her?

As always, Bryce heard the still small voice loud and clear, but instead of responding, he closed his eyes in an attempt to prevent the truth from spilling from his lips. He wasn't ready to face the truth. He didn't really know what the truth was anymore. He believed he could stop his extracurricular activity any time he wanted. Bryce just didn't want to, but for Denise's sake, he was going to try.

"I promise I'll work on giving you more attention." Then after a prolonged silence Bryce added, "I love you."

Denise didn't respond. The words, meant to be enduring, sounded void and hollow, but they were better than nothing. Bryce tightened his hold on her and she relaxed in his arms and fell asleep.

Bryce mounted the podium and quickly scanned the audience. Something was not right. He closed his eyes tightly then reopened them just to make sure he was seeing correctly. He was. "Oh, God," he gasped, surveying the congregation. He stepped toward the edge of the platform, hoping to see Denise, but she wasn't there. His eyes frantically searched for his mother-in-law. She wasn't there either. The elders and deacons weren't there to offer him the much needed prayer and support. Bryce slowly walked back to the podium, bowed his head and wept.

"Bryce."

At the sound of her voice, Bryce's cries stopped and he jerked around to find Daija occupying his leather chair, beckoning him with her index finger.

"No!" Bryce screamed, but the congregation, filled with the faces of the many women with whom he'd found pleasure, cheered him on.

"Daija, you can't be here! Not in the church!" Bryce's attempt to sound authoritative amused Daija and the rest of the congregation.

Daija stood on Bryce's chair, and after throwing her long black hair over her shoulder, gestured toward the congregation. "Why not, Bryce; you brought us here." Daija smiled and struck one of Bryce's favorite poses.

"Pastor Hightower, why don't you save us?" someone in the audience mocked.

Bryce fell to his knees and sobbed uncontrollably. "God, help me!"

Bryce bolted from his bed, dripping with perspiration and shaking. The dream, like the one two nights ago, frightened Bryce with the implications, however true they were. Bryce was polluting the house of God and his addiction rendered him defenseless to stop the infection from spreading. This morning, Pastor Hightower had a reality check as images captivated his mind and lured him into lust as he sat in the pulpit, the holy place, waiting to present the Word of God. Never before had he been overtaken in the House of God. His prayers were rendered useless. In the past, he'd do his business, ask God to forgive him, then mechanically fulfill his pastoral duties. That didn't happen today, and now, his demons haunted his dreams.

After stumbling into the master bath and splashing water on his face, Bryce studied his mirrored reflection. Except for the extra inch around the middle and short haircut, Bryce looked the same as he did seventeen years ago, at age seventeen, when he was forced to face life alone following the unexpected and tragic death of his parents. It was while sorting through his father's belongings that pornography was officially introduced to him.

He'd known about the "business" his father kept in the bottom nightstand drawer most of his teenage life, but assumed the magazines were nothing more than women in string bikinis. He soon found out differently and discovered porn was "therapeutic" in helping him deal with the loss of his parents. In some distorted way, when Bryce carried out his secret acts, he felt close to his father.

It didn't start out as a daily ritual; maybe once a month to help relax him on days he felt overwhelmed. When that wasn't enough, he added masturbation. Eventually, the old magazines weren't enough to satisfy Bryce; he began purchasing his own collection.

At age twenty-one, he gave his virginity to a woman without knowing her real name. For the right price, she was willing to do the things he requested without complaining.

After joining the church at age twenty-five, Bryce felt convicted about his habit. He began to feel dirty after every encounter. For a while, he stopped the acts of self-gratification and magazine collecting, but one session with his pastor changed his mind. Following Bryce's confession, the late Reverend Daniels brushed off the habit as if it were no more than a piece of lint.

"Son, ain't nothing wrong with looking at a beautiful woman," Reverend Daniels had said, "just as long as you don't touch. When you get a wife to enjoy, the need for those pictures will go away." Reverend Daniels gave him a look whose meaning could only be interpreted between men.

Bryce soon learned that the church that he attended had its own version of the "good ole boys' club." It was a common thing for preachers and elders, not only to lust with the eyes, but to also sleep with the sisters in the church. The indiscretions were usually swept under the rug unless the sister in question became pregnant or if her husband discovered the affair. Then the woman would be shunned from the church, but not without being labeled a "loose Jezebel" or a home wrecker. The preacher, however, would continue preaching, and in some cases, be elevated to a higher office in the church.

Bryce didn't buy into the double standard and the tolerated behavior set forth by his spiritual fathers. Eventually, Bryce lost respect and moved his membership after enrolling in Seminary. There, Bryce was too busy focusing on the Word of God and praying constantly for his imagination to run wild. The more he prayed and read the Bible, the less of a desire he had to fulfill the lust of his flesh. The day Bryce graduated Seminary, he vowed to parallel his life with the standards set forth in the Bible. Bryce was determined to be a true man of God. "If I can't live this Gospel, I won't preach this Gospel," was his slogan. He recited those eleven words faithfully before every sermon. The more he preached, the purer the pictures in his mind. The more he fasted, the less he fantasized, until eventually, the imagery stopped. That's when he met Denise.

From the day he saw her standing before him at the altar, giving her life to God, Bryce loved her. Actually, he'd noticed her before mounting the podium. She carried her curves well with her five-foot seven-inch height. Bryce loved the fullness of her body, but even more so, the sweetness of her spirit. He still loved her, but he'd allowed himself to become comfortable in his walk with God. Now, he was paying the price in his bedroom, in the pulpit, and in his dreams.

"Are you sick?" Bryce was too engrossed in his thoughts to notice Denise standing in the doorway.

He turned and stared at his wife hard and long as she leaned against the door frame. She'd put on a robe and her hair hung wildly at the nape of her neck. Her face, void of make-up, allowed Bryce to see the genuine love she held for him. A love that said, "Whatever it is, I'm here for you."

When he didn't answer, Denise asked the question again. Bryce slowly made the three steps that placed them an inch apart. He wanted to tell her that he was, in fact, very sick. That he had broken fellowship with God and that the line between reality and fantasy was so blurred, he couldn't tell the difference anymore. He wanted to tell her the reason for his inattentiveness, and reassure her of his love for her. Bryce didn't say any of what made his heart ache to have released. He simply kissed her forehead and went back to bed.

Chapter 2

Rolling her eyes at the ceiling while switching the sweaty telephone receiver to the opposite ear, Denise wondered again why she had bothered making the call. She'd asked that question three times during the hour-long one-sided conversation. Why did she bother calling her closest friend? Erin was a caring and sensitive person. The problem was, Erin loved to talk. She was the perfect Public Defender for Santa Clara County.

Being from the South, Erin talked faster than most people. She could beat any opponent ten to one when it came to spitting out words. Most people gave up after the first conversation, but not Denise. That's why she'd spent the last hour hearing a play-by-play recap of Erin's cross-examination of a witness who'd falsely identified her client as the shooter in a grocery store robbery.

Normally, Denise wouldn't discuss her marriage with Erin, who was single and also a member of Word of Life. Granted, Erin graced Word of Life with her presence only twice a month and on special occasions. She didn't participate in programs or ministries, but Erin was a faithful tithing member.

Denise never needed to solicit advice concerning her marriage. She thought about calling her mother, but that would prove to be a waste of time. Lucinda Sanders would defend Pastor Bryce Hightower against anyone, including her daughter. Denise couldn't trust any sisters in the church to confide in for fear they'd use the opportunity to replace her as first lady. Her mother warned her severely against sharing anything with what Lucinda called, "nosey church folk." The first six months of her tenure as first lady, Denise was afraid to address the congregation.

This morning during her prayer time, Denise felt the spirit leading her to call the church mother, but a flashback of Lucinda's warning prevented her.

"I don't care how hard it gets," her mother cautioned, "don't tell nobody but God. He can fix anything. These nosey church folks will try to fix you right on out the church!"

Lucinda's stern advice left her sitting in her downtown Oakland office overlooking Lake Merritt, half focusing on the hospital conglomerate's proposed budget for the upcoming fiscal year and half listening to Erin's Perry Mason imitation. Denise glanced down at her desk clock, she knew she'd come up empty. In less than five minutes, the first casualty of her purposed cuts was due in. She hated this most about her job as budget director.

"So, girl, what's going on with you?" Erin finally asked.

Denise rolled her eyes as if Erin could see her frustration. "Never mind."

"Come on, Denise, you didn't call for nothing."

"You're right, I didn't, but it's too late now." Denise sighed. "I have a one o'clock appointment with Doctor Allen."

Erin gasped. "Are you referring to Dr. Jonas Allen, the gorgeous gynecologist at Jefferson Memorial?"

Denise hadn't personally met Doctor Jonas Allen, but from his picture in the company directory, she couldn't second Erin's description. "He's the department chair."

Erin went into overdrive, leaving Denise in need of an interpreter. "What did you say?"

Denise chuckled listening to Erin inhale and exhale then pronounce her words so slowly, one would have thought Erin had taken a sedative.

"I said, 'Tell him your available best friend would like to meet him. I'm on my way. Don't let him leave before I get there." The volume of Denise's laughter surprised her. "I'm not playing!" Erin warned.

"I know you're not, but I am not about to hold a man hostage while you make an hour's drive just so you can drool." Denise's intercom sounded. "I have to go and you need a shower." Denise rose to greet her visitor, but before disconnecting the call, advised Erin to remain in her downtown San Jose office.

Denise fastened the last button on her navy blue blazer a second before Doctor Allen trudged into her office, obviously perturbed by the budget cuts she proposed in her email.

"Good afternoon, Dr. Allen." Denise smiled, hoping to diffuse his anger. It didn't work.

Doctor Allen slammed the folder onto the oak desk. "Look, Ms. Hightower, I didn't graduate medical school to balance budgets. I'm a doctor and I treat patients."

And I didn't save myself for a husband who doesn't notice I exist anymore, but that's life. That's what Denise wanted to scream, but what she verbalized was, "I understand, Dr. Allen, but if you don't balance your budget, the only way you'll treat patients is for free."

Denise took a gamble that Doctor Allen was like every other doctor she knew. If she wanted their cooperation, threaten to stop underwriting porches, vacation homes and leisurely afternoons on the greens. It worked.

Denise took her seat and waited for the doctor to do the same. After a few huffs, Dr. Allen sat down and listened to what Denise had to say. By the end of the meeting, the doctor's demeanor had softened and his attitude was quite pleasant. The cuts Denise suggested weren't nearly as deep as he'd envisioned. He would have known that if he'd bothered to read the entire proposal.

"Ms. Hightower, I apologize for my behavior earlier," Doctor Allen said as he rose to his full six-foot height.

"No problem, but next time I suggest you not only read the first and last pages, but also the ones in between." Denise hoped her smile didn't betray the message she wanted to convey. "After twelve years of schooling, you don't want to give the impression that you can't read."

Doctor Allen erupted in laughter, and for the first time, Denise had to agree with her friend. Doctor Jonas Allen was gorgeous with his dark chocolate complexion and solid upper body. Denise guessed his age at 45, but he could compete, and probably win, against guys half his age.

"Dr. Allen, are you married?" His eyebrows shot up. "If you're not, I have a friend who would love to meet you."

Living up to his reputation as a ladies man, Jonas was curious. "Tell me about her."

"Her name is Erin Reynolds. She's single, size six, no kids, and loves to have a good time. She's a Public Defender in Santa Clara County."

Doctor Allen frowned, took a step back and held out his hands. "You almost had me sold. Sorry, but I don't do lawyers."

Denise made pun of his resolve. "Why not? Next time I'll have her read my proposal and then have her explain it to you." Denise laughed although she doubted if Doctor Allen would be able to understand one word from Erin's faster-than-the-speed-of-sound mouth.

"You're a funny lady, Ms. Hightower. But I still don't do lawyers. Accountants, maybe, but never lawyers."

The flirtation went over her head. "I don't know any single accountants," Denise gave him a dismissive smile.

Doctor Allen wasn't gone five minutes when Erin came bursting into her office unannounced, panting for breath and dripping with sweat. "Where is he?"

After the initial shock, Denise laughed until tears rolled down her cheeks and merged under her chin. "Thank you, girl," Denise managed after cleaning her face. "I owe you one."

Erin was puzzled and speechless, but Denise didn't care. Without trying to, her friend had provided just what she needed – a way to rid herself of frustration without exposing her marital business.

"God, please let this work," Denise mumbled, picking up the loaded picnic basket from the kitchen table.

This morning during her prayer time, the idea of surprising her husband came to her. The official start of spring was only one week away. Flowers were blooming and trees blossoming. Maybe if she tried something new, the spark would return to her marriage. She'd taken the day off and spent the morning making Bryce's favorite meal and preparing a surprise indoor picnic for the two of them. Bryce spent his Wednesday mornings conducting church business with the administrative staff. The meetings usually left him drained, so Denise thought an unexpected interruption would be just what he needed. Plus, it would give them some quality time together, a chance to talk. More than anything, today, she wouldn't complain or nag him about his behavior; just minister to his needs.

It had been three days since she voiced her concerns to him. Denise had to give her husband some credit, he was trying. Bryce brought home flowers two nights in a row, and last night, they made love. It wasn't the best, but it was enjoyable. And this morning before he left, he kissed her, something he had stopped doing. Denise grabbed the basket and her coat, then started for the door.

Bryce sat at his desk fighting the urge to seek out Daija. For three days, he fought against his will and won. But today, it was nearly impossible to keep his mind off the woman who could make him do things and feel things he never thought possible. His eyes scanned his desk; they landed on a photo of him and Denise then moved to a picture of him in his black ministerial cassock. That's when he felt like weeping. "God, why can't I stop this? How did this get control over me?" Bryce had asked those same questions a thousand times. How did his once "therapy" turn into a habit that controlled him like crack controls a drug addict? How did just one look, turn into a desire that drove him out of himself and away from God? And when did it become so comfortable that he didn't mind defiling the church's office? "How did it all come to this?" he mumbled.

With each question, Bryce took another step into his bathroom and to his hiding place. With Daija in hand, Bryce leaned against the wall and allowed his hands to succumb to the place his mind wanted to go. He hurriedly unzipped his pants and moaned when he cradled himself. That's how Denise found him; leaning against the bathroom wall holding Daija in one hand and himself with the other. Bryce was so caught up, he didn't hear Denise unlock his office door and come inside.

"Oh, my God . . . Bryce . . . Wh-What are you doing?" The picnic basket slipped from Denise's hand, causing its contents to crash to the floor.

Hot lasagna and garlic bread stained the grey carpet. Neither one noticed the mess, just stared in disbelief at one another. Denise couldn't believe her husband, Pastor Bryce Hightower, was standing there fondling himself. Bryce couldn't believe he'd been caught with his pants down.

"What are you doing?" Denise asked again.

Bryce couldn't verbally respond. He just stood there with his mouth open, still holding himself. The porn magazine containing Daija's spread fell from his hand onto the floor. That's when Denise fully understood what she'd walked in on. Denise picked up the magazine and had to remind herself to breath. It was obvious Bryce looked at the woman's nakedness often. The ends of the pages were curled and the pages wrinkled.

"Oh, God," she whispered. The woman in the photo was everything Denise was not. The unknown woman was lighter, taller and much thinner than she. Her hair was even longer and she did things in those photos Denise didn't think were possible.

"Bryce, how could you?" Denise threw the magazine at him then willed her eyes to look at her husband. It was hard; in a matter of minutes, she'd lost all respect for him. Bryce had also broken her heart.

Bryce still didn't answer; he still held his mouth open. In his mind, he wondered why he didn't hear the door. Why didn't he hear her walk into the office?

"Pull your pants up and answer me!" Denise screamed, wiping the tears that had settled at the tip of her chin.

"D-Denise . . . it's not . . . it's not what it looks like," Bryce stammered.

"Oh, it's not?" Denise questioned sarcastically. "So, you're not standing here masturbating in the church's bathroom with a porn magazine?"

Bryce quickly zipped up his pants. Somehow hearing his wife say it, made his actions seem dirty. For the first time, he felt shame. “Look, Denise, I don’t want to talk about this now.” Bryce washed his hands without looking at his reflection in the mirror.

“I do!” She said firmly. “How long have you been doing this?”

Bryce dried his hands and walked out to his desk. He wasn’t ready to answer her questions, so he took the defensive approach.” Why didn’t you knock? Why didn’t you call before you came waltzing in here?” he yelled.

“I was trying to surprise you!” she shot back, “But instead, the surprise is on me!”

“Next time call!”

“Next time don’t get caught with your pants down!”

Hearing his wife belittle him made him angry, even if he was wrong. He had to make this her fault. How else could he face his congregation if he took responsibility for his sins? If he verbally admitted his addiction to pornography, he’d have to admit that he was a fake and a cheat.

“I will do whatever I want to do. Maybe if things were more exciting in our bedroom, I wouldn’t need this magazine.” His cold stare made her shiver. “Maybe you should take the magazine home, you might learn something.” He then turned his back to her.

Bryce’s harsh words caused Denise’s anger to leave only to be replaced by hurt. She had to lean against a chair to keep from falling. Bryce knew she was crying, so he didn’t turn around. Only after he heard the door close did he allow himself to feel remorse. It was then he fell to his knees and wept like a baby.

“Why, God!” Denise lost track of how many times she’d asked that question in the last two hours. “What’s so wrong with me?” She was now standing in front of the full-length mirror that hung on her bedroom door.

She barely could see her reflection through her puffy wet

eyes, which was a good thing. She couldn't stand to look at herself now that her husband had so eloquently informed her he preferred a nameless woman in a magazine over her. He preferred to play with himself than to play with her. All the things she'd done to satisfy him; the costumes, the phone sex and other creative things. None of that was good enough for him. "Maybe I didn't do it right," she mumbled.

Denise stumbled over to the bed she shared with Bryce, but didn't allow her body to touch the bedding. What was once a place of warmth and comfort was now dirty and defiled. Was I that bad in bed? Does he think my body is disgusting? Was he thinking about other women when he was with me? Was he faking all this time? Denise couldn't stop the questions from coming or the tears from falling.

None of it made sense to her. During their courtship, Bryce constantly complimented her fullness. Whenever she suggested losing a few pounds, Bryce always protested, saying he loved her just the way she was. It was Bryce who showed her how to appreciate her body. It was his constant loving that made her secure with her size and her sexuality.

Denise's tears subsided as anger took over again. Bryce had committed adultery. He was a liar. She reasoned out loud. "Bryce didn't cheat because of my inability. Pastor Hightower plays with himself because he wants to! It is not my fault he can't control himself."

With her peripheral vision, Denise glimpsed at the framed picture of Bryce she kept on her nightstand. Without a second thought Denise grabbed the photo and banged it against the wood repeatedly, shattering the glass. "How could you do this? You're supposed to be a man of God!" she screamed and dropped to the floor. The admiration she once had for him was now gone. Soon, so would she.

Without hesitation, Denise retrieved a suitcase from her closet and began packing. First, she packed slowly, as if she wasn't sure she wanted to leave. But the more Bryce's words echoed in her head, the faster she shoved her belongings in the case, pulling and yanking clothes from the hangers and throwing the garments into the designer luggage. In the bathroom, with one sweep of the hand, her toiletries spilled into her travel bag. Denise slammed the mirror so hard, a hairline crack appeared. She then snatched the dresser drawers off the rollers and dumped every thing onto the floor. She haphazardly sifted through the undergarments she wanted to take, stuffing them into the smallest suitcase. Inside the walk-in closet, she picked shoes at random and threw them into the open luggage. Denise didn't know where she was going, but one thing was certain, she couldn't stay there.

"What are you doing?" Bryce's voice startled her and she stopped abruptly.

"What does it look like I'm doing?" she scoffed.

"It looks like you're leaving."

"I am. I'm leaving your dirty-lying-adultery-committing-perpetrating-man-of-God behind." Denise turned away from him and continued packing.

The words had the same effect on Bryce as if someone had punched him in the gut. His knees buckled, causing him to use the doorframe for support. He couldn't let this happen. Denise couldn't leave him. She was his covering. What would the church think if she left him behind his habit? He loved her, but his reputation before the church was first priority. He needed his "amen corner." He needed her.

"Please don't leave."

At first, Denise thought Bryce's request was a figment of her imagination; he'd said it so low. When she didn't respond to him, Bryce crept to her, grabbing her arms from behind.

"Denise, please don't leave."

"Take your dirty hands off me!" Denise snatched away from him. Turning to face him, she yelled, "Don't ever touch me again!"

"You don't mean that, baby," Bryce pleaded and reached for her again, but she pushed him in the chest and he retreated.

"I do mean it!" Denise scolded. "Just like you meant it when you decided you wanted porn over me! You can have your *little* slut!" She used her fingers to emphasize the word little, then folded her arms across her chest, waiting for Bryce to deny it was an issue of size. He didn't.

"I don't want Daija."

Denise's arms fell and her head jerked upward. "You know her?"

Bryce massaged his temples as fantasy and reality intertwined. "No! I don't know her outside of those photos. I promise."

Denise pushed him in the chest. "Liar! If you don't know her, how do you know her name?"

Bryce didn't know how to tell his wife he'd been having imaginary sex with women for so long that he developed make-believe relationships with them, to the extent of naming them; women who didn't have a clue to his existence. Women who, had he seen them on the street he wouldn't have given them a second look because of their size. While Bryce enjoyed fantasizing with petite women, his real-life preference was thick, full-sized women.

The reality of the person he'd become was too much for him. He was controlled by lust. He was guilty of the very things he preached against. Shame flooded his soul as Bryce slumped down on the bed he'd shared with his wife; the same bed he refused to find satisfaction in.

"Bryce, answer me! How do you know her name?" Denise demanded.

When Bryce finally raised his head, Denise wished he

hadn't. He had that look of helplessness that made her want to comfort him. She wrapped her arms around her body to keep from reaching out to him.

"I don't know her name," he began, his voice nearly breaking. "That's the name I made up for her." Bryce's head fell again with his hands resting on his knees.

Denise pushed Bryce so hard he almost fell over. "Are you crazy? How could you make up a name, and then gratify yourself using the photo of a stranger?" She pushed him again. Bryce still didn't answer. He wouldn't make eye contact either. "For three years, I have done everything you requested in bed. I have worn trashy clothes. I have contorted this big body into all kinds of embarrassing positions. I even learned how to perform acts that were once taboo in my mind. Thanks to you, I can earn a living on any 1-900 chat line. After all that, you want an imaginary woman?" Denise threw her hands up, shaking her head. "You can have her, I'm out of here!"

Denise was about to zip the small suitcase when Bryce stood up. "Baby, please!"

"Don't call me baby!" she screamed.

Bryce inhaled deeply before responding. He had to gain control of his emotions before he lost it completely.

"Alright, Denise, please don't leave. I love you. I don't want you to go. I need you."

"Bryce, what do you need me for?" Denise was curious now, but before he could answer, she answered for him. "That's right; you need me to sit in your amen corner at church, so your dirty little secret won't be exposed. You can forget it! I'm not a perpetrator like you!" Blinking her eyes rapidly, Denise thought she was seeing things. Bryce fell to his knees, begging.

"Denise, please! I know I have a problem, but please don't leave. I'll get help. I'll go to counseling, whatever you want. Just please don't leave me."

Denise closed her eyes and inhaled deeply. "No!" she screamed as she felt her resolve and anger evaporating.

Seeing her husband literally begging and pleading pulled her heart into a place she no longer wanted to be. It was the place in her heart that she knew no one but Bryce could occupy; a place of unconditional love and acceptance. She couldn't allow herself to go there right now; not after Bryce had been unfaithful and demeaning.

"Denise," Bryce continued, "I didn't mean what I said earlier. I am satisfied with you; you're my heart. I enjoy making love with you." Bryce looked down. "I just have this problem."

Denise fought with her arms to keep them from reaching out to him. She folded them then interlocked her fingers behind her back. When none of that worked, she grabbed her keys from the nightstand. "I've got to get out of here," she grumbled, running out of the bedroom.

Chapter 3

Parked along the bank at the San Leandro Marina overlooking the Pacific Ocean, Denise shed tears at a rhythm parallel to the raindrops that beat against her windshield. She couldn't see the ocean in front of her any clearer than she could envision her once happy life returning. "What did I do wrong?" she asked again audibly, and like the countless times before, the confines of her Lexus didn't provide her with an answer.

Denise continued the conversation as though she had an audience, using her fingers to add up the points in her favor. "I pray everyday. I attend church every Sunday. I am faithful to Bible Study. I visit the sick. I give to the poor and just about anyone who asks. I don't gossip. I don't backbite or sow discord. I tithe faithfully." Sighing heavily, Denise came to the conclusion, "God, I don't deserve this! This is not the life I signed up for. Love isn't supposed to hurt like this." Denise repeated several times while shaking her head. "I've done things for which I deserve punishment, but not this time." Looking up at the cream leather on the car roof, Denise pleaded her case. "I kept my body pure when I wasn't

As long as he lived, he'd never forget the pain etched on Denise's face or the hurt that laced her voice. Hurting Denise was something he never intended to do. Contrary to Bryce's abrasive attitude, he really loved his wife. She was his soul mate. He loved everything about her, from her thick black curly hair to her cute painted toes. He would give his life for Denise in less than a second. She had to know what she meant to him. She had to know how much he needed her. Aside from distant relatives, Denise was his family.

Denise entered the house to find Bryce standing near the door waiting for her. The brief eye contact was too much. She quickly looked away and brushed past him.

"Thank you for coming back," he called after her.

Denise remained silent as she kept moving down the hall to the linen closet. There she retrieved extra pillows and a blanket. Bryce followed her into the den.

"Don't you want to sleep in our room?" he asked, watching her turn the couch into a makeshift bed.

Denise finally spoke to him, but didn't face him. "Bryce, I'm not sleeping with you. Tomorrow, I'm purchasing a bed for the spare room. That's where I'll be sleeping from now on."

Bryce wanted to protest, but didn't. The spare room was designated for a future nursery; it wasn't supposed to be a hide-away for his wife. At least she came back and wasn't leaving him, not at the moment anyway. "Denise, I really am sorry. We're going to work through this."

Denise walked over to the archway and gestured for him to leave. "Goodnight, Bryce."

Before exiting, Bryce stopped in front of her, "I love you," he whispered before leaning in to kiss her lips. Denise turned her head. His lips landed on her cheek. Bryce left without another word.

saved because the church mothers told me you would bless me if I did. They told me you would bless me with a good husband. I believed them; now what?" When the answer didn't come, Denise beat the steering wheel in frustration.

She needed to talk to someone, but to whom? The mothers of the church were sweet and always supportive, but Denise doubted they could handle knowing their beloved pastor was a pervert. That might be enough to send a couple of them home to glory sooner than expected. The younger women in the church would use the information to pounce on her inability to satisfy her husband and solidify their contention that Bryce married the wrong person. Denise came to the conclusion that she couldn't share with anyone in the church. Not even her mother. Despite how wrong Bryce was, Lucinda would find a way to make everything Denise's fault. Lucinda always said, "It takes a wise woman to build a happy home. Show me a man that's not happy at home and I'll show you a silly woman." Denise couldn't handle her mother's narrow-mindedness right now. Her self-esteem had suffered enough for one day. That left Erin.

Denise retrieved her cell phone from her purse and punched her friend's number. Erin's voicemail greeting broke the dam and Denise yielded to another round of crying.

Bryce didn't get up off his knees until he heard the garage door open. He'd been praying since Denise left over three hours ago. Bryce prayed harder tonight than he had the last two years. He prayed for two things: that Denise would be safe by herself in the streets of Oakland at night and that she would return to him. Bryce's worry intensified after placing calls to both her mother and Erin. Neither had seen or heard from Denise. To make matters worst, Denise wasn't answering her cell phone. He started to go look for her but was afraid she'd return in his absence and leave again.

* * *

"Denise, wake up," Bryce said, shaking Denise for the third time. He had allowed her to sleep as long as he could.

Denise yawned and stretched before asking, "What time is it?" without opening her eyes.

"It's eight in the morning. You're going to be late for work."

Denise squeezed her eyes to push back the tears that threatened to escape. She'd taken the day off with the expectation that after the indoor picnic, they'd spend most of the night making love, leaving her too tired for work. She'd hoped they'd spend the day talking and planning for the family they wanted to start. Maybe yesterday had been just a dream? Denise squeezed her eyes again, praying that is was. Her eyes flickered open only to see Bryce standing over her holding a washcloth.

Slowly beholding her surroundings, it was confirmed; yesterday was not a dream. It was her reality. She'd caught her husband pleasuring himself with pornography and now didn't know if she wanted to be with him or not. Denise slowly positioned herself so that her back was resting against the arm of the couch. Bryce offered his assistance, but she pushed his arm away.

"What do you want?" she asked, with less concern she would give an ant crawling on the ground. Her impetuous tone caused Bryce to flinch. Never had she shown him so little regard and he didn't like it. His first impulse was to remind her he deserved respect as her husband and pastor. That thought dissipated as quickly as it had come once he remembered how much he needed her to stay around.

"I made you breakfast."

Denise slowly turned her head then forced back the sadistic smile that threatened to invade her face. Stationed to the right of her pathetic husband was a cluttered wooden tray. Bryce cooked. He made her favorite breakfast; blueberry pancakes and turkey sausages accompanied by cranapple juice. Bryce hadn't made breakfast or any other meal for her in over a year. He barely remembered to open doors for her anymore.

"Here." Bryce handed her the wet washcloth, but she continued starring at the wooden tray accented with a yellow rose that she recognized from the rose bush in the front yard.

Reluctantly, Denise accepted the washcloth. When she was done cleaning her hands and face, Bryce carefully maneuvered the tray directly in front of her, and cautiously, Denise began eating after silently saying grace.

Bryce figured since he had created the mess, he'd be the one to break the silence. "I unpacked your bags and placed your things into the spare room." He hadn't slept last night; too afraid he would wake up and find Denise gone.

She hoped he didn't expect her to thank him. Denise continued to eat in silence, not bothering to ask about the bandage on his left thumb. She figured it was from the shattered glass she'd left in their bedroom the night before.

When she didn't respond, Bryce continued. "Denise, I know this is a little late, but I understand now."

Denise started to ask him just what did he understand, but was too emotionally drained to care.

Bryce would have preferred she slap him over the vicious look she shot at him. Her eyes encased daggers that pierced his heart.

"I know what I was doing was wrong. In a sense, I was unfaithful and a hypocrite. I haven't been fair with you or the church. I pray you give me the chance to make this up to you." Bryce paused, waiting for her to say she understood and accept his apology.

Denise choked, swallowing the cranapple juice. "What do you mean, in a sense you have been unfaithful? You committed adultery! I have grounds to divorce you!"

Bryce pushed the lump in his throat down before continuing. "Denise, I promise I haven't committed adultery. I have this problem, but I have been faithful to our marriage vows."

Denise set her fork down, shaking her head from side to side. "You are the biggest hypocrite."

"What do you mean?"

Denise gave in to her frustration. "Don't play stupid, Pastor Hightower! You know the Bible better than anyone. You tell me what is says about looking on a woman with lust and adultery."

Bryce knew verbatim what Matthew 5:28 stated; he just refused to apply it to his circumstance. "That's not the same kind of adultery you can divorce over," was his rehearsed defense.

"Well excuse my ignorance. I didn't know there were different types of adultery. Excuse me for thinking all sexual activity a married man has should involve his wife." Denise was smiling, but her words dripped with sarcasm. "Forgive me for thinking I should be the only one to blow your mind." Denise patted his hand. "Thank you so much for clearing that up for me." Bryce didn't respond, and Denise took advantage of the moment. "I guess this means I can go to the strip club and get off too, just as long as I don't physically touch. Maybe I'll stash some magazines in my desk at work. Better yet, why don't I just go to the adult video store and buy DVDs to watch here at the house? You can have your collection and I'll have mine and we'll live happily ever after. I'm sure you won't mind since you don't consider that being unfaithful."

Bryce's nostrils flared. "That's not what I mean and you know it!"

"You're right, Pastor Hightower; what you mean is you can do whatever you want and I should sit back and take it! That's what you expect; me to just look the other way."

"What I expect is for you to understand and allow me time to work through this."

Denise raised her voice to match his. "And I expect my husband and my pastor not to cheat on me!"

Realizing he wasn't making any headway, Bryce plopped down next to her on the couch, leaning his head back. Denise positioned her body, making sure he couldn't touch her.

"Bryce, how long has this been going on?"

Denise studied her husband carefully as he inhaled and exhaled deeply. He then changed positions. His thumbs cradled his forehead while his knees supported his elbows. That was his classic body language for when he really didn't want to give an answer or when he knew the answer would be hurtful. "I want an answer and don't lie to me."

"It started years before I met you, when I was seventeen."

Denise gasped. "That's half your life."

He sighed, "I know."

Denise listened intensively as he shared about discovering porn after his parents' death and how he lost his virginity.

"After we got married, I stopped. I thought the desire would leave, but soon I found myself sneaking peeks at magazines. Shortly after, I resumed my habit. I wouldn't use the computer because I was afraid you would find out. I have magazines concealed in the car, the bathrooms both here and at the church and in my study."

Bryce watched the tears slowly stream down his wife's face, wanting to wipe them away, but he couldn't. He also couldn't lie to her anymore.

"Did you ever think about those women when you were with me?" The sudden onset of nausea gave her the answer before he did.

"Not in the beginning and not all the time," Bryce answered honestly. "The occasions when I made odd requests of you, I was trying to recreate what I'd seen and the feeling I had while fantasizing and . . . well, you know." Bryce lowered his head in his hands and wept after he watched Denise knock the tray over and run into the bathroom. Just vocalizing his actions opened his eyes to how far he had fallen.

Inside the bathroom, Denise relieved herself in a vicious bout of heaving. Once the gagging subsided, she remained in the restroom. Bryce found her there on her knees with her face leaning into the toilet bowl, whimpering like a wounded animal.

"Denise, I'm so sorry."

"If you didn't want to be with someone like me, why did you marry me? If that type of woman turns you on, why did you marry me and make me a substitute?" She asked the question, pointing at herself. "I'm not what you want. I'm not skinny; I don't have a weave down my back and I don't wear colored contacts. If I'm not appealing to you, why did you ruin my life by marrying me?"

Denise refused his assistance and pulled herself up so that now she was standing over the sink. He waited until she finished rinsing her mouth before answering.

"Denise, you are—"

She cut him off. "I was a virgin when I married you. I gave you the best gift I could give you: me, pure and undefiled. All I was to you was a legal way for you to fulfill your raunchy fantasies and remain the pastor!" Her tears were hot, heavy and continuous.

"Denise, that's not true. You're everything I want." Bryce tried unsuccessfully to keep the lump in his throat from escaping. His voice broke as slight tremors shook him.

"Don't lie to me!" Denise screamed. "Tell me the truth, for once!"

Bryce sighed deeply while running his hand over his head. "I'm a pastor and your husband and I love you, but I'm addicted to pornography. That's the truth." Denise didn't respond, just turned her back to him. “Niecy.” Bryce hadn't called Denise by his pet nickname for her in so long she almost didn't recognize it. “Please, don't leave me,” Bryce begged. “We're the first family and we have to set the example for the rest of the congregation.”

She turned to face him. “So you want me to be a fake like you?”

“What I want is for us to work through this together.”

“What does ‘work through’ mean? The only way we can stay together is for you to give up porn and I can't make you do that. You have to do that on your own because you want to.” For the first time since catching Bryce in the act, Denise made eye contact with him. “Do you want to give it up?”

Bryce exhaled, and for once, felt the heaviness lift. “Yes, I do. It's going to take some time. Can you give me time to work on this?”

Denise didn't answer, she just solemnly walked away.

Chapter 4

"Saints, it's time to go before the throne and invoke God's presence in our worship service this morning."

From her front row seat, Denise solemnly watched as the 500 plus membership of Word of Life crowded the altar and side aisles at the deacon's request. Seven short days ago, Denise would have been the first one standing at the altar with arms raised, ready to praise God. Today, the only reason she was at service was because for two days straight, Bryce had begged her to come. Not only did Denise not feel like praising God, she didn't want to. She couldn't praise a God who'd deceived her. She had prayed, fasted and read her Word and was certain the Lord told her Bryce Hightower was her ordained husband. If her mother constantly filling her ears with how great a first lady Denise would make wasn't persuasive enough, the Lord confirmed it through a visiting evangelist by a word of prophecy. "Somebody lied," she mumbled.

Bryce emerged from his office, another indication he was worried Denise would leave him and expose his secret. Bryce never joined the congregation before the choir's second selection. He smiled at Denise and she pretended not to see him, focusing her attention on the deacon as he sang, "I Need Thee."

Listening to the deacon belt out the words with his heart and soul, Denise shed silent tears of her own. The elderly gentleman reminded her so much of her late father. Denise could almost feel Deacon Jeremiah Sanders' presence there with her on the front row. More than anything, she wanted to be held by her father's strong arms and hear his baritone voice whisper, "Everything will be all right." If her father were alive, he would have a talk with Bryce and make him do right by her. Better yet, Deacon Sanders wouldn't have allowed Bryce to come within arm's reach of his baby girl. Jeremiah Sanders could spot a cheat a mile away. He was the main reason Denise didn't have male callers until she went away to college. Towering just over six-feet-three-inches tall and weighing in at 250 pounds, all muscle thanks to his job as a firefighter, Jeremiah intimidated young boys, and most adults for that matter.

"I need you, Daddy," Denise whispered as the deacon finished the second chorus. She closed her eyes and listened to the deacon pray, too disillusioned and hurt to offer an Amen at the closing. After accepting tissue from an usher, Denise wiped her eyes, stood to her feet and put on her church face for Praise and Worship.

Aside from preaching, Praise and Worship was Denise's favorite part of the service. The Word of Life singers were anointed to usher in the presence of God and destroy yokes with their melodious voices. Most Sundays, Denise would lose herself in the worship to the point of losing her hat and some rhinestones from her Sunday-go-to-meeting suits. Today was no exception. The first stanza of "I Love You Jesus" *Jesus* tore down the wall of resentment she'd built toward the Lord. Denise repented for using her frustrations with her husband as an excuse to boycott God. Praise and

Worship continued and Denise seized the opportunity to cry out to God for help. That was one of the benefits of corporate worship. Anyone involved could weep like a baby and everyone would just assume that their tears were attributed to being satisfied with Jesus.

Praise and Worship shifted gears with "Victory." While the congregation clapped, swayed, and jumped, Denise attempted to dance her sorrows away.

"Go ahead, First Lady. Praise Him!" Someone cheered when Denise lost her hat.

Bryce rose to his feet, doing his dance to demonstrate that the first family was on one accord. Tired and breathless, Denise slowly made her way back to her seat. She'd lost her hat and one shoe, but she retained her burdens.

"God, please help me deal with this," she prayed after cleaning her face again. She was about to sit down when Mother Gray, the church mother, gripped her, pulling Denise into a tight embrace.

Mother Gray held Denise like she was a baby, cradling her head and stroking her back. Denise didn't know how to respond to the tenderness. What would the congregation and her mother think if she broke down in the church mother's arms?

"Hold on baby. God is going to heal him," Mother Gray whispered in her ear while squeezing her tighter.

Denise's head snapped up and she gasped, shocked that Mother Gray knew about Bryce's illness, but was too afraid to ask the woman just how much God had revealed to her. She lowered her head in shame as fresh tears fell. At that moment, Denise couldn't care less what the people thought. She returned the mother's firm embrace and wept on her shoulder until the wells of her eyes were dry.

Back in her seat, Denise whispered a prayer of thanks to God for providing her with the strength to continue. She still wasn't sure of what to do about her marriage, but it was comforting to know God loved her enough to send her a word, through the saintly mother, to ease the heaviness. To let her know He had heard her cry and felt her pain.

For the first time in three days, a smile creased her face. It quickly disappeared upon making eye contact with Lucinda. Her mother's face displayed a stern look of rebuke. Lucinda's dislike for Mother Gray wasn't exactly a secret. Most of the congregation was aware of the age-old feud between them that stemmed from what Lucinda referred to as Gray trying to stick her big nose where it didn't belong. In actuality, Mother Gray had shared with her some concerns she had about Deacon Sanders and Lucinda didn't like it and stopped speaking to the woman whom she once considered a friend. Denise anticipated a lecture would immediately follow the benediction, but she didn't care. Ignoring her mother, she directed her attention to the platform.

The high-spirited service prompted Pastor Hightower to skip the choir selections and mount the podium. This was his routine when the Praise and Worship was extremely high.

As always, before beginning his sermon, Pastor Hightower acknowledged his beautiful and loving wife. Denise didn't want to, but with the help of the two big-screen wall monitors making it so that all eyes were on her, she didn't have a choice but to play the role. She weakly smiled and blew her husband a kiss. That gesture was the assurance Bryce needed to preach what he hoped wasn't his last sermon.

Denise watched and listened in awe as Bryce preached what had to be one of his best messages. Pastor Hightower's revelation about the woman with an issue of blood was so profound, most of the women and a large percentage of the men were driven to tears crying out to God for deliverance.

During the prayer line that followed, Pastor Hightower laid hands and the power of God manifested, leaving people slain in the Spirit and crying out to God for healing.

Denise leaned back on her front row seat, shaking her head in amazement. She couldn't understand how God could use Bryce to that magnitude considering his sins. How could God bless him in his wrong and yet let her suffer for doing the right thing?

"I thought You were a just God," she grumbled.

Denise knew her mother well. No sooner had the congregation recited the *May the Lord watch between me and thee . . .* dismissal, Lucinda pounced on the first lady.

"What is your problem? How many times have I a warned you about letting nosey church mothers in your business?"

Denise downplayed her mother's tantrum. "Mother Gray was not being nosey, she simply prayed for me. Is it a crime for the church mother to pray for the first lady?" Denise glared at her mother. "Someone needs too."

Lucinda didn't like the implication. "Just what do you mean by that?"

"You know what I mean, Mama." Denise repositioned her hat and adjusted the strap on her Bible.

Lucinda leaned in closer, but to further make sure she wouldn't be heard, lowered her voice. "I know something's going on with you. I'm not blind. Whatever it is, hurry up and fix it before you damage Bryce's ministry."

Denise's jaw fell. "Me?"

"You heard me. Bryce is a good man and he has a lot on his plate with this church. He doesn't need you acting a fool and adding to his stress. There are plenty of women who would love to offer him a "stress-free" life. Now get yourself together!"

Denise backed away from her mother so quickly, she tripped over her feet.

"Baby, be careful!" Bryce said, catching and preventing her from falling backward.

Denise hadn't notice Bryce behind her. For the first time in days she was happy to feel his arms around her. All she needed to make her day perfect was to fall and make one of the congregants the $10,000 winner on *America's Funniest Videos* or have her mishap appear in a YouTube blooper special.

"Are you all right?" Bryce asked, helping her straighten her clothing.

"I'm fine," Denise responded, avoiding being singed by her mother's hot glare.

Aware of the audience and camera phones, Denise pasted on her best smile, thanked her husband for the rescue, then slowly headed for the door. Knowing Lucinda would follow her, once in the parking lot Denise increased her pace. Denise had locked her doors by the time Lucinda breathlessly banged on her window. After turning up the radio volume, Denise pretended not to hear her and drove away.

Bryce entered the dark 3,000 square-foot home carrying curbside takeout from Denise's favorite restaurant. It was a safe assumption Denise wasn't cooking for him; she hadn't cooked a thing since preparing the ruined surprise picnic five days ago. Stepping into the kitchen, his assumption proved correct.

Not only hadn't Denise cooked, the kitchen was clean enough for a photo shoot in *Gourmet Kitchen* magazine thanks to Bryce. In an effort to gain Denise's allegiance, he'd been house cleaning for three days; stopping only for prayer and to prepare his Sunday sermon. Every floor in the five-bedroom three-bath home was mopped and the baseboards scrubbed. Walls were washed and the windows glistened with a streak-free shine. Bryce finally got around to hanging paintings Denise had been nagging him about for months.

If Bryce was waiting for an affirmation from Denise, he wasn't going to get one. Although she listened to his pleas for her to stay, outside of church today, Denise hadn't spoken ten words to him. Most of the time she remained in the spare bedroom with the door closed, crying. During the long nights in his lonely king-sized bed, Bryce cried too, and prayed. He didn't pray for himself; choosing instead to center his petitions on Denise, asking God to soften her heart.

He'd become accustomed to her disregard of his presence, but he called out to her anyway. "Niecy, I'm home." Bryce allowed a moment to pass before continuing. "I brought your favorites from Outback. I'll set the table; we can eat in the dining room. We haven't done that in a while. I also got some of that pear cider you like."

Bryce set the table complete with candlelight, then went to search for Denise. His heart raced and the lump in his throat prevented him from breathing after opening the spare bedroom door only to find it empty. Bryce frantically searched each room, including the bathrooms, without success. "She has to be here", he mumbled, remembering her car was parked in the garage. He then panicked. What if Denise had taken a taxi to the airport and purchased a one-way ticket out of town and away from him? He loosened then snatched off his tie. The cold January thermostat registered 50 degrees outside, but Bryce perspired so heavily he grabbed a towel from the linen closet to dry his brow.

Giving in to his anxiety, Bryce plopped down on the couch in the den. That's when he saw her. Denise was sitting outside in their enclosed patio on the futon wrapped in a blanket. "Thank you, God," Bryce whispered, at the same time making his way to the sliding patio door. "Niecy, it's time to eat." Careful not to invade her space, Bryce came close enough to see if she was awake. She was. "I set the table," Bryce shivered. "Baby you should come inside. It's cold out here." Bryce offered his hand to assist her, but she refused it. Before he formulated another thought, Denise brushed past him and went into the house.

The sound of Tim Bowman's guitar, radiating from the sound system, substituted for dinner conversation. Bryce was afraid the wrong word would send her back into hibernation inside the spare bedroom, so he remained quiet. Having Denise beside him this way was better than the alternative. Between bites of rib-eye steak, Bryce studied his wife's face. Missing was its normal radiance, but she was still beautiful. Also missing was her appetite, she'd barely touched the crab cakes and cider she loved so much.

"When did you become such a hypocrite?" Denise asked without warning.

Bryce chewed his food slower than normal, then sipped cider before answering. "I'm not a hypocrite."

Denise dropped her fork and pushed her plate away. "I can't wait to hear this. I'm just dying to hear you twist the Word to explain how you had the audacity to stand before the church, knowing you just finished playing with yourself."

Bryce's flinched at her words but held his ground. "I've been clean for three days, and in that time, I have done nothing but clean this house and pray. When I mounted the podium today, God anointed me because He knows my heart is right."

Denise cocked her head to the side. "Can you pray and ask Him to make your hand right so you can stop playing with yourself?"

Bryce pushed his plate back and stepped away from the table. "I know I have a problem, but you don't have to be so cruel."

"Forgive me for having a hard time accepting that my

husband likes to have sex without me!" Denise yelled after him.

Watching her husband walk away from her, Denise wanted to shed more tears, but none would come. They wouldn't come on the patio either where she longed to bury herself underneath the blanket until freezing to death. Bryce's interruption was proof that God wasn't going to grant her wish. There was no escaping the veracity of her situation.

Her marriage was damaged; she just wasn't sure as to what extent. Did she want to take the 'out' the Bible clearly gave her? Did she want to stay as Bryce requested and help pray him into his deliverance? She didn't know, but one thing was certain; she needed to set some ground rules until she figured it all out.

After clearing the table and storing the half eaten meals inside the refrigerator, Denise stalled by taking a shower first. She then checked her email and chatted with Erin for a few minutes. Finally, Denise fastened her robe and went looking for her husband. She found him in the den sitting on the couch with his eyes closed.

Standing over him, Denise admired his features. Bryce had always been handsome in her eyes, he still was. Brushing her tongue slowly across her lips, Denise scolded herself for wanting to kiss his full set of lips. Closing her eyes tight, she counted to ten to regain her focus.

"I will not live in the same house as your trash. I want all of it out of this house tonight." Bryce's eyes bucked at the request, but he knew better than to protest.

"Okay."

Her next statement was a test of Bryce's level of commitment. "Now, Bryce! And I want to see them burn." She said pointing to the fireplace.

"Whatever you say."

Bryce inhaled deeply before slowly rising from the couch. He stood there momentarily looking around as if he were lost, before finally retrieving a magazine from behind the sixty-inch flat screen television. His head hung in shame and Denise leaned against the marble fireplace for support, when he unzipped the couch cushion and removed the forbidden contents. He produced magazines from his car and his study, but Denise was blown away when he lifted the carpet in the den. He had them everywhere.

Denise stepped away from the fireplace and leaned against the wall after Bryce dumped the second armful of magazines into the orange flames. The once hidden arsenal opened her understanding. Bryce didn't just have a problem; he was truly addicted to pornography. It was no ordinary addiction. Bryce was controlled.

"How did I miss this?" Denise wondered out loud. When Bryce didn't answer, Denise turned to the wall and the tears returned.

"Are you planning on divorcing me?" he asked pitifully.

"Bryce, I don't want a divorce," she admitted. "What I want is a husband who will not cheat on me." Turning around to face him she continued. "What I want is the husband that vowed to love and cherish only me."

Bryce made slow deliberate steps toward her.

"I want the husband who used to make me feel special and loved. I want the husband who made me feel safe and secure." Only inches separated them now. "I want the husband God sent to me." Denise used the back of her hand to wipe her chin.

"Oh, Niecy," Bryce whispered when she allowed him to cup her face and wipe her cheeks. "I am the man that God sent you, but I have flaws. I'll correct them, but it's going to take some time. Can you love me in the meantime? Can you give me another chance?" His questions, laced with desperation, reached that part of Denise that only he could touch. "Eventually, I'll be everything you need me to be."

Denise closed her eyes, lowered her head and took a step

back. Bryce made a bold move, stepping to her and wrapping his arms around her waist. "Niecy, I know I hurt you; let me love the pain away," Bryce whispered in her ear. His petitions were answered the moment Denise raised her chin and allowed him to kiss her. Bryce responded by deepening the kiss.

Denise's heart eventually prevailed over the battle in her mind. The love they made on the floor of the den in front of the fireplace was more like a tug of war. It was sweet and sour; bitter and sweet. It was difficult for Denise to completely open up to her husband again. He sensed it and constantly reassured her of how beautiful she was and how much he loved her. She wanted to believe him. Still joined together, Bryce kissed away the steady trail of tears from her cheeks.

"I love you, Niecy. I'm going to make this up to you. I promise."

Later, Denise faced the fireplace with her back to him, wondering which woman he'd been fantasizing about while making love to her.

Chapter 5

The pillow beside him, void of dents or imprints, didn't bother Bryce so much this morning. His wife hadn't shared his bed with him last night, but Denise had given him her body, and for Bryce that was enough. She didn't kiss him goodbye before leaving for work this morning, but that was minor. His marriage was back on track. Glancing to his nightstand at her picture he whispered, "Thank you, Father for touching her heart. Thank you for blessing me with a loving and understanding wife."

Leaning against the headboard, Bryce exhaled heavily several times. As embarrassing as it was having his secret exposed, it felt like someone had lifted a 200-pound barbell from his neck. He could breathe again without the tightness in his chest. He slept better too; his demons hadn't invaded his dreams in three nights. Not once had Daija or the 100's of other nameless faces he'd been intimate with beckoned him to dance. Shaking his head, Bryce made a declaration. "I'm not masturbating ever again. It's not worth it."

Walking into the bathroom, Bryce wished he had someone he could talk to. An older man, perhaps, from whom he could seek advice on how to avoid self-induced sexual gratification. A man to help him understand his addiction and not judge and belittle, or worst, assassinate his credibility as a man of the cloth.

Christian-dome mastered the restoration and love speeches, but from Bryce's observations, failed miserably in the application. He could count his circle of preacher friends on one hand. Mainly because older preachers were intimidated by younger and more innovative pastors, and the younger preachers were too busy competing with one another to care about each other's spiritual well-being.

Bryce longed for the days when the late Reverend Daniels was alive. Pastor Daniels may have tolerated questionable behavior among his young preachers, but he kept their secrets and didn't believe in open exposure.

After getting dressed, Bryce walked out onto his front porch. Inhaling the fresh after-the-rain mid-March air, he thought of his mother. She had loved the rain and he benefited from it greatly. On rainy days, Mavis Hightower literally baked all day long. With what seemed like nothing more than a mixing bowl, flour and vanilla extract, she made enough sugar cookies, lemon pound cakes, pecan pies, and chocolate cakes to feed all the neighborhood kids and the Port of Oakland where his father worked as a Longshoreman.

Bryce closed his eyes, imagining sitting at the table with a tall glass of milk and walnut brownies melting in his mouth.

"You better not spoil your appetite," his mother would warn at the same time, allowing him another serving.

Mavis couldn't help spoiling her only child. An emergency hysterectomy after Bryce's birth robbed her chance of having the three children she'd planned for. As a way to cope, Mavis smothered him, permitting him to nurse until age five, much to his father's angry objections. Mavis didn't care; she kept her little man close to her as much as possible.

In elementary school, Bryce got teased everyday because his mother volunteered in all his classes. Mavis served as chaperone for his Junior Prom, and sure enough, when it was time for pictures, it was Mavis standing beside him.

His father loved him, but wasn't nearly as smothering. Thomas Hightower felt a man's number one priority was making money and providing for his family, not all that mushy cuddling stuff his wife complained about not receiving. Thomas didn't give many hugs or compliments. Doing well was expected, not something to be rewarded for. As a child, Bryce didn't understand his father's emotional constipation. As an adult, Bryce often wondered if his father's pastime drained him of his ability to meet his family's emotional needs.

"Good morning, neighbor." It was the elderly gentleman, who walked the neighborhood every morning, interrupting his thoughts. Bryce waved back at the always cheerful man and offered him a smile. "How's life treating you today?"

Bryce smiled and answered the man honestly. "Life is good." In his opinion, life was great. He expected Denise to return to their bedroom after wooing her with the evening he had in mind. Denise loved candlelit bubble baths and hot oil massages.

The older gentleman stopped his brisk walk, and from the sidewalk, studied Bryce for a long hard moment before continuing his morning exercise. "Be praying for you, son."

Bryce's eyes followed him until the grey jogging suit disappeared around the corner. Turning into his house, Bryce thought the man was a little more than peculiar, but figured prayer couldn't hurt.

By noon, Bryce had prayed and completed his research for Wednesday night Bible study. He then dressed in his black suit complete with ministerial collar. With his Bible lying face up in the passenger seat, Pastor Hightower headed for Summit Hospital to visit sick parishioners.

* * *

Even as a child, Denise hated Monday mornings. In church, the preacher said Sunday was supposed to be a day of rest for the saints, but the only rest young Denise saw saints take was between dancing breaks. Like most church kids, Denise danced and imitated the older saints until she was exhausted. Her strenuous activity continued after service as she helped her mother serve dinner in the fellowship hall. Twice as much dancing went on Sunday nights; so much that the pastor rarely preached, choosing to dance along with the congregation. Monday mornings, Denise was so tired, she needed her own Sabbath. Many times she crossed her fingers behind her back and faked being sick.

Now, looking out over Lake Merritt from her thirty-second floor office window, Denise concluded not much had changed. Word of Life no longer held Sunday night service, but Sundays were still strenuous and Denise was still exhausted come Monday morning.

The emotional category five hurricane caused by her beloved husband only added to her physical fatigue. She sighed, and used her fingertips to ease the tension mounting in the back of her neck before positioning herself in her leather executive chair behind her mahogany desk. She turned on the computer and at the same time wished she didn't love Bryce so much. That futile thought had filled the darkness of the spare bedroom as she lay in bed unable to sleep the night before. Without love, it would be easy to make a decision about her marriage; she would simply walk away. But she did love Bryce, always would. That's the reason she allowed him to make love to her.

The wounded and vulnerable man, who so readily burned his habit for her, touched her heart and she thought she needed him to physically touch her back. Denise thought loving him would help ease the pain. She was wrong. The second she exposed herself, insecurity she'd never known overwhelmed and paralyzed everything but her mind. Her head filled with voices that mocked her for believing her plus size body was stimulating to her husband. With all the women he'd played with, certainly he wasn't referring to her as beautiful. Bryce's body may have been on the floor with her, but his mind was among the ashes in the fireplace.

This morning, after stepping from the shower, she took extra time to critique her body in the full-length mirror attached to the bathroom door. After a critical inspection, Denise decided it was time for her to lose some weight. Her size had never been an issue for her, but suddenly, her thick curves weren't an asset anymore. In five short days, her perception had been so damaged that the only thing Denise admired about her body was the set of acrylic nails glued to her fingertips. Her ample thighs weren't luscious anymore and she carried enough junk in her trunk to have a yard sale. There was a time when walking past a construction site filled her ears with whistles and cat calls. Thinking back now, Denise wondered if the men were collectively making fun of her instead of admiring her.

Bryce declared he loved her body, but that was a lie. Her husband's true taste in women was evident on the pages of the magazines he found pleasure in.

"I'll probably never be a size six, but with Jenny Craig and exercise, size ten is possible." Denise sighed, while browsing the weight-loss website. "It may take awhile, but I'll get there. If Kirstie Alley can do it, so can I. As for hair, I can join the other eighty percent of the African American female population in the Bay Area by getting a weave." Before figuring on a solution for lightening her mocha complexion skin, the intercom sounded, ending the conversation she was having with herself.

"Mrs. Hightower, your mother is on line one, she says it's urgent."

Denise thanked her secretary, but before answering the

line, prayed for strength. Lucinda was still hot over Denise's behavior in church the day before. Denise only added fuel to the fire by ignoring her persistent cell phone calls. Denise cleared her throat and prepared for battle.

"Hello, mother, how are you today?" Denise was caught off guard by Lucinda's calm demeanor.

"Baby, I'm fine. I know I came at you hard yesterday. I'm sorry. I just want the best for you."

Before Denise could voice her acceptance of the apology, Lucinda turned a curve, laying another brick in her new insecurity wall.

"It's not easy being married to a preacher, a pastor at that, but you have to watch how you carry yourself. Stop all that crying and moping. People are always watching you, waiting for you to make a mistake. You can't let them know you're weak, or they'll take advantage of you, just as sure as my name is Lucinda; and I know that's my name."

"But Mama, you don't know what I'm dealing with." Denise's voice was so low she wasn't sure if she voiced the words or just thought them.

"It doesn't matter; you need to be strong for Bryce. You have to be everything he needs, especially at church. If you don't, he'll find happiness someplace else."

Denise switched the receiver to the opposite ear, and at the same time pondered her mother's implication. If Bryce isn't happy with her, did that give him the right to practice porn? "Mama, I can't be solely held responsible for our problems." Denise paused. "Bryce has problems—serious problems. He's not perfect."

Denise wished, for once, her mother would ask her what those problems were. Just once she yearned to talk woman to woman with her mother about the turmoil racking her mind without the burden being placed back on her shoulders.

"Baby, of course he's not perfect; he's human. But it's your job as his wife to cover those imperfections."

Denise didn't realize she was crying until she felt the tears on her hand that held the receiver. After using a tissue from the dispenser on her desk, Denise remained quiet as Lucinda went into her don't-tell-nobody-but-God-speech.

"I love you, baby and I'm praying for you," Lucinda said before disconnecting.

Reading the desk clock, Denise groaned. Just a mere 15 minutes separated her from her next visitor. She'd let two valuable hours pass without giving Dr. Allen's revised budget a glance.

She wished all the department heads were as proactive as Dr. Allen. Most doctors procrastinated until the very last moment to review their proposed new budgets and submit the requested documents. Then they would have the audacity to barge into her office before the deadline, begging for alterations. She'd just finished calculating the last column when her secretary announced him.

"Ms. Hightower!" Doctor Allen greeted her as if she was an old friend. Denise stood, and after a quick handshake, went right to business. Once seated, she laced her fingers together on the desk and leaned forward.

"Dr. Allen, I hope you took the liberty of reading the complete final proposal?"

"Of course, after your strong rebuke last time, did I have a choice?" Denise afforded him a slight smile. He continued. "I'm quite pleased with your sensitivity to my department's needs."

"Since we agree, I'll print two hard copies for you to sign. One for your records and the other one I'll forward to the chief financial officer for the upcoming fiscal year."

Doctor Allen agreed, and after obtaining the signatures and handing Dr. Allen his copy, Denise closed down the file then stood signifying the end of the meeting. Before she could dismiss her present visitor, an unexpected one arrived.

"Ms. Hightower, Erin Reynolds is here to see you," the secretary called over the intercom.

I can't believe this girl! Denise laughed out loud. She'd totally forgotten mentioning Doctor Allen's visit to Erin the night before. Erin promised she would make an appearance, but Denise didn't believe her. Erin not only appeared, but made a production out of the "chance" meeting.

Erin stepped into her friend's office wearing a black Dolce & Gabbana silk suit with both the skirt and jacket stopping just low enough to cover the important parts, and topped it all off with matching designer four-inch stilettos. Gone was the bun she wore for court. Erin's natural long, thick, black hair flowed loosely midway down her back. She always reminded Denise of Pocahontas whenever she let her hair down.

"Oh, Denise, am I interrupting something?" Erin's attempt at being remorseful was pathetic at best. "Do you need me to come back later?"

Denise cleared her throat, mainly to stifle the laughter that threatened to erupt from the pit of her stomach. "Come on in. Dr. Allen was just leaving."

Erin gasped. "Are you the famous Dr. Jonas Allen from Jefferson Memorial?" He nodded. "I didn't recognize you from television." Doctor Allen, along with two other gynecologists, was recently featured for their work with infertility patients on a local health channel. "I can't believe I'm standing next to you."

Denise asked the Lord to please forgive her friend for lying. Denise leaned against her desk with her arms folded and watched Erin put on a performance that would have beaten Halle Berry for the Oscar.

Erin spoke very clearly, almost seductively. "I'm Erin Reynolds, Denise's oldest and best friend." She extended her freshly manicured hand and Doctor Allen casually shook it. "Your wife must be very proud of your accomplishments?"

Doctor Allen was keen to the game and cut to the chase. "I'm not married, Ms. Reynolds."

"Then you won't mind joining me for lunch?"

Doctor Allen smiled, admiring the bravado of this woman who was just a few inches over five feet with heels. "Ms. Reynolds—"

"Please call me Erin."

"Erin, I usually don't eat in the company of lawyers, but since it's lunchtime, I'll make an exception. That is, providing Ms. Hightower can join us."

Erin corrected him. "That's *Mrs.* Hightower, and we don't need a chaperone."

"With your prowess, I can't be sure. I write alimony checks to the last lawyer I shared a meal with."

Erin lowered her lashes. "Dr. Allen, I promise one meal with me and you'll lose the grudge you have against lawyers."

"We'll see." Doctor Allen then turned to Denise. "Will you please join us, my treat?"

Denise looked from Doctor Allen to Erin. Her friend obviously expected her to come up with an excuse and send them on their way. "Sure, why not?"

Denise sat in the booth of the Italian restaurant picking at her fresh baby spinach and mixed greens salad, and wondering what possessed her to play third wheel. She picked up another lemon wedge and squeezed until the leaves wilted, then slowly placed another forkful into her mouth. After a lunch like this, the food she'd get from her appointment at Jenny Craig later that evening would taste like a gourmet meal.

Watching Erin woo Doctor Allen, for the first time ever, Denise was jealous of her friend. By society standards, Erin was gorgeous. With her petite figure, everything looked great on her. Erin's double-creme coffee skin was smooth and flawless. Denise never understood why she used foundation when she really didn't need it. Erin was also very courageous. Denise would have never mustered enough nerve to chase after a man. Worst of all, Denise couldn't keep her own husband interested in her. She attempted to push thoughts of failure to the back of her mind and listened to Doctor Allen discuss his television appearance.

Denise knew for a fact, Erin had watched at least three re-runs of the show. She'd phoned Denise every time inquiring about Doctor Allen, yet, Erin appeared fascinated by his every word, until her cell phone vibrated.

"Excuse me, I need to return this call," Erin said after checking the Caller ID on her cell phone. Doctor Allen stood and allowed room for her to leave the booth.

"Dr. Allen, I know my friend is a little pushy, but Erin really is a good person. You should give her a chance. You never know, you might be a match," Denise suggested after taking a sip of water that she'd also spiked with juice from her lemon.

Doctor Allen leaned back and stretched his long arms. "Ms. Hightower," he stopped; "or do you prefer *Mrs.* Hightower?"

"Actually, I prefer Denise."

He smiled. "Good. I prefer Jonas." She nodded and he continued. "Like I was saying, Denise, I don't doubt your friend is a nice person, but she's not my type. Aside from being a lawyer, she's too pushy and she talks too fast."

Denise didn't mean to laugh so loud, but it was too late; her high pitch caught the attention of fellow patrons. "I was hoping you wouldn't notice," she whispered after apologizing to the table directly in front of them.

Jonas made a face that said, 'Be for real,' then joined in with her laughter.

Denise was too busy laughing to see the unexpected visitor who walked up to the table. The tap on the shoulder nearly startled her. "Bryce?" she spoke.

"Your secretary told me you were having lunch here. She didn't tell me it was a business lunch," he answered, acknowledging the tall muscular stranger, who moments earlier, had made his wife laugh the way he used to make her laugh.

"It's not business. Actually, I'm chaperoning for Erin." She snickered then introduced Jonas to her husband.

"Hello, Reverend," Jonas said in reference to the clergy collar. Bryce cordially greeted him with a light handshake. "I didn't know I was speaking to *the* first lady," he teased.

"I hope Ms. Goody Two Shoes didn't bore you to death," Erin said jokingly upon returning.

Jonas rose to let Erin into the booth and continued standing. "Ladies, I've enjoyed the company, but I have clinic this afternoon." He placed enough bills on the table to cover the check and a nice tip. "Denise, I'll be in touch." He looked at Erin. "Ms. Reynolds, take care."

Before Erin could think of a way to keep him there, Jonas was gone.

"What happened, the cat finally got your tongue?" Bryce teased Erin.

Erin rolled her eyes at Bryce then made a dash for the door.

Bryce position himself in the spot Doctor Allen had vacated. "That woman is going to find her a husband at the risk of becoming a stalker."

Denise sipped water during the uneasy silence that followed. "Bryce, why are you here?" she finally asked.

"I was hoping to spend lunch with you, but I see I'm too late." He gestured at her half eaten salad.

Denise sighed heavily. "Maybe next time." She flinched

when she felt his hand on top of hers, all the while speculating what defiled things he used that very same hand for.

"What would you like to do about dinner?" Bryce was determined to press forward. "I thought maybe we could have Thai food then a DVD. I'll even watch *Pretty Woman* with you." He decided to keep the bubble bath and massage plans to himself.

Denise smiled weakly. "I'm sorry, but dinner is out. I have an appointment this evening." She wasn't ready to tell him about her date with Jenny Craig. "It'll probably be too late to watch a movie when I return; maybe another night." She stood to leave. "I'd better get going. I have a busy afternoon."

He stood and followed her out of the restaurant. Outside, Bryce attempted to kiss her lips, but Denise offered her cheek instead. Feeling rejected, Bryce somberly walked back to his vehicle and removed his clergy collar.

"What's this?" Bryce asked, relieving the boxes from her arms.

Denise couldn't keep her planned metamorphosis a secret any longer, but she didn't have to reveal everything just yet. She threw her purse and keys onto the kitchen counter. "There are more boxes and bags in the car," she called over her shoulder, before heading back to the garage.

Bryce followed her, repeating his original question.

"After my meeting, I picked up a few things," she finally answered after dropping the last bag on the floor.

"*A few things?*" Bryce raised an eyebrow and surveyed the now cluttered counters and floor.

"Yeah, I'm starting a weight loss program." She shrugged her shoulders nonchalantly. "I have enough food here for the first month buried in these boxes. Over there," she gestured toward the heap of retail bags that cluttered the floor. "That's my new workout wardrobe."

Bryce stopped unpacking fresh produce, and leaning back against the refrigerator with his arms folded asked, "Why do you want to lose weight, and how much do you plan on losing?"

Enough to make you stop looking at naked women and playing with yourself, is what she wanted to say, but what she verbalized was manufactured and well rehearsed. "I'll be thirty in a few months and I want to be in shape before we have kids," she answered over her shoulder as she stocked the freezer with pre-packaged meals.

The joy ignited by her answer overshadowed the guilt and shame Bryce carried from the activity he had indulged in that afternoon after Denise's rejection at lunch. Her mention of children was a clear indication that she planned to stay committed to their marriage.

Knowing at the precise moment her husband was smiling, Denise resisted the urge to turn around. She hadn't completely bought into the idea that her job was to cover her husband's sin. While arranging her nutritional snacks on the counter, Denise had to remind herself that pornography was part of Bryce's past. "Or is it?" she wondered out loud. She could no longer ignore the gnawing feeling in her gut, the darkness she'd felt the second she entered Bryce's presence.

"Bryce, did you look at pornography today?" she whirled around and asked without warning. He appeared taken aback by the question.

"What?"

"You heard me. Did you look at pornography today?"

Bryce raised his voice and threw his hands up in an effort to sound convincing. "Why would you ask me that? You saw me burn all those magazines last night."

Denise started to apologize, but her intuition wouldn't allow her. "Bryce, did you play with yourself today or not?" Bryce hesitated too long. "How could you? You promised me."

Denise paused to wipe the tears that instantly pooled her eyes, with the back of her hand.

"I didn't mean to, but you brushed me off and I . . . I don't know what happened after that." Bryce shrugged his shoulders in resignation.

Denise turned her back to him, leaning on the counter for support and continued talking, barely audible. "You promised . . . you made love to me . . . you said things . . . you didn't mean it . . . you lied to me."

With the sanguinity that fueled her only moments before gone, Denise drearily stepped from the kitchen.

"Where are you going?" he called after her.

"I'm going to my new room and do what a good Christian wife should do; I'm going to pray."

Chapter 6

Denise made one last check of her daily meal schedule before zipping the insulated cooler she'd purchased on her shopping spree. The cooler was heavy, loaded with bottles of water, three pre-packaged meals, salad, fruit, and two snacks. The gym bag she threw over her shoulder was just as weighted with walking shoes, ankle and arm weights, a jogging suit and pedometer. She had a plan.

Denise vowed to follow the weight loss plan, and to increase the results, she created her own exercise regiment. She would workout everyday in addition to walking around Lake Merritt on her lunch break and the San Leandro Marina trail in the evenings. Last night, after loading her car with low-calorie and probably tasteless food, she made an impromptu visit to the mall.

There she purchased exercise wear, resistance balls and band, and a membership at the 24-hour gym. She was on a mission: transform into a size 10 by the end of summer. Dropping three sizes in six months was ambitious, maybe unrealistic, but what choice did she have? Bryce had already demonstrated her body wasn't appealing enough to hold his attention for twenty-four hours.

"Let me help you with that." Denise hadn't seen him standing under the archway in the silk pajama set she'd given him for Christmas. Her first thought was to refuse assistance, but Bryce snatched the bags before she voiced her objections. After securing them in the trunk of the Lexus, she expected him to disappear, but he didn't.

"Baby, we need to talk," he said, blocking the driver's side door with his body. "I'm sorry about yesterday, it won't—"

Denise cut him off. "Don't say that. Don't lie to me. Tell the truth. You had a need I couldn't fill." Determined not to cry, she inhaled and exhaled deeply. "I have to go. I have a busy day at the office."

Bryce pressed her to his chest and held her tightly. "Baby, I don't want to be the cause of your tears. I don't want you to run from me," he whispered in her ear.

She raised her head, hoping to convey how deeply her wounds ran. "Then stop piercing my heart. Stop cheating and expecting me to understand. You're a man of God; a man of the cloth. If you don't love me enough, think about the flock you shepherd over."

"I do love you, don't ever doubt that." The words fell on closed ears. "I'm trying to beat this, but I need more time."

Denise treated him to sarcasm. "You're the man; take all the time you need. What do I care if you play with yourself everyday?"

Bryce's jaw flexed rapidly and his nostrils flared as he slowly backed away from her. Denise took the opportunity to quickly jump into the vehicle and secure her seatbelt. After pressing the garage door opener, she backed out and sped away without giving her husband a second glance.

For the second time in as many days, Bryce found himself standing before the fireplace burning pornography. To save his life, Bryce couldn't explain how he had fallen the day before. All he remembers after Denise's rejection are the forbidden acts he performed in his car while parked at Point Richmond. He couldn't even recall driving to the adult store ten miles away, which he frequented.

With his mouth he recited the same prayer he'd been praying since the day his dark sin was brought to the light. "Father, forgive me for my sin. Help me to walk worthy before the people you've placed me over. Help Denise to understand. Heal her heart and give her patience as I work through this."

What about your heart; is it healed?

The audible voice startled Bryce to the point he turned around expecting to find someone standing in the room with him. Frantic eyes scanned the den, confirming that he was alone. No other human was present, but Bryce knew beyond doubt the presence of God was there and he didn't have an answer to the question being asked. Bryce fell to his knees in reverence, weeping like a baby to avoid dealing with the truth. He was still sitting on the floor when the doorbell sounded an hour later.

"Hello, neighbor." Up close the strange man looked much younger. Bryce had guessed the man to be in his 70s, but now standing face to face, he placed the man no older than 60 and he appeared to be wearing the same jogging suit as the day before.

"Hello," Bryce answered in his preacher's voice. "What can I do for you?"

He stared at Bryce for a long hard moment before replying, "I was in the neighborhood." The older gentleman laughed at his own pun, not offended by Bryce's stone-faced stare. "Like I was saying, thought I'd stop by and see if you need my help. I have a lot of free time on my hands since selling my business and retiring."

Not exactly sure of what services were being offered,

Bryce respectfully declined. "Thank you, but I don't need anything."

"Son, you do need my help and you need it now." He let those words sink in before continuing. "Unless you have a gardener, and if you do, I suggest you fire him."

"I don't have a gardener." Bryce wondered where all this was going. "I take care of the yard myself." Bryce placed his hand on the doorknob. He didn't know who this man was and he wanted him to leave. "Look Mr.—"

The senior cut him off. "Let me properly introduce myself. My name is Bernard Johnson, retired horticulturist. You can call me Benny like everyone else does." Bryce reluctantly accepted his extended hand. He wasn't prepared for what happened next.

Benny placed his hand on Bryce's shoulder before speaking. The father's touch—at least that's what Bryce assumed it was—unnerved him. The simple affectionate contact was firm and caring; corrective, yet reassuring.

"Your job as pastor doesn't allow you time to tend to the yard properly. I bet you haven't planted spring bulbs yet?"

Bryce look perplexed, "Huh? Bulbs? I didn't know light bulbs could be planted."

Thunderous laughter poured from Benny, but Bryce was still confused. "Just as I thought; you don't have a clue. Whoever heard of such a thing as planting light bulbs?"

Bryce joined in with the laughter. He didn't like being the subject of stupidity, but detected Benny didn't mean any harm.

Benny abruptly stopped laughing and looked Bryce dead in the eye. The jovial voice was replaced by an authoritative tone that didn't allow for debate. "Don't worry, I'm here to help you." He paused to let the words settle. "Come spring, you'll have the nicest yard, outside of mine, in the entire subdivision. I'll even plant you a vegetable garden in the back. Come on, I'll show you."

He didn't know why, but Bryce decided right then that he liked his peculiar neighbor. Bryce obeyed by following Benny around the front yard and trying to envision the ideas Benny saw in his head. Benny was correct in his assessment; Bryce didn't know anything about yard upkeep outside of watering, and he couldn't even remember to do that on a regular basis.

"Mr. Benny, this all sounds fantastic." He was actually smiling. Denise mentioned upgrading from the one sparse rose bush; this would make her happy. "Let me go inside and get my checkbook."

Benny grabbed Bryce's shoulder and stopped him. Benny the authoritarian was back. "Son, don't worry about your checkbook. Continue studying the Word of God and stay on your knees in prayer so you can obey the Lord when He speaks to you." With that, Benny turned and started down the brick walkway, then paused. "You might want to tell your wife. I work with the sunrise; wouldn't want to frighten her."

"Mr. Benny, how did you know I'm a pastor?"

"The Lord told me," Benny answered, but continued walking.

For the second time, Bryce watched the grey jogging suit until it disappeared around the corner. He still considered his new friend strange, but also wondered what else the Lord had revealed to the man.

"Father, please give me the strength to make it through this." After mumbling the prayer, Denise took a swig from her water bottle. Looking down, she frowned.

Bryce wouldn't be happy with her attire. He warned her constantly against dressing so casually in front of the congregation. "You represent me," is what he drilled into her. Tonight she didn't care what he thought of her nylon warm-ups and Nikes.

The two-mile walk around the Marina took longer than

she anticipated, leaving her with not enough time to change and make it to Bible Study on time. Bryce would just have to deal with it the same way she'd been forced to deal with his extra-curricular activity. After taking another swig of water, Denise plastered on her 'church face', and entered the sanctuary and began making her way to her front row seat.

Pastor Hightower's displeasure was evident when he didn't return the fake smile she offered him. At the last second, Denise decided to test her husband's tolerance level. Instead of using the side aisle, First Lady Hightower sauntered down the center aisle, stopping every few steps to wave at and greet congregants.

Finally reaching her reserved seat, Denise slowly finished her water bottle then sat down. Pastor Hightower opened his Bible and began his lesson without acknowledging his wife.

Denise felt Lucinda's hot gaze from across the aisle. She also heard the snide comments from several females who, from the beginning, thought she wasn't first lady material. Leaning back in the padded chair, Denise didn't care what Bryce, her mother, or the members of Word of Life thought of her. Right now, her feet hurt and her leg muscles had begun to stiffen. To make matters worse, she'd finished her daily food allotment and was still hungry.

"Baby, how are you doing?" The benediction had barely been given when Mother Gray approached. Denise produced her church smile, but this time she didn't resist Mother Gray's hug.

"I'm blessed."

"I didn't ask if you are blessed. I asked how you are doing. How is your mind holding up?"

Denise wasn't prepared to respond to a direct question about her state of mind. She refused to lie, so she didn't say anything with her mouth. The tears that welled in her eyes spoke the words her voice held hostage. She didn't know how to verbalize the inadequacies she now felt as a woman.

Mother Gray offered Denise a tissue. "I don't know what you're going through, but hold on. God will work it out."

"Sweetheart, how was your workout?" Neither Mother Gray nor Denise saw Pastor Hightower walk up.

"Good," Denise answered, at the same time wiping her eyes. She wasn't fooled; Pastor Hightower asked the question not because he was concerned, but as a way of justifying her attire to Mother Gray who couldn't have cared less.

"I enjoyed you tonight, Pastor. God bless you." Mother Gray shook her pastor's hand and left, leaving Bryce guessing at their conversation.

Denise read his thoughts. "Don't worry, I didn't say anything." He was about to thank her, but Lucinda interrupted.

"Pastor, do you mind if Denise stops by my house for a few minutes?" Lucinda was smiling but Denise knew the conversation would be anything but pleasant. Bryce readily agreed, appreciating the ally he had in his mother-in-law.

"I'll see you at home." He kissed his wife's cheek then proceeded to greet waiting parishioners.

"What is your problem?" Lucinda asked for the third time without receiving an answer. "Didn't you hear anything I said to you the other day?"

Seated at her mother's kitchen table eyeing the sweet potato pie only inches away, Denise rested her chin on her fist.

"What is going on with you? That open display of disrespect you put on tonight was too much and totally uncalled for." Lucinda paused. "If you're not careful, you're going to run a good man away."

The tears began to flow before Denise could stop them. The tremors and sobs followed shortly after.

"What is it, baby?" Lucinda softened, finally seeing the depth of her daughter's pain. She walked around the table and embraced her.

For once, Denise heard the voice of the mother who loved and supported her; the woman who had given birth to her and nurtured her. The woman who would sacrifice her life for her daughter. Denise let down her wall and opened up. "He committed adultery." she managed between sobs.

Lucinda was stunned by her daughter's revelation of the son-in-law and pastor she loved. "How can that be?

"He was cheating before we got married," Denise continued, "but I didn't discover it until recently."

Lucinda refused to believe it. "How do you know?"

"I caught him." Denise broke down again and Lucinda comforted her before continuing.

"Did you see this with your own eyes or are you assuming he's cheating? The imagination is a powerful thing."

Denise lifted her head from her mother's shoulder. "I caught him red-handed, gratifying himself with the help of a porn magazine." To Denise's surprise, her mother laughed as if what she'd just revealed was some kind of joke.

"Is that what this is all about?" Lucinda questioned. "Pornography?"

Denise didn't respond; she'd been thrown off balance by her mother's passiveness.

"Baby, if that's the case, you need to go home to your husband and apologize for all this drama."

Denise gasped, "Mama!"

"Look, Denise, I could understand if Bryce was sleeping around, but he's only looking at pictures. A lot of men do that. It's their pastime, like baseball and apple pie."

"But he's a man of God!"

Lucinda smirked. "Baby, being a man of God doesn't stop him from being human first. Sexual sins and preachers are almost synonymous."

Denise wasn't buying it. "But Mama, he's looking at women and doing things in his mind with them that he should be doing with me."

Lucinda tried another approach. "Baby, Bryce is a man and a man has needs. Would you rather he actually sleep with other women?"

Denise snatched away from her mother. "I would rather have him come to me to fulfill his needs. I would rather have my husband's mind filled with thoughts of me and not strangers!" With every word, Denise grew angrier at her mother. "Mama, how could you think that? How would you feel if Daddy had given his mind to some strange naked woman?"

Lucinda blinked quickly and turned her head away. Five years after his death, it was still hard for her to hear him spoken of in the past tense.

"How would you feel if Daddy was making love to you, but thinking about some woman on the page of a magazine that doesn't even know he's alive? How would you feel if Daddy used you as a substitute for the women he couldn't have?"

"I know how you feel, but it's not as bad as you think," Lucinda said once she composed herself enough to face her daughter.

"Mama, you can't possibility know how I feel." Denise shook her head. "You and Daddy had a wonderful relationship. Daddy adored you."

Lucinda closed her eyes, exhaling and inhaling deeply. She had to make her daughter understand. "We did have a wonderful relationship. Your father was a devoted deacon in the church and a great provider. He was my best friend and my only lover. Your father was an excellent husband and father. But, he was also a charter member of *Playboy's* fan club and every other dirty magazine."

"What?" Denise was flabbergasted by the last part of her mother's statement.

Jeremiah Sanders was the most loving man she'd ever known; always handling her with extreme care. Towering over six feet tall, Denise saw her father as a pillar of integrity and strength. Head Deacon Sanders was an excellent student of the Word and was a Prayer Warrior, long before the term became popular.

"How can you say something so horrible about Daddy?" Denise's brown eyes pleaded with her mother to tell her she'd made a mistake, that she hadn't meant to tell her an untruth about her beloved late father. "Daddy loved us and you know it!"

Lucinda nodded. "Yes, your father loved us, but he also enjoyed his "playtime." That's what he called it."

"Mama, I don't believe you!" Denise stepped away from her mother, not wanting to be near the woman who'd just tarnished the golden image she had of her father. "Daddy was saved; he went to church three times a week."

"Baby, I wouldn't lie to you." Lucinda reached for her daughter, but Denise took another step back. "Do you remember the boxes that used to be stacked in the front left corner of the basement?"

"Of course I do. That's where Daddy kept his important papers." As she said those words, Denise wondered why her father would keep important papers in the basement where the chance of water damage was probable.

"Those important papers were his magazines he brought home every other week. I told him I didn't want to see them, so that's where he kept them."

For the second time in one week, Denise's heart was broken by a man she loved. Denise fell to her knees, weeping like a baby. "Mama, how could he do this to us, to you? How could you let him get away with it?"

Lucinda responded by placing her arm around her daughter. "I didn't let him get away with anything, but I couldn't stop him either. I couldn't stop your father from doing something he really wanted to do."

"But didn't you hate him for it? Didn't you think it was cheating?" Denise inquired.

"I didn't see it that way. I didn't like what he was doing, but at the end of the day, Jeremiah Sanders came home to me. For thirty years, he came home to me, not to one of those loose women on them pages."

"But he did, Mama; he kept the other woman in the basement!"

Denise's revelation hit Lucinda in a place she didn't want touched. "Look, Denise, I did what a good wife is supposed to do, I prayed for my husband. That's exactly what you need to do; go home to your husband and pray for him until he gets delivered."

Denise maneuvered herself upright; she hated it when church folks, especially her mother, tried to hide everything behind prayer. If Lucinda was purposefully tripped or kicked by a sister, she would pray about it instead of calling the sister on it. There wasn't any doubt in Denise's mind; Lucinda did more praying than talking to her husband about his habit.

"Bryce is the head of the home, Mama. If I'm praying for him, then who's covering and praying for me?" Lucinda didn't answer. "Tell me, Mama, if I was spending all my time lusting after some strange man, do you think Bryce would just stay there and *pray* for me? He gets jealous when I comment on Morris Chestnut."

"All I'm saying is you can't leave him. You have to stay there until he's healed."

Denise threw her hands in the air. She had to get out of there before she really said something to hurt her mother. "Did Daddy ever get healed?" Denise didn't wait for an answer. "Of course not. Those boxes were in the basement the day he died. I thought it was strange how you opted to burn the contents." Denise stopped and faced her mother, never removing her hand from the doorknob. "Mama, I'm not you. I can't spend thirty years of my life playing understudy to a photograph and an imagination. If I can't have Bryce exclusively, I won't have him at all. I deserve to be the only woman in my husband's life. There's no amount of praying that will change how I feel." Denise slammed the door so hard, the *Praying Hands picture* near the door, fell off the hook.

"Denise, wait!"

Alone in her car, the tears flowed again, but for a different reason. A cloud of hopelessness, mingled with depression, rained violently over her, drenching her spirit. Jeremiah Sanders was the strongest man she knew, and he couldn't stop the wiles of pornography. What chance did her husband have? Maybe her mother was right; being ensnared with sexual sin came with the territory of being a man of God. The Father obviously didn't mind; He continued to anoint Bryce to preach. Maybe she was over-reacting. Maybe she should calm down and conform to the 'man's world' ideology. "Maybe this is as good as it gets," Denise mumbled, pulling into the garage.

Once inside the house, she shivered. The place she called home didn't feel like home anymore. The building still stood, but the foundation had been shattered; respect and trust were gone.

Dragging her gym bag and briefcase behind her into the spare bedroom, she pondered her next move. It didn't take long for her to accept the fact that she was stuck in a hopeless situation. Like her mother, Denise couldn't control her husband; neither could she make him stop. After seventeen years, the addiction had become part of who he was. If

God allows him to continue in his mess, what was she supposed to do?

Denise mechanically began removing her clothes from the drawers then walked down the hall.

Bryce sat straight up on the king-sized bed when she entered the room. Denise didn't stop, but continued to the mahogany bureau she loved so much and placed her clothes inside. She didn't bother asking what magazine he was looking at; it didn't matter anymore.

Upon realizing what was happening, Bryce got up and helped her move back into their bedroom, all the while talking about things Denise's mind was too cluttered to comprehend. She vaguely heard the words neighbor and yard, but couldn't figure how the two were related.

Her extended shower afforded Bryce the opportunity to thank God for restoring his marriage. His joy was somewhat deflated when Denise climbed into bed and scooted to the edge. He moved next to her, resting his arm around her waist.

"Niecy, thank you for sticking this out with me," he whispered in her ear.

Denise didn't have any words for her pastor and husband, just her silent tears falling against his arm.

Chapter 7

The best part of the grueling weight-loss program Denise subjected herself to was her Saturday morning walks around the Marina. Unlike the rushed weekday evenings when the trail consisted of mostly business people racing against the sunset to get at least one mile in, Saturday was leisurely and relaxed. Almost like a social gathering, full of regulars, some Denise had come to know by name.

With the San Leandro Marina pouring into the bay, the panoramic views of the great Pacific Ocean in the backdrop were breathtaking. On sunny days, the blue sky and clear blue water blended so well. It was sometimes difficult to tell where one ended and the other began. All along the mile trail, groups of nature lovers would line up and watch the huge, but gentle, waves crash against the rocks or take photos of the big Boeing 747's landing and taking off from the Oakland Airport, which sat less than a quarter mile away.

Every ten yards or so were exercise stations and apparatuses complete with billboards containing detailed instructions, based on individual levels of fitness. Leg lifts and stomach crunches weren't so difficult when accompanied with cheers from groups of strangers and well-wishers. Nature lovers and exercise fanatics weren't the only creatures that enjoyed the trail. At any given time, just as many squirrels as humans darted around the trial. This morning, the squirrels outnumbered the humans probably due to the dark clouds that loomed out over the ocean.

"I'd better hurry," Denise mumbled, adjusting her fanny pack. After a brief stretch session, she gripped her water bottle and started down the trail. In no time, she'd reached her pace.

Only six weeks into her body makeover and already she could see results. She'd lost fifteen pounds, her clothes were fitting looser and she had more energy. Denise had gotten use to the pre-packaged meals too. Erin downplayed her progress by saying it was probably just water weight, but Denise was satisfied.

"Erin, you wouldn't understand. You're already small," is what she told her friend after her constant nagging about Denise's reasons for wanting to lose weight.

"You're already married to a man who likes *all that.*" Erin used her hands to demonstrate the vastness of Denise's body.

Denise didn't respond to her friend's assumption. How could she say, 'I'm losing weight so I can compete with my husband's paper mistresses,' without sounding like a fool? She couldn't, so she said nothing.

Rounding the first curve, as always, her mind wandered to her husband-pastor. When Denise first began taking these walks, she prayed for him to change. After learning of her father's addiction, she stopped. Figuring, what's the use; it is a man's world. In Pastor Hightower's world everything was perfect.

At church they were the ideal pastor and wife. Denise resumed her 'amen corner' duties with what appeared to be joy. She dressed appropriately, and when asked to speak, honored Bryce as if he were a king. The women stopped snickering and Lucinda beamed with pride. At home, Denise didn't question him about his 'activity'; in fact, she rarely addressed him at all.

She spent most of her down time reading or working on projects from work. Bryce found solace in his study. When he wanted sex from her, Denise obliged without participating and with the lights off. She'd lay there until he finished, then tip to the bathroom to camouflage her sobs underneath the shower head.

Denise stopped at the exercise station and positioned her body flat against the support beam. After gripping the side bars, she closed her eyes, inhaled, and pressed her legs to her chest. During the third repetition she heard her name.

"Denise?"

Denise opened her eyes to find a familiar face staring down at her. If her legs weren't in mid-air revealing her expansive behind, she would have been happy to see him. Instead, she was embarrassed. "Jonas?"

"I thought that was you," he smiled. "How is my favorite budget director?"

"What are you doing here?" she asked, returning to the upright position.

"From the looks of things, the same thing you are." Jonas assisted her to her feet. He studied her closely. "Are you losing weight?"

Denise's face flushed with embarrassment. Jonas was the first person to acknowledge the weight loss without her having to point it out. She relegated her accomplishment. "I haven't lost much; just fifteen pounds. I have a *very long* way to go." She then resumed walking; he joined her pace.

"That's wonderful, you should be proud."

"Thanks. I am," she admitted, bracing for the next incline.

They walked in awkward silence. Denise found conversation with Jonas outside of work difficult. "Jonas, what are you doing out here? Shouldn't you be getting ready for your big date?" she smiled.

Jonas looked perplexed. "Huh?"

"Come on, Jonas; don't down play spending an evening with a beautiful woman just because I'm her pastor's wife and she's my friend." His face softened. "Just keep the evening holy," she warned with a raised eyebrow.

"You have nothing to worry about, First Lady. As I told you before, Erin is not my type."

Now Denise was confused. "Then why did you invite her on a date?"

"I didn't," he answered frankly, reaching for the chin-up bar at the next exercise station.

Denise positioned herself and reached for a lower bar. "I don't understand."

"Denise, your friend has been hounding me for weeks. Calling the hospital, leaving messages on my car windshield, and I don't know how she obtained my home address. Then again, you know lawyers. I agreed to one date with the promise that after this she'd back off. Erin is under the impression that one date with her will change my mind about lawyers."

Denise completed the set in silence. Erin conveniently omitted the details leading up to what she called her date with destiny. As outrageous as Erin's behavior was, it really didn't surprise Denise. Erin had always been aggressive. The day they met at Fresno State, Erin was arguing with the dorm director over the curfew rules. Erin told the middle-aged African-American woman in no uncertain terms that she was an adult who didn't need rules. If she wanted to be treated like a child, she would return home to her mother. The dorm director agreed with Erin and had her removed from the dorm. It took three days of sleeping in her car for Erin to apologize and beg for another chance.

"Jonas, I'm sorry for my friend's behavior," Denise said once they resumed the trail. "But could you answer something for me?" he nodded. "Aside from her being a lawyer, why aren't you attracted to her? I mean, she's gorgeous and accomplished."

Jonas didn't hold back. "Erin is gorgeous, but by whose standards? Personally, I prefer women with more substance." He touched her shoulder. "Don't take this the wrong way, *Mrs. Hightower*, but I consider you the perfect size just the way you are." Denise tripped at that statement; Jonas steadied her with his arm. "Don't worry." He winked. "Pastor Hightower has nothing to worry about. I am a ladies man, but not a married ladies man."

Firm on her feet again, Denise shared a nervous laugh with what appeared to be her new exercise buddy. Inside, she worried about Erin's impending disappointment.

With the end in view she asked, "Jonas, do you come here often?"

"Four times a week, usually in the early mornings."

"Maybe we'll meet again; if not here, in my office for sure."

"I guess that's my cue to leave," he said, zipping up his fleece.

"Oh, no—"

"Don't fret over it." He was smiling. "I have two miles to run anyway."

"I'm sorry, did I hold you up?"

"I enjoyed the company. See you around."

Denise watched him sprint across the grass and take off in the opposite direction. It wasn't until the cold air fanned her teeth did she realize she was smiling.

"Mr. Benny, it looks great out here," Bryce commented from the porch.

In the six weeks his neighbor had been working for him,

Bryce learned two important things about Bernard Johnson. One, don't interfere with his work, and two, Benny loved to talk. Bryce thought Benny had the DNA of a preacher the way he had three points with supporting evidence to every story.

The first day, Bryce made the mistake of asking Benny about the soil. By the time Benny answered his question, Bryce not only knew the three basic types, but how it was formed and the details of its composition. That day, walking back to the house with a major headache, Bryce vowed never to ask Benny anything he really didn't want the answer to.

Benny beamed with pride before responding to his young neighbor. Even retired and after 40 years in the business, Benny reveled in his customer's satisfaction. "Son, you haven't seen anything yet; wait until the rainbow of poppies, calendulas, and ranunculas blossom. The irises and daffodils will be fabulous."

Bryce leaned against the brick pillar that supported his front porch and folded his arms. He prayed the new yard and garden would make Denise happy. Lately, the only time Denise displayed any sign of happiness was on her way out the door to work or to the Marina. She didn't hold conversation with him unless it was absolutely necessary, and even then her answers were short. Church was the only place Denise responded to him without contempt. What he viewed as her wifely duties had all but ceased with her spending more time away from home than at home.

To his knowledge, the congregation was clueless to the dysfunctions behind closed doors.

Thanks to Denise's weight-loss program, home cooked meals were nothing more than a distant memory unless he stopped by his mother-in-law's house. His vocabulary didn't contain an adjective to adequately describe what their sex life had dwindled to. Denise's physical body was present, but void of emotion. The only movement from her was the trip to the bathroom afterwards. At first, Bryce was understanding, but after a few tries, he used his imagination to soar to the heights his wife refused to take him to, justifying the guilt that followed on her non-responsiveness.

Bryce sighed louder than he realized. Mr. Benny walked over and laid the trowel on the bottom step.

"Son, what's on your mind?" Benny asked, removing his gloves.

Bryce shifted his weight from one foot to the other, debating the best way to answer without falling into a long conversation with Benny. He hesitated too long.

"It's your wife, isn't it?"

Bryce's mouth gaped, confirming Benny's guess. Benny slapped him on the shoulder to reassure him. "Don't worry, son, I'm not going to tell anyone the pastor can't keep his wife happy."

Bryce brushed Benny's hand away, "Now wait a minute; my wife's happiness is my business, not yours!"

Benny's suggestion that he couldn't keep his wife happy irked Bryce, but that loud laughter that erupted from his gardener infuriated him.

"You're right; it is your business and you manage the business with your wife like you manage this yard; haphazardly and ignorantly. It's no wonder your wife walks around here sad and depressed all the time."

Bryce felt his jaw flinch and his hands ball into fists. If Benny had been younger, Bryce would have punched him. But Bernard Johnson wasn't younger; he was an older man who saw right through him. The words spoken by Benny, the truth, seared Bryce's conscience faster than an iron. Bryce couldn't hit him, but he could get rid of him. "Mr. Benny, your services are no longer needed!"

Benny was still laughing when Bryce stormed into the

house. Benny bowed his head briefly before picking up his tool and starting down the walkway.

Bryce returned with checkbook and pen in hand. "How much do I owe you?" he barked.

Benny paused just long enough to shake his head at what he considered juvenile behavior, then retraced his steps. "Son, did I tell you I was once married?"

Bryce expected a direct answer, not an irrelevant question. "No, and I don't want to hear about it!" The harshness in his voice was uncharacteristic, but Bryce didn't apologize or back down.

"Hear about what?" Benny asked as if he didn't understand.

Bryce's patience ran out when Benny accurately analyzed his marriage. Whatever happened or didn't happen in Bernard Johnson's life was of no concern to him. "Your marriage!" Bryce yelled.

Benny smiled, "Well since you asked, I'll tell you." He then placed his tool on the porch and after downing half of his water bottle, sat down on the steps, totally ignoring Bryce's attitude.

"Mr. Benny, I'm warning you. I will—"

"I was married to a great woman named Loretta," he said, looking up at Bryce. "She was the best; devoted to me and one of the best cooks this side of Texas. We married at age nineteen with ambitious dreams of starting a business and raising a family." Bryce exhaled loudly but didn't interrupt. "Loretta didn't complain. She worked right alongside me, slinging a hoe and rake, then after feeding me a meal fit for God Himself, she would allow me to make love to her like Armageddon." Benny paused and enjoyed the memories with a smile pasted across his face. "Loretta didn't ask for much, but the one thing she did ask for I failed to give it to her and that destroyed us."

Knowing he'd probably regret asking, Bryce inquired anyway. "What was it?"

Benny slapped Bryce's leg with his glove. "I knew you'd be interested."

Bryce smirked and shook his head in anticipation for the answer.

"Like I said, we married at nineteen. I loved her and thought I was ready to be a husband to her, but unfortunately for the both of us, I didn't know what being a husband meant. I thought a husband meant paying bills and providing. It's so much more than that." Benny paused. "Now, don't look down on me, pastor, but at the time I didn't know God; hadn't accepted His love. Although I loved Loretta, I didn't love myself. In turn, the love I offered her was tainted and painful." Benny looked up at Bryce who appeared to be in deep thought. "The one thing Loretta asked for, no, begged for, was *me*."

"I don't understand," Bryce asked, now squatting down next to him. "You married her; she had you."

Benny smirked. "You're right, Loretta had me and I had nearly every female in Kern County."

"What?"

"Believe it or not, I cheated so much I'd forget whose bed I was in." Benny stifled a grin. "I got Dorothy mixed up with Ada, and Corrine confused with Nadine. I stopped addressing women by their first names and labeled everyone as 'baby'."

"Well, I'll be," Bryce said, slapping his knee. "I would have never guessed you were a—"

"Cheat?"

Bryce shrugged his shoulders in agreement.

"Four years into the marriage, Loretta got tired of me spreading myself like jelly with the population and left me. I begged and behaved until I convinced her to come back, but that didn't last long because I still had that ivy. She divorced me after only six years of marriage. I believe she tolerated my foolishness for as long as she did because she was saved."

"Ivy? Huh?"

"I'll tell you about the ivy later. The bottom line is, I ran a good woman away. I was too selfish and too concerned with my agenda to see the pain I caused her every time I laid with another woman. Yet, I expected her to be available to me whenever I wanted. I looked the other way, knowing that every time I found pleasure with a strange woman, a piece of Loretta died. Good thing she had enough sense to leave me before I demolished all of her self-esteem."

While pondering Benny's words, Bryce gently massaged the ache that suddenly gripped his chest. "What happened to her?"

"She's married to a preacher and they've got five children. Go figure; six years I tried to give her a baby and nothing." He leaned close to Bryce as if revealing a secret. "I know your wife doesn't, but do you have any kids running around?"

Bryce rose to his feet, waving his hands. "No, no."

"I have three girls by three different women. If Maury Povich was around back in my day, I'm sure I'd have some more," Bryce chuckled. "I love my girls; can't say the same about their mamas."

Bryce inattentively listened as Benny bragged about his daughters. Two were teachers and the other a nurse. Bryce wanted to ask him how was a man to know when he's about to run his wife away. How does a man stop placing his needs before his wife? How does a man learn to love himself? He had so many questions; questions he would have asked his father if he were alive.

His hard gaze traced Benny from head to toe. Could this strange, nosey, pushy, peculiar man be the answer to his prayers? Benny had been down the dark road and wasn't afraid to light the way for the next guy. Could this be the one person he could reveal his charred inner self to? Bryce pondered too long. Denise pulled into the driveway before he could make up his mind.

"Son, I'm going to get back to work." Benny rose to his feet. "I'll tell you about the ivy later. You need to figure out how to put a smile on your wife's face, and I don't mean in the bedroom. Any pair of pants can do that, but it takes a real man to keep his wife happy once she's upright."

Bryce grinned, watching Benny as he strutted away with a new level of respect. Never before had Bryce seen a man so transparent and yet proud. "And to think I was going to fire him," he grumbled, looking down at his checkbook.

Bryce rubbed the spot where Benny slapped his shoulder, trying to recall his own father's touch; he couldn't. It was then that Bryce realized Benny's preferred name for him was *son.* Bryce doubted if the man knew his name.

Walking over to assist Denise with more pre-packaged meal boxes from her trunk, Bryce watched as his wife treated the gardener with a smile. Benny explained his plans to her, and Denise shrieked with excitement, rewarding him with a big hug. Instantly, Bryce became jealous; his wife hadn't smiled or grinned at him outside of church in weeks.

He had to clear his throat twice before they released the embrace. Even then, Denise didn't address him, just pointed to the trunk where the boxes were. "Mr. Benny, I love what you've done," she said, resuming the conversation as though Bryce weren't present.

"When you get time, I'll show you the vegetable garden." Benny winked.

"I have plenty of time." Denise interlocked her arm with his and the two left Bryce standing alone in the driveway.

Thirty minutes later, Denise skipped into the kitchen ready to restock her prepackaged meals and prepare a salad for lunch. She came to an abrupt stop when she rounded the island and found her husband seated at the kitchen table.

Bryce had not only stored her boxed meals inside the freezer, but had also prepared them each a salad.

Denise was tongue-tied as she racked her brain for sufficient words. 'Thank you' would have been appropriate if this morning she hadn't discovered the magazine concealed behind their wedding portrait. The deed wasn't fueled by his supposed love for her, but guilt. She wasn't going to reward him with appreciation.

"You didn't have to do this; I could have stored the food and prepared my salad," she finally responded, after washing and drying her hands.

He motioned for her to sit. "I know I didn't, but I wanted to."

"Really?" She rolled her eyes, which was totally out of her character. Denise considered neck and eye-rolling distasteful and juvenile. "I thought the only person you cared about is yourself. You know; what you want, how you look," she said, placing the napkin in her lap.

As it had done so many times over the last six weeks, bitterness hung in the silence that followed. Bryce watched, tight-lipped as she said grace and began eating as if he wasn't in the room. *Is this how it starts?* Bryce considered in reference to a man losing his wife. True, Denise kept physical residence with him, but apparently her emotions lived elsewhere. At first he thought that was enough; that he could handle the posturing, but after hearing Benny's saga, the realization that he may end up alone sobered him. He could no longer sit back and wait for God to 'fix' him; Bryce needed to put in some work.

Denise attempted to block her husband's presence completely from her mind by focusing on the kitchen she once spent so many hours in. It had been her place of solace. Every detail had been hand picked by her. That was Bryce's wedding present to her; a house decorated to her specifications. The country sized eat-in kitchen, which was rare in the Bay Area, was where she'd spent the most money customizing everything; pecan-colored oak cabinets, mauve granite countertops, double stainless steel refrigerator, double ovens, granite floor, and a center island with a sink. It all seemed foreign to her now.

"The weight loss is progressing well. You look good, but then you've always been beautiful to me." Bryce spoke the words at the same time a cherry tomato exploded in her mouth. Denise slowed her chewing and raised her head.

"Is that so?" she asked after washing the tomato down with Crystal Light.

With hunched shoulders, Bryce lifted the glass to his lips. "I don't think you need to lose weight, but if that's what you want."

Denise cut to the chase. "Bryce, if you want sex, then say so, but don't sit in my face and lie to me." She then continued eating.

Exasperated, Bryce slammed his fork down, "I don't want sex; at least not the way you're giving it! I was trying to pay you a compliment!"

What he meant to be insulting, Denise laughed at. She laughed so hard tears rolled down her cheek, but they weren't tears of joy from comic relief. They poured from the hollow empty place that had once housed her spirit. "Of course, you don't want sex from me," she managed between giggles. "I'm sure you get enough of that from the women you keep behind our wedding picture."

Bryce angrily pushed away from the table. "My problem is not funny!"

"You're right, honey," Denise still snickered. "It's very sad for a grown man to play with himself on a regular basis then preach the Word of God." Denise's giggles followed Bryce into their bedroom where he slammed the door.

Chapter 8

"I am so sorry," Denise apologized profusely for almost hitting the elderly Hispanic woman in the crosswalk with her car. She'd been so excited about reaching her 20-pound weight loss mark in nine weeks, that Denise didn't see the red light or the woman creeping along with the aid of a walker, until the very last second. She was too 'caught up' singing "Victory" with Tye Tribbett and GA on the satellite radio. The tires screeched and came to an abrupt stop just inches away.

If the woman was fearful, Denise couldn't tell. Before Denise could get out and assist her, the woman began yelling things she couldn't understand. The woman raised her fist in the air and Denise decided it was best if she remained in her car.

"I am so sorry," she attempted again.

The woman continued yelling until she made it to the other side of the street. There she turned and offered Denise an offensive gesture.

"Great," Denise laughed out loud. "It's not even 9:00 A.M. and I've been cursed out."

Beep! Beep! The blaring horns from behind directed her attention back to the intersection, and Denise crossed just before the green light turned yellow. Just before turning into the company's parking lot, her cell phone sounded for the third time. Like the two previous times, she let the call go to voicemail without checking the Caller ID, figuring it wasn't anyone other than Bryce or her mother. Outside of Erin's occasional call, those were the only two people who called her.

Denise thought to trash the cell phone, but Bryce said as the first lady, she needed to be accessible at all times. What he should have said was, "I need to know where you are so you won't catch me with my pants down."

Denise entered her office suite smiling and greeted her secretary and at the same time, wondered why she hadn't fired her a long time ago. The woman never had anything good to say unless it pertained to company gossip, and sometimes ordered Denise around like she was the employee.

"Good morning, Jennifer."

"What's so good about my morning? I went to bed with David Letterman and woke up to *Good Morning America*."

"At least you had a warm place to sleep and food to eat this morning."

"What good is a warm bed if the house is empty?" Jennifer said, rolling her eyes.

Denise, determined not to allow Jennifer's pessimistic attitude bring her down, retrieved her messages then went to her office without responding. An hour later, in the midst of running reports for her afternoon meetings, her cell phone sounded again. She reluctantly unclipped the phone from her waist and viewed the incoming number. Since she didn't recognize the number, Denise decided to answer the call.

"First lady, I have been calling you all morning," the female said on the other line. "This is Melanie Anderson." Melanie was on the praise dance team and also a newlywed.

"Hello, Melanie," Denise said, using her church voice. "This is a surprise; is everything all right?" The prolonged silence that followed made Denise think the call had dropped. "Melanie?"

"I'm here, First Lady." Another pause. "I need to talk to you."

"Okay," Denise answered slowly, thinking about Melanie. She was an introvert. She kept to herself and only spoke when spoken to or if she had something important to say. If she was calling, something was very wrong. "Do I need to pray now?"

"No, but I'd like to say what I need to say in person." Melanie explained, "It's too hard to say over the phone. Can we meet for lunch? I really need to talk to someone I trust."

The last sentence touched Denise and she regretted her work schedule wouldn't allow her to meet with Melanie today. With back to back board meetings, her afternoon didn't allow for flexibility. "I'm sorry, Melanie, but my afternoon is booked with meetings. Can we meet tomorrow, say one o'clock?" When Melanie didn't immediately respond, Denise suggested meeting over dinner later that evening.

"That won't work; Clay will be home then." Clay was her husband. "Tomorrow will be fine. Where?"

"Across the lake at Fresh Greens."

Melanie agreed, but before disconnecting, Denise said a quick prayer, hoping to put Melanie's mind at ease.

Stopping mid-stride, Denise switched the cell phone to her right ear. "Huh?" Erin was too excited for Denise to understand. The only words she could make out were *date* and *Jonas*. "I'm so sorry," Denise said, assuming Jonas had let Erin down gently.

"My man may not be a pastor, but Chief of Gynecology is not what I would call a consolation prize."

"What?" Denise was more confused, but before she gained clarification, Erin shifted into overdrive. She resumed her evening walk, half listening to Erin rant and rave on and on about Jonas for the last quarter mile. Every twenty steps or so, Denise interjected an "Uh-huh."

Erin, being used to carrying the bulk of conversation, didn't notice Denise's inattentiveness. "So what should I wear?" Erin slowed the tempo to ask.

"When?" Denise asked, walking across the parking lot.

"Weren't you listening to anything I said?" Erin snapped.

Denise fumbled over the right words that wouldn't offend her friend. "You know there's the noise from the airport and . . . and . . . how am I supposed to keep up with your motorized mouth? You talk so fast I need a teleprompter to keep up."

Erin laughed. "Girl, if you weren't the pastor's wife and my friend, I'd hang up on you."

"Whatever. Now tell me again, very slowly."

Unlocking her Lexus, Denise was surprised to learn Jonas had invited Erin to the hospital's annual party at the end of the month.

"Jonas told me to wear white. What does that mean?" Erin inquired.

Denise used her hand to stifle her laughter. Erin was obviously reading more into the invitation. "It means it's a White Linen party. The conglomerate holds one every year as a charity fundraiser. The Chiefs are required to purchase a table for ten. Most give the tickets away to staff."

"This year will be unforgettable with me on his arm," Erin shrieked.

Denise laughed along with her friend but for a different reason. Jonas had left out one important detail. "I'm sure you'll have a good time, but I doubt if Jonas will be there."

"And just how would *you* know where he will and will not be?" Erin said, smacking her lips. Her attitude was lost on Denise.

"When we met on Saturday, Jonas mentioned visiting his kids in San Diego around that time. You do know he has two teen-aged sons?"

Erin lied. "Of course he told me about his children. What he didn't tell me was that the two of you have been seeing one another outside of work." Her voice changed from one of excitement to that of a calculating litigator going in for the kill.

Until then, Denise didn't find it necessary to tell Erin about running into Jonas at the Marina three weeks ago or the subsequent planned exercise sessions. She hadn't told Bryce either. "Jonas jogs the Marina," she answered nonchalantly.

"I didn't know you were that serious about your little weight loss thing that you worked out on Saturdays."

"It's not *little*. I'm down twenty pounds!" Denise hollered.

"Good for you." Erin faked sincerity.

Denise continued boasting about her success, totally oblivious to her friend's discomfort.

"I have to go," Erin abruptly interrupted. Before Denise could say good-bye, Erin had disconnected.

Seated near the window facing Lakeside Avenue in the restaurant overlooking Lake Merritt, Denise thought of a happier time. The four-mile man-made estuary in the heart of Downtown Oakland was a common spot for everyone from joggers to children. Joggers loved it for its ability to build one's endurance. Children flocked to the lake because of Fairyland, a place where fairytales literally came to life. Lake Merritt was special to Denise for a different reason. That's where Bryce had proposed.

During their courtship, they spent countless hours strolling around the lake while holding hands. Sunday afternoons, if Bryce didn't have a preaching engagement, they'd pick up fried chicken meals from Merritt Restaurant and have a picnic. It was on one of those lazy Sunday afternoons that Bryce asked her to be his wife.

Bryce had just spoon fed her the last of the potato salad. Wiping the corner of her mouth with his thumb he asked, "Niecy, are you happy with me?"

She nodded yes.

"Would you like for us to be this way forever?"

Denise lowered her eyelashes. "Pastor Hightower, what are you asking me?"

Bryce held her left hand in his. "Denise, I love you and I want you to be my wife."

"I love you too," Denise responded, using her free hand to wipe the tears that trickled down her cheeks.

"Will you marry me and let me love you forever?"

Denise didn't hesitate. "Yes, Pastor!" she screamed. Watching Bryce retrieve the black box from his jacket, Denise wiggled her finger in anticipation.

"After I place this on your finger, you have to stop calling me Pastor and use my name," he teased, knowing Denise preferred the title.

"After you say 'I do,' I'll call you King Bryce if that's what you want!"

"Bryce will do," he said, reaching for her finger once again. He was serious again. "I meant what I said; you're the only woman I'll ever love. I won't purposefully hurt you. I'll cherish you as my queen," he said once the one carat diamond was secure.

At that moment, Denise trusted her king totally. She had patiently waited, prayed and fasted for her Boaz to come. Finally God had answered her.

"What happened to him?" Denise mumbled, blinking back tears. "What happened to my king?"

"I'm her," the voice said, ending the reminiscing. It was Melanie. "Sorry I'm late. I couldn't find a parking spot."

Denise quickly smiled, transforming into her first lady face. Standing, she hugged the young woman, but Melanie didn't embrace her fully.

"Melanie, what's going on?"

The young woman nervously scanned her surroundings, biting her lower lip and fidgeting with her hands. "First Lady—"

"Denise is fine," she interrupted.

Melanie hesitated before addressing her by her first name. "Alright, Denise—"

Her inexperience showed when Denise interrupted Melanie the second time. "Before we begin, let's pray."

Melanie agreed. Denise gathered her hands, bowed her head and said a quick prayer. When she opened her eyes, the waitress was standing at the table tapping her pencil against her pad.

"Can I have your drink order please?" the waitress asked.

"Water is fine," Denise answered, in hopes of shooing her away.

Melanie ordered a Diet Coke then excused herself from the table. "First Lady . . . Denise, let me build my salad, then we'll get started."

Now Denise felt like a moron. She'd suggested the self-serve soup and salad restaurant and was sitting at the table waiting for someone to serve her. Trying to save face, Denise agreed that was a good idea and joined her.

Melanie loaded her tray with two plates, one with cold pasta salad selections and the other with mixed greens. Denise settled on a simple spinach salad and a small cup of mixed fruit. Both skipped the dessert bar on the way back to the table.

"Denise, I see how you've lost weight; you don't eat very much," Melanie commented, inspecting Denise's baby spinach and apple salad. "You look good, but then again, I thought you were nicely proportioned before."

Denise, sensing the genuineness of the compliment, graciously smiled back. "Thank you, Melanie, and for the record, I eat plenty. It's the middle of the day; I have five hours to go."

They ate in silence. Denise didn't want to rush her. Melanie's anxiety showed in her hands; they constantly shook.

"Denise," she said half-way through her salad. "I called you because I didn't know what else to do. I have tried everything, but nothing's working . . . it's like . . ." Melanie's lower lip quivered, causing her to pause.

Denise pushed aside her salad and moved to comfort Melanie. "What is it? You can tell me."

After sniffling and wiping her eyes, Melanie locked eyes with her first lady. "Denise, you have to promise not to tell anyone what I'm about to tell you. Not even Pastor."

In Melanie's eyes, Denise saw so many emotions. Emotions that were familiar to her: hurt, longing, desperation and helplessness.

"Unless it's something detrimental to the church, whatever you tell me stays between us," Denise assured her.

Melanie drew a long breath before continuing. "It's not detrimental to the church, but it's lethal to my young marriage."

Denise softened her grip on Melanie's shoulder as she wondered how she of all people could help anyone with marital issues when hers is a hot mess. Melanie could probably teach her a thing or two. "Are you and Clay having problems?"

"Denise, don't get me wrong, I love my husband. God knows I do, but I can't do what he's asking of me. For five years, I've listened to what church elders and mothers have said about how a wife must submit to her husband, but what my husband is asking of me is not right. It's not Godly and I'm not doing it."

Denise assumed she was referring to an act of a sexual nature. A lot of women have a hard time with certain forms of sexual expression. "Maybe if the two of you discuss it, you'll feel more comfortable." Nothing could have prepared Denise for what Melanie revealed next, almost in a whisper.

"I will never feel comfortable watching pornography."

Denise's throat suddenly became parched and the ache she'd been suppressing resurfaced with a vengeance. She sipped water to keep from crying out, "Oh God!"

"Denise, I didn't want to say anything. I was afraid of damaging Clay's character. He's not a bad person; he just has this thing with pornography. He wants me to watch movies with him before we have sex. He says that helps to stimulate him. Shouldn't I be enough to stimulate him?"

God, what am I going to tell her? "Yes. As his wife you have everything he needs inside of you. It's up to him to receive it or not."

"We talked about sex during marriage counseling and we agreed; we would only do things both of us are comfortable with. Now three months later, he wants to change and demand that I do what he wants."

Denise pushed the bitter thought back. She considered it was better for Melanie to find Clay is a pervert now and not three years from now.

"The way I figure, I was deceived and he's committing adultery."

"Do you know if he's sleeping around?" Denise reviled herself for sounding like her mother.

"Don't you think if a married man willfully participates in sexual stimulation by a woman other than his wife, he's committing adultery?"

Denise swallowed hard then answered honestly. "Yes, I

do," she paused. "But unfortunately, a lot of people, women included, don't."

Melanie gasped. "Both Clay and I are saved. We don't follow the standards of the world. The Bible says, if a man even looks, he's committed adultery. He's supposed to find satisfaction in my breasts, not the breasts of some strange woman on a television screen."

God, I can't do this. "Melanie, I'm not sure what it is you're looking for. I agree; what Clay is asking of you is wrong, but I can't tell you to divorce him over it. Is that what you want?"

Melanie lowered her head as if in deep prayer; then slowly lifted her head and made her request known. "I don't want a divorce; I love my husband. I just need to know what I can do so he won't desire other women. I need to know as a wife what I can do."

Denise filled her mouth with water to keep from screaming out to God, "You are not fair!"

She contemplated Melanie's words and at the same time mentally argued with God about how unfair it was for Him to send Melanie to her. What advice could she give? She was experiencing the same thing; the only difference being Bryce is the pastor; Clay the youth minister. Both were addicted to pornography. She couldn't instruct Melanie to lose weight as she had done. At one hundred fifteen pounds, Melanie was already slender. It was futile to suggest a hair weave like the style she had planned on getting when Melanie's hair already flowed down her back. Should she tell her the truth; that it's a man's world, especially in the church? That nothing would change until Clay was willing? How could Denise expose to Melanie that her very own pastor is addicted and still effectively preaches the Word of God every Sunday?

As hard as Denise tried to formulate the perfect answer, something deep and revelatory, she couldn't. Melanie's pleading wet eyes pulled her heart strings for an answer. Denise knew she would hate herself later, but she had to offer Melanie some type of hope. Exhaling deeply, she gave it to her.

"Melanie, you need to pray for your husband. Pray that God heals him. Aside from that, it's really not much you can do." Denise would remember the defeat that snapped every drop of hope from Melanie for many days to come.

Ten . . . nine . . . eight, Bryce anxiously counted the seconds for the dismissal bell. Grinning and hugging the blue first place ribbon close to his chest, Bryce bolted from the classroom, through the crowded hallway and down the front steps. Bryce didn't stop running until he found his father cutting a piece of sweet potato pie at the kitchen table.

It took Bryce less than a minute to catch his breath. "Look, Daddy, I won!" Bryce yelled at the same time thrusting the first place ribbon in his father's face. "I won!"

"Boy, what are you talking about?" his father asked before lifting a piece of pie into his mouth without acknowledging the ribbon.

"I won first place in the school's Science Fair." Bryce waved the ribbon back and fourth. "I'm the best in the whole school!" He waited excitedly for a hug or a high-five from his father.

"You should be the best; as much as it's costing me every month. Get upstairs and do your homework. The next time I catch you running in this house, I'm going to take off my belt." He pointed toward the stairs and Bryce knew better than to test him. Eleven-year-old Bryce moped from the kitchen without his father mentioning one word about his accomplishment. As far as Bryce could tell, his father hadn't looked at the ribbon.

Bryce sat up straight and wiped his face. Thinking back to that day in fifth grade always triggered emotions in Bryce that he couldn't explain. It was a turning point for him.

Bryce never ran home to share anything with his father again. During puberty, his mother forced him to ask his father about the changes occurring in his body. His father's response was a box of condoms.

"You better not slip up and leave something behind," his father warned.

It was his mother who explained how to handle his night and morning surprises. Mavis taught him what to do about the constant itching caused by sweating. Mavis' love and over attentiveness, however well intended, couldn't satiate the hunger for his father's validation. It wasn't a substitute for fatherly instruction and advice. He would give anything just for one memory of his father's hug, or a recollection of hearing him say, "I'm proud of you."

That's what he was hoping for that day so long ago. Bryce wanted to make his father proud. He wanted to hear his father brag about his prize at the barber shop like the other dads, but it never happened. In spite of his best effort not to emulate his father, he failed.

Not only was he forcing Denise to accept his addiction; he wouldn't emotionally open up to her. He'd never shared with her the relationship with his father. She didn't know that his insecurity and fear of failure was the driving force behind him always wanting everything his way and why they had to look a certain way in public. He let her believe he was just selfish. He was her king, how could he show weakness? Men didn't do that, at least not the man who held the greatest influence over him.

"*I didn't know how to love her; I didn't love myself.*" Bryce recalled what Benny had said and wondered if he really loved himself. The surface answer was 'yes,' but then Bryce questioned why he would risk his soul for a few minutes of self-gratification.

Lately, it wasn't about pleasure. This addictive act had become more of a habit; something to do just because.

Since being exposed, the highs were shorter and the lows longer, but he couldn't stop. He would do well for a few days, then as routine as blowing his nose, he'd masturbate with one of his favorite magazines. Although it took longer to become aroused, he continued until catapulted into a world of fantasy; a world where King Bryce ruled.

"Father, you have to help me," Bryce mumbled, at the same time tugging at his zipper.

Watching Bryce struggle with his zipper, Denise quietly entered the study. At first she started to turn and run, but Melanie's face flashed before her. She couldn't avoid or ignore Pastor Hightower's addiction now that a member of the church was suffering with the same evil.

"We need to talk," she said, kneeling beside his chair.

Relieved his wife's sudden appearance prevented him from once again yielding to temptation, he tried to explain. "Denise . . . I . . . I"

She quieted him by placing her right index finger to his lips. Once he relaxed she closed his zipper then rested her head on his lap.

Bryce received the gestures as an invitation and gently stroked her hair. When she didn't flinch, he expanded the territory to include her neck and back.

"I ate lunch by the lake today," she started, still lying in her husband's lap. Bryce knew his wife well enough to know more was coming. "Overlooking the lake, I thought about us. I recalled the day you asked me to marry you. I remembered every word you said, every promise you made." Bryce remained quiet, envisioning the moment. "Before you made love to me on our wedding night, you told me I was your queen. I experienced such joy that night; I was afraid to fall asleep. Afraid I wouldn't wake up on earth." Denise repositioned herself so that her forearms rested on his lap and drew her face closer to his, before asking, "What happened?"

Starring into her beautiful, yet pleading eyes, Bryce moved his lips to speak, but the words cemented in his throat.

"I can't go on like this," she continued.

His breathing accelerated and his chest muscles tightened as anxiety gripped him.

"I—we can't keep living this lie. We can't keep pretending we're happy for the sake of people. It's not helping us and it's certainly not helping the church God has placed in our care. How can we help anyone in our condition?" She lifted her left hand to his chest, covering his hand. "Can you honestly tell me you're happy with our marriage? Are you content living a lie before God's people?"

"No," he responded, shaking his head slowly. "But I don't know how to fix it."

"One of our church members came to me for advice today and I couldn't freely help her."

"Why not?" Bryce interrupted. "You know the Bible and you know how to pray."

"But I haven't mastered being phony," she replied. "I couldn't help her because she's battling the same evil as I. Like you, her husband is addicted to porn and expects her to accept it." Bryce sank back into the chair, but didn't have a response. "I couldn't tell her that I understood her anguish firsthand, because it would have devastated her to learn the happy and loving couple portrayed every Sunday is just an illusion. I couldn't assure her that you would talk to her husband and help him get delivered because I know you're not willing to do that. You're not willing to expose your weakness to anyone. I only know about your transgressions because I caught you."

"Who is it?' Bryce wanted to know.

"What difference does it make? You can't help him until you help yourself."

Bryce persisted. "I can talk to him without exposing myself. I can tell him what the Word says."

She answered shaking her head from side to side. "You speak every Sunday from the pulpit, but it's not effective because the man you present is not who you are."

Bryce bowed his head as her words added more weight to the heaviness in his heart.

"I can't do this anymore. I thought I could fake it until I make it and look the other way, but that was before this afternoon. Until now, I thought our dysfunction was exclusive to us, but the truth is, we can't effectively minister to the congregation if we're sick."

"Denise, I am trying. I need more time." The frustration seeped through his usual cool demeanor.

"Are you really?" she asked, leaning back against her legs. "If I'd been a minute later, I would have walked in on you in the middle of the same sin that you repeatedly claim to be working on freeing yourself from."

Rubbing his forehead, Bryce swallowed hard. How could he reveal to his wife that deep down he was helpless against the allure and seduction of his fantasy world?

Denise debated her next question, but pressed him away. "Have you considered outside help? A therapist, maybe?"

Bryce exhaled loudly. "If I find a Christian therapist I feel comfortable with, I'll consider it."

Denise pushed harder. "What about the Church Council; maybe there is someone—"

Bryce cut her off. "Under no circumstances will I expose myself to anyone involved in the church!" He was adamant. "No buts!" Bryce added, rising to his feet. "My frailties will not be the topic of discussion at anyone's dinner table."

"The elders wouldn't expose you."

While shaking his head, Bryce folded his arms. "Denise, you have to trust me on this. I know first hand how the elders "handle" issues of this nature. I will not set myself up to be a spectacle." Bryce walked over to the window and gazed at the bright half moon. Denise stood, but didn't follow him.

"I know I need help, but I don't know how to get it," he said in resignation. "I can't tell you how many times I've prayed, read scripture and made proclamations. With the best intensions, I only last a few days." He paused to swallow the lump bulging in his throat. "I wish I could tell you it'll get better, but I don't know if I believe that anymore. Don't get me wrong, I am not happy and I know it's impacting the ministry, but I don't know how to stop it. I want to, but I can't."

Hearing movement from Denise, he assumed she was leaving the room. He jumped when he felt her embrace from behind.

"I love you," she said, resting her head against his back. "We'll figure this out together."

Chapter 9

Bryce leaned against the counter, starring aimlessly at the coffee maker. The percolating had ceased and the rich bold Columbian fragrance saturated the house, but Bryce couldn't get his bearings together to taste his morning staple. He was still spent from the previous night's lovemaking session with his wife.

After admitting his resolve and failure to overcome his addiction, he expected her to leave him. Denise's actions contradicted everything he believed about women and their need for a knight in shining armor with all the answers.

She didn't berate him for admitting his failure. Instead, she led him by the hand to their bed and made love to him as if he was a soldier coming back from war. Skillfully, she tended to his exposed wounds with the healing balm of her sweetness, and at the same time, shaking his protective emotional wall.

He'd awakened in the middle of the night still connected. He'd been so fulfilled with her warmth, he drifted into a peaceful rest before he could disengage.

He shifted positions, and in the still darkness, Bryce gave

way to the tears he bottled at the end of every trip to fantasy land. *You deserve much better than this*, he thought looking into his wife's serene face. On his best day, Bryce wasn't worthy of the love she had unselfishly given him. He didn't know how, but he was going to conquer his demons.

Now leaning against the counter, he adjusted his stance and stroked his left cheek with the back of his hand. Denise had kissed him before leaving after praying for him. She hadn't done either in weeks.

"Good morning, son." Benny entered the kitchen through the back door. He reached into the cabinet for a mug, then poured a cup of coffee like he lived there. Shaken from his daze, Bryce peered at the uninvited visitor.

Exasperated, Bryce turned and leaned against the counter with his arms folded. "Mr. Benny, since when did the kitchen become part of the yard?'

"The moment you forgot how to fill a cup with coffee," Benny laughed. "I saw you through the window; standing here just dumbfounded." Benny added cream and sugar to the coffee then gestured for Bryce to sit down at the table. Bryce obeyed. "Good thing I'm here; you need help." He handed the cup to Bryce.

"Thank you." Bryce reached for more sugar, but Benny shooed his hand away. "Too much sugar is not good for you."

Bryce placed the cup on the table. "Mr. Benny, how is it you always know what kind of help I need and what's good for me? Do you pay this much attention to your own life?"

"Since you haven't had your coffee yet, I'll let that remark slide," Benny said at the same time, opening the refrigerator. "Before you attempt to smart mouth me again about looking in the refrigerator, your wife, who's a lot nicer than you are in the mornings, told me I can help myself to anything I want. Now deal with that."

Bryce studied the pushy old man through the steam rising from his mug. For a man who worked outdoors, Benny was well groomed down to his physique. He guessed it was Benny's physical characteristics, not his personality, that helped him score with the women. With his pushy behavior, Benny was a prime candidate for a pot of hot grits or chicken grease. Bryce considered the man over zealous, watching him remove pots and pans from *his* cabinet and turn on *his* stove.

"I see you've been working around here," Benny said, filling the pot halfway full with water.

"I haven't touched that yard," Bryce insisted, placing the mug down.

"Make sure you don't," Benny responded after placing the pot on the burner. "I was referring to your wife. When she left this morning, she wasn't frowning. She wasn't beaming, but at least she wasn't frowning. That tells me you've been working." Benny glanced over his shoulder at Bryce with a furrowed brow. "Either you've been working or she's finding joy somewhere else." Benny laughed out loud, hearing Bryce choke on his coffee. "Son, stop being so serious all the time. If you do your job, you won't have to worry about that. Trust me, I know." Benny turned his attention back to looking for salt and pepper.

Silently watching Benny fry bacon and scramble eggs, Bryce second-guessed his appraisal of Benny. Maybe he didn't like him so much. Bryce was a grown man and the pastor of a growing congregation, but Benny had a way of making him feel like a child. Around Benny, his authority meant nothing. Bryce didn't like that. Could he have an ulterior motive for offering his gardening service? After all, Benny had been working for nearly three months and had yet to accept one dime from Bryce for services rendered.

"Mr. Benny, why are you here?' Bryce asked plainly. "Your interest in my yard is just the vehicle you used to butt into my personal business. What is it that you really want from me?"

"Certainly not your cooking and gardening skills," Benny snapped and continued cooking.

"Mr.—"

Benny held up his open palmed hand as a warning for him to be quiet. Bryce got the message and didn't utter another word. Benny placed the plate of scrambled eggs, bacon and grits in front of Bryce. "Eat up; maybe you won't be so grouchy then."

"Where's your plate?"

"I eat with the sunrise. I cooked breakfast for you. I reckoned, if you couldn't figure out how to pour coffee, you'd starve to death trying to figure out how to cook."

Ashamed, Bryce swallowed the lump in his throat. No man had ever shown him that much consideration. "Thank you."

"To answer your question, I like you, Bryce." Bryce's mouth gaped. "You didn't think I knew your name did you?"

"No."

"Well I do, but I like calling you son. If I had a son, he'd be around your age. He'd be more handsome like me, but you do get my point. Anyway, the only thing I want from you is for you to be a better man than I was. That's my God-given assignment: train men to be great while they're young and not wait until they're old like me to realize they've been fools."

Bryce suppressed the spark of hope he felt rumble in his belly. "You know I'm a pastor and—"

"What's that supposed to mean?" Benny interrupted. "Pastors need more help than the congregation. You can take the "holy roller" mask off. God sent me here for you. You need some serious help before you lose your marriage and church to the devil. Now stop playing games and eat your breakfast before it gets cold. When you get ready to stop playing, I'll be in the yard. And wash the dishes," Benny called over his shoulder.

Watching Benny stomp out of the kitchen, Bryce didn't know if he should laugh or cry. Maybe Benny was an answer to his prayers. He definitely had a way of pulling truth from him. Pushy or not, he decided he liked the old man. Could he trust him with his secret? That remained to be seen.

"Where did the time go?" Denise mumbled, glancing down at her watch.

She'd given up her evening walk for research at the library. For two hours, she pulled up article after article about the evils of pornography. It didn't take long to learn pornography addiction wasn't just a physical act, but an emotional attachment as well. She read several testimonies of recovered addicts who used pornography as a way to soothe the emotional scars caused by the lack of love or validation from one or both parents. Reflecting on what she knew of Bryce's childhood, she felt that didn't apply to her husband. Being an only child, he was the center of attention. She'd seen the pictures; his mother was always there. She continued reading, looking for something to relate to her husband. One article featured the stories of a father and son who battled the same addiction and won.

In the story, the father, who was a pastor, started with pornography as a way to cope with his wife's sudden death, then introduced it to his son as a means to celebrate his sixteenth birthday. The son, now in his mid-thirties, had lost his wife and kids behind the resulting addiction. After successful therapy, the son begged the father to get help. According to the feature, the two now ran a successful treatment program for addicted males.

In the photo accompanying the article, the father stood with his arm affectionately around his son's shoulder. Denise focused on them for a long moment and was about to move on to the next article, when the thought came to her. Whereas Bryce constantly spoke proudly of his mother, Denise could count on one hand how many times she'd heard his father's name mentioned. She made a mental note to ask Bryce about the disparity.

Before leaving, she wrote down the names of books to order from Amazon.com. She also printed a second copy of the articles for Melanie. Driving home, Denise couldn't remember the last time she was happy to return home. Last night, they connected on a deeper level. For once, Bryce released the control reins he held onto so tightly and Denise recognized how much he needed her. Denise needed him too. Good or bad, they were a team.

She hadn't comprehended how much she missed him being a part of her life until he phoned her earlier that day. Her husband called her three times just to say 'hello' and that he loved her. The first call made her cry, but on the third call, she giggled uncontrollably listening to his cracked voice sing the words.

"Hey beautiful." Bryce accosted her from behind the second she stepped into the house.

"Hey, yourself." Denise didn't waste any time. "I have some information to share with you," she announced, holding out her briefcase. Bryce placed the briefcase on the floor then drew her close to him for a kiss. After the kiss, Denise looked into her husband's eyes with more hope than she'd had for the past three months. "Was today a good day?"

Bryce massaged his chin using his thumb and index finger. "Today was great." He went on to tell her about his hospital and convalescent home visits and his meeting with the Dean at a local Christian College. "If all goes well, I'll start teaching in the fall," he proudly announced.

"That's great," she half-smiled.

"I didn't revert back to any old ways, if that's what you want to hear," he added after a prolonged silence.

Denise made no attempt to hide her relief. "Good, that's

what I want to talk to you about. I learned a lot today." She reached for the briefcase, but he interfered.

"Can we eat dinner first?" He motioned toward the dining room. It was then that Denise noticed the candles everywhere. She followed him into the dining room where Bryce had the table set with candlelight and china.

"You didn't have to do this," she commented when Bryce placed a cloth napkin in her lap.

Bryce waited until he served her food from her favorite Chinese restaurant before responding, "Yes, I did. I wanted to celebrate our new start." Denise smiled and joined hands with him for grace. After blessing the meal, Bryce kissed the back of her hand before releasing it.

"You know this is not on my meal plan," she said of the dry fried ribs, sweet & sour chicken and fried rice. "I can eat the green beans."

"You can eat whatever you want," he said, feeding her a chunk of chicken. "I like you just the way you are. Actually, I liked you before, but this is nice too."

Denise chewed the chicken slower than normal. Bryce's comment, however well intended, made her wonder if he'd like her more after reaching her goal. The articles she read emphasized that pornography addiction was not due to deficiencies from the significant other, but Bryce's sudden attentiveness made her wonder about the theory.

"What's on your mind?" he asked.

Denise raised a fork loaded with green beans. "I have an appointment tomorrow. I'm getting a weave," she said quickly, then stuffed her mouth. Bryce continued eating as if he hadn't heard her. "I was thinking of something long and wavy, similar to Beyoncé," she continued after sipping water.

"It's your hair, do whatever you want with it," he said before leaving the table. "Just remember, if I wanted a woman who looked like that, I would have married one."

Denise quickly filled her mouth with water to keep from voicing the nasty thoughts that instantly formed. *I don't want to be married to a pervert, but I am.* She knew then that last night was a good start, but they had a long way to go. "I'm just trying to keep you from looking elsewhere." She mouthed the words low, thinking he wouldn't hear, but he did.

"Is that what you think?" he asked, now standing over her. "Is that what the weight loss is about?'

Denise didn't answer. It was one thing to admit the truth to herself, but to verbalize it was unbearable. Her silence was all the answer he needed.

"Do you honestly think I got caught up into this craziness because of how you look?" Still silence. "I told you I started that long before you."

"But you weren't satisfied with me enough to stop." Denise turned away to hide the tears that instantly pooled her eyes.

"Honey, my addiction has nothing to do with you." He squatted down beside her.

"How can you say that? I saw the magazines; those women are nothing like me. You found pleasure in them before me and continued to after. Face it, Bryce, those types of women have something you like."

Bryce couldn't formulate a response. There was something drawing him; he just didn't know what it was.

"Think about it," she continued after drying her cheeks. "You're always telling me how to dress, because as you say, I represent you. My standing hair appointment is more to keep you quiet than for me."

Bryce hung his head to hide the tears that welled in his eyes. He mentally berated himself for being so selfish and for hurting her. Being one-dimensional, he managed to rob a beautiful and self-confident woman of her natural security of womanhood.

Slowly and somberly, Bryce blew out the candles then cleared the table. Denise remained in the dining room alone, wondering how a day that started so good could end so badly. She pushed away from the table, just in time for Bryce to lift her from the chair.

"Niecy," he began, balancing her weight. "I didn't mean to make you feel inadequate. I don't know what it is that compels me to fantasize about strange women. I am going to find out, but in the meantime, know that you are everything I need."

"Prove it."

After a prolonged kiss, Bryce carried her to bed.

Chapter 10

Bryce spent most of the night convincing Denise she satisfied his sexual appetite. Bryce persuaded her enough for her to make the decision to cut back on the prepackaged meals. Instead, she would consume portion-controlled healthy meals. Under no circumstances would she give up exercising. "I like walking," is what she told him when he tried to talk her into skipping this morning's session.

The time spent at the Marina was therapeutic for her. The waves helped her relax and the exercise couldn't hurt. Watching Jonas jogging toward her, Denise wondered if that was the complete truth.

Jonas slowed into a walk and the two exchanged greetings.

"How was the visit with your kids?" she asked him.

Denise listened with excitement to Jonas brag about his boys. Both were honor students and excelled in sports. The oldest, soccer and the youngest, track.

"If I didn't have to see their mother, the visit would have been perfect," he added, approaching the first exercise station.

"She can't be that bad; you once loved her enough to make her the mother of your children."

Jonas positioned himself on the work bench, "I liked her a lot, once. I'll always love my kids." Denise remained quiet until he asked, "Why doesn't your husband accompany you on your walks? Don't tell me he's too busy with the church?"

"No, he's not. I've never invited him." Denise resumed walking, a clear indication she didn't wish to discuss her husband.

"Hey, guys, wait up!"

Thinking she recognized the voice, Denise paused momentarily then continued walking.

"What's it like being married to a pastor?" Jonas asked.

"Denise!"

Denise stopped dead in her tracks. She did know that voice; it belonged to Erin.

Astonished, Denise turned around to see her friend fitted from head to toe in red and black spandex workout wear. Erin actually resembled a Barbie Doll in the shorts and midriff top. Her hair was pulled back in a ponytail with matching headband. The red and black Reebok's looked fresh out of the box. Denise guessed if Erin was dipped in oil, she'd weighed no more than one hundred ten pounds. Why had she driven twenty miles on a Saturday morning to walk when it was obvious exercise for her wasn't a necessity? There was only one answer to that question: Jonas.

"Hey guys," Erin said after catching up to them. She then went into a quick stretch routine, allowing Jonas to view her from all angles.

"Forgive her, Lord," Denise mumbled under her breath then said out loud, "Erin, what are you doing here?"

"Exercising, of course," she answered as if she worked up a sweat everyday. "How are you, Jonas?"

He smiled, but Denise could tell he wasn't excited about seeing Erin. "I'm good; you?"

"I'm better now." Her flirtation fell on deaf ears. Jonas resumed walking with Denise.

Erin joined their pace, being sure to stand beside Jonas. "What were you guys talking about? I had to yell twice to get your attention."

"Denise was about to tell me what it's like being married to a pastor."

"Well—" Denise started.

"That's easy," Erin interrupted. "All she has to do is sit on the front row and holler 'Amen.' Every Sunday she wears a new suit and Pastor draws attention to her with his silly comments about their relationship. Then on special days, the congregation showers her with gifts. How hard can that be?"

"Erin!" The summation astounded Denise. She nearly screamed the woman's name.

"Girl, you know I'm just playing," Erin said and playfully pushed Denise's shoulder. Denise half returned that smile. "Being married to Pastor Hightower must be *hard.*" Erin's smirk reminded Denise never to share her marital problems with her.

"I'm sure that's not the answer Jonas was looking for." Denise looked to him. "Was it?"

"No, but we can discuss that later." Jonas glanced at Erin. "Aren't you cold?" he asked, looking at the bumps on her arm.

That's what you get for coming out here half-naked, Denise thought.

"I'm fine," Erin insisted, although the clatter of her teeth betrayed her. For a moment, Erin thought he'd offer her his fleece, but he didn't.

Denise and Jonas continued walking at a brisk pace, passing up the exercise stations; mainly to bring the walk to an end as soon as possible. The Marina had lost its serenity now that Erin was there running her mouth non-stop about her latest case. When Jonas couldn't take anymore, he zipped his fleece, excused himself, and then sprinted off.

"What's wrong with him?" Erin asked, frowning.

"Nothing," Denise responded, still disturbed by Erin's earlier comments. "He usually jogs the trail. He only walks to keep me company."

Erin's eyes followed Jonas's tall muscular physique down the track until he was nearly a speck. "Does he talk about me often?" she asked expectantly.

Denise increased her pace and looked out over the Pacific to keep from facing her friend. "He has mentioned you a few times."

"What did he say?" Erin couldn't keep pace, so she grabbed Denise's arm, forcing her to stop.

Denise starred at her friend, debating the best way to tell her the man she'd shamelessly thrown herself at on more than one occasion didn't consider her anything above a nuisance.

"Denise, tell me," she whined.

"Maybe you should ask him?" Denise suggested.

"I did, but all he keeps preaching is he doesn't do lawyers, then he stood me up at that party."

"He never stood you up," Denise corrected. "He never said he was coming."

"Whatever." Erin said as she waved her hands. "How does he feel about me?"

Gazing at her friend, Denise was aware for the first time that for a lawyer, Erin was lacking in common sense. "Jonas thinks you're intelligent, pretty and very aggressive. However, he's not interested in having a relationship with you."

"He told you that?"

"Yes, but only after he told you first."

Denise thought she saw tears in her friend's eyes before Erin took off running.

"Erin! Erin!" she called after her. Erin ran across the track, through the parking lot and to her car.

"Denise, who is that outside talking to Bryce," Lucinda asked, entering the kitchen.

Denise stopped washing dishes long enough to hug her mother.

"Hey, mama," Denise looked down at the foil covered pan her mother held with the aid of pot holders. "Let me guess . . ." Denise inhaled deeply. "Peach cobbler!"

"Somebody has to make my pastor something to eat," Lucinda replied, placing the pan on the stove. "Just because you're on a diet doesn't give you the right to starve the man."

"Mama, please, don't use my diet as an excuse to cook for Bryce. Truth be told, you'd feed him before feeding me."

"You're exaggerating now." Lucinda walked over to the kitchen window. She repeated her original question. "Who is that with Bryce?"

"That's the gardener, Mr. Benny."

Lucinda grunted. "He's doing more talking than working.

Denise finished rinsing the sink before responding to her mother's nosey, but correct, observation. "Bryce complains that he's pushy and nosey, but he likes him."

"The yard does look nice." Lucinda observed them a while longer before sitting down at the kitchen table. "How are you and Bryce?"

"We have an understanding," Denise answered, joining her at the table.

"Good. I've been praying for you." Lucinda patted her hand in show of support. "I know it's hard, but it's not too hard for God."

Denise asked the question that had gnawed her for weeks.

"Mama, how is it you can still respect Bryce as your pastor, knowing about his addiction?"

Lucinda answered without hesitation. "That's easy. The same way I respected your daddy. I knew he had a good heart, and deep down, Jeremiah loved me. He just had a struggle. Everyone struggles with something; drugs, cigarettes, alcohol; for your daddy it was pornography. It's the same with Bryce. His heart is good and he really loves you. He just needs help with his issue."

Denise remembered Bryce telling her those exact same words.

"It's hard being married to a pastor," Lucinda finished.

"Not everyone believes that." Denise went on to share Erin's insensitive remarks from earlier.

Lucinda helped herself to some grapes hanging over the side of the fruit bowl centered on the table, before commenting, "That's because the congregation only sees the glamour." She used two fingers to emphasize the word glamour. "That's all they need to see. If they could see Bryce's faults, they wouldn't respect him."

"Mama, that's not fair; he's human."

"I'm not saying it's fair, but that's the way it is. The church has a way of robbing preachers of humanity almost to the point of placing preachers in the place of God." Lucinda let the words marinate before adding, "I wouldn't worry about Erin; she's always been jealous of you."

Denise gasped. "Mama!"

"It's the truth. I see her rolling her eyes every time Bryce acknowledges you. And I haven't forgotten all the trouble she caused leading up to your wedding."

Denise remembered too. Erin complained about everything. Her dress was the wrong color and style, the shoes weren't her type; the hairstyle Denise chose made her look like an old woman, the music was too slow. Whatever

Denise liked, Erin hated. The greatest monstrosity of all was the day Erin accompanied Denise and Lucinda to the bridal shop for a dress fitting.

Never believing for a second Denise was still a virgin, Erin mocked her openly for choosing to wear white. Although Denise recalled all those things, she still couldn't quite share her mother's conclusion. She and Erin's friendship had been solidified through eight years of joy, sadness, and death. For her, Erin was more like the sister she never had. Erin went as far as to call Jeremiah, dad.

"Mama, I don't believe that," Denise said, shaking her head. "I'll admit Erin is a little self-centered, but jealous is a stretch."

"If you say so." Lucinda shrugged her shoulders. "Some things are only learned in time."

Pondering her mother's words, Denise couldn't help but wonder if her mother was right. After determining she didn't want to deal with the reality of it, Denise pushed it to the back of her mind, opting to figure it out later. Right now, her marriage was first priority.

"Hello, mother." Bryce entered the kitchen followed by Benny. After kissing his mother-in-law, he introduced Benny. "Mom, this is Bernard Johnson, our gardener."

Benny extended his hand. "Hello. You can call me Benny."

Lucinda, smirking and rolling her eyes, ignored his hand. "My name is Lucinda Sanders. You can call me Mrs. Sanders."

"How about I don't call you at all?" Benny shot back.

Both Denise's and Bryce's mouths hung open.

"How about you go outside and do some work. From what I can see, you do more talking than working."

"Mama! Benny!" Denise and Bryce said simultaneously, but they were ignored.

"Why don't you go buy you some business and keep your nose out of mine?" Benny replied.

"That's enough!" Bryce raised his voice. Both Benny and

Lucinda heeded the warning, but not without giving one another the 'evil eye.' "What's this all about? The two of you haven't known each other five seconds and already you don't like each other?"

Lucinda grunted. "I know a bad seed when I see one."

"If that bothers you so much, stop looking in the mirror," Benny rebutted.

"Enough!" Bryce warned again.

Denise was speechless. She'd never seen her mother act this rude.

"Benny, have a seat! Mom, be quiet!" Bryce ordered, although he wanted to laugh. Watching two senior citizens roll their eyes and pout like two-year-olds was quite amusing.

Attempting to defuse the tension, Denise offered the men some peach cobbler and vanilla ice cream. They quickly accepted and sat down at the table. Watching them devour the dessert like vultures and moaning with pleasure, Denise prematurely allowed herself to relax.

"Mom, you outdid yourself this time," Bryce said, licking his spoon.

"Thank you, baby." Lucinda blushed. With that, Benny stopped eating.

"How was it, Mr. Benny?" Denise made the mistake of asking.

"I've had better," he replied dryly.

Lucinda's head shot up.

"Come on, Benny; back to the yard." Bryce pulled his arm and directed him outside before Lucinda could lay hands on him.

"What was that all about?" Denise questioned after Benny and Bryce were beyond ear shot.

"I told you, I know a bad seed when I see one!"

"You're wrong about him. Mr. Benny is saved."

"That's good," Lucinda said, folding her arms across her

chest. "He's going to need Jesus if he insults my cooking again."

Denise threw her hands in the air. For the second time today, someone close to her displayed behavior totally out of character. If she didn't know any better, she'd think both her mother and friend were after the same thing: a man.

Out in the yard, Benny put an end to Bryce's cross-examination before it got started. "Son, I like you and your wife, but your mother-in-law needs an attitude adjustment."

"How can you say that? You just met her."

Benny gave him one of those looks a father would give his son. The look said, 'I'm not going to tell you again.'

Bryce shied away, leaving Benny alone in the yard.

Chapter 11

"Daddy are you coming to my game?" seven-year-old Bryce asked his father at the dinner table. He begged his parents to sign him up for baseball after watching his father play for his job's softball team. His dad could hit the ball to Neverland. That's what little Bryce called the land beyond the left field fence. Bryce wanted to be just like him.

"Are you coming?" Bryce asked again.

"I'll be there," his father finally answered without looking in his son's direction.

In a semi-conscious dream-state, Bryce wiped the sweat from his forehead then turned onto his left side, wrapping his arms around his abdomen.

Little Bryce poked his head through the fence and waved to his mother who was sitting in the stands wearing a shirt with his picture on it. "Where's Daddy?" he yelled.

"He's coming," Mavis assured him.

Bryce nodded, then focused his attention back on the game. The bases were loaded with one out. Bryce was up next. Practicing his warm up swings, Bryce spotted his dad taking a seat beside his mother in the stands. He waved frantically at his dad.

"Pay attention to the game!" his father yelled. Bryce obeyed.

Young Bryce lost his courage, watching his teammate, Tim, strike out. Tim was the best hitter on the team.

"Take your time and watch the ball," the coach instructed from the coaches' box.

"Hit it out the park!" he could hear his father yelling.

Bryce's palms were sweaty and sweat from his brow dripped into his eyes; stinging them. Bryce held his swing for the first pitch to see how fast the ball was coming. His strategy failed; strike one.

"That's just one strike; you've got two more," the coach encouraged him.

"What are you standing there for? Hit the ball!" his father yelled.

The sweat and stinging combined with two different directives proved too much for little Bryce. He swung wildly at the next two pitches which missed the strike zone by at least two feet. Ashamed for striking out, young Bryce cried on his way back to the dugout.

"Don't worry, you'll get 'em next time," his coach said, patting him on the back. When Bryce looked back toward the stands, his father was gone.

Bryce awakened to an empty house, sweating and shaking. Denise and Lucinda had gone shopping, leaving him home alone. "Why am I remembering this now?" he directed his question to the air. As expected, there wasn't a response.

He hadn't recalled that memory in months, but whenever he did, Bryce would take a trip to his fantasy world to escape the pain of it. He hadn't masturbated in three days and he wasn't going to now. The first thing he needed to do was to leave the confines of his study and do something to chase away the loneliness that threatened to swallow him.

On his way to the kitchen, Bryce turned on the sound system, filling the house with John P. Kee. He enjoyed another serving of Lucinda's peach cobbler and laughed out loud, reminiscing over the earlier fiasco. "My friend has met his match," he chuckled.

Friend? Where did that come from? Referring to Benny as a friend caught him off guard.

Benny was many things: wise, knowledgeable, aggressive and today, rude. His revelation of the Word fascinated Bryce to the point he'd have to reread scripture in order to hold a conversation with Benny about the Bible. Benny knew twice as much about life as he did the Bible, and he didn't mind sharing. That's what kept drawing Bryce closer to him.

Before the disaster in the kitchen, Benny had been sharing memories of the day he met the legendary Jackie Robinson. Bryce was just as surprised as Benny to learn they shared a love for baseball. "I have season tickets to the Giants. From here on out, you are my game buddy," Benny decided without asking Bryce's opinion. "When they're away, we can watch the games on my big plasma surround sound screen. That way we won't disturb your wife."

Benny went on and on about his autographed baseball collection, but Bryce wasn't listening. He checked out after Benny invited him to watch a game.

Spending a leisure afternoon at the ballpark with friends was a desire he aborted long ago. After accepting his call into the ministry, his late pastor advised him to associate with fellow ministers. It wasn't until after disconnecting from his high school and college friends that Bryce learned most ministers had little or no time at all for sports. Most felt leisure activity was a waste of time because it didn't hold spiritual value.

Ironically, those same spiritual ministers fathered numerous illegitimate children and indulged in multiple affairs. Needing to fit in, Bryce gave up his pastime, settling for a game occasionally on the television. He thought the desire no longer existed. Today, he learned he'd simply suppressed it. *That's why I had the dream*, he reckoned.

"Is Benny my friend?" he asked audibly.

A friend was something he needed, but Benny? Bryce attempted to shrug away the notion, but Benny's words pounded his head like waves rolling in from the Pacific. "*I'm here for you. God sent me here for you.*"

"Where are you now when I need to talk?" Bryce grumbled, walking to the sink after finishing the cobbler. The plate and spoon slipped from his hand, tumbling and clattering into the stainless steel sink. Bryce blinked and strained his eyes to make sure he wasn't experiencing an illusion. Benny was standing in his backyard, watering the vegetable garden.

His gardener had left two hours ago, why had he come back? He could have given Bryce instructions to water the garden. Benny waved for Bryce to join him.

"What's on your mind?" he asked, once Bryce was standing beside him.

Bryce pierced him with his eyes, trying to decipher his real intentions. How did Benny always know his thoughts? How was Benny able to reach him in places his father never could or wouldn't? Not quite ready to trust him, Bryce downplayed his need.

"What makes you think something's on my mind?"

Benny smirked. "Still playing games, huh? You're a pastor. That means your mind is always flooded with somebody's, if not everybody's business, plus your own."

"You're right about that," Bryce chuckled.

Benny drove the point home before Bryce could send a smoke screen. "What I want to know is, where does the pastor go when he needs help?" Benny leaned in closer. "In other words, who heals the physician? Or does he suffer silently until the cancer kills him?"

Bryce immediately turned his back to prevent the emotional release he needed so badly, but refused to allow.

"'I guess you're trying to figure out how I know you're sick?"

Bryce, back still turned, hunched his shoulders for an answer.

"Son," Benny said, placing his arm around Bryce, "all of us have struggles. That's normal. The problems come when we don't trust God to handle our struggles."

Bryce quietly watched the water flow through the dirt and form puddles, providing the ground with life-saving nutrients. That's what his soul needed; to be nurtured. What formula could assist him with his addiction? Praying plus fasting plus reading the Word didn't equal deliverance for him. Perhaps his soul would never receive the vital nutrients it needed to heal.

"How do I trust God with my struggle?" Bryce asked, barely audible. "I've tried everything." After exhaling deeply, his muscles relaxed. Just sharing that little information relieved some of the heaviness.

"Son, God always answers prayers. The problem is most of the time we're not listening or we don't agree with His methodology." Benny shut off the water valve then insisted Bryce join him on the bench. "Now is a good time to tell you about the ivy."

Remembering Benny's long and drawn out method of answering questions, Bryce contorted his face.

"Don't look at me like that!" Benny scolded. "I can't mess you up any more than you already are." Bryce continued standing. "That's the problem with preachers; they make you listen to them babble for hours on Sundays, trying to prove three points, but can't give you five minutes unless you have an offering in your hand."

"Your personality could use some work," Bryce said, positioning himself on the bench.

Benny lifted his hands in the air as if in a prayer line. "Lay hands on me, preacher."

They shared a hearty laugh then drifted into a friendly silence.

Benny leaned back and rested both arms against the bench. "Two of my old customers had a fence dividing their property lines. They built the fence twenty years before I became their gardener. One guy made the mistake of planting ivy right alongside the fence; thinking the ivy would be a nice addition to his yard."

Bryce sighed at the same time wondering what a fence and ivy had to do with his issues.

"Over the years, the plants' small manageable vines transformed into what they referred to as the Green Monster. The ivy grew taller than the fence, entwining itself between and underneath the wood. The neighbors took turns trimming the vines only to have fresh ones appear with the first rain. Then they realized too late that humans aren't the only species that use ivy for a covering. After the rodent invasion, both owners agreed they'd had enough and hired me to get rid of the ivy."

Bryce shifted positions, resting his elbows against his knees.

"At first I didn't want the job because I don't like destroying things." Benny held his opened palms out. "These hands were made for nurturing and growing, and in my younger days, loving." Benny laughed out loud, drawing a grin from his student. "Anyway, I was just about to walk away when the Lord told me to take the job."

"Really," Bryce smacked. "The Lord told you to destroy a plant?"

Benny narrowed his eyes. "Make fun all you want to, I know what I heard. It was the same voice that told me to walk down the block and teach you some sense." When Bryce didn't respond, Benny continued. "Like I was saying, the Lord said He wanted to show me something with the ivy. I took the job for half the cost, figuring whatever the Lord wanted to show me was worth more than a paycheck.

"As I began working, I realized I couldn't remove the ivy without removing the entire fence. Whereas on the outside the vines were small, the hidden vines were thick as branches. The oldest vines were now as thick as a tree trunk. The mature vines had not only entangled themselves with the fence, but had uprooted it. The strong branches were literally holding the fence up."

"Wow," Bryce commented, finding the fact interesting.

"The ivy was literally suffocating the fence; decreasing its lifespan by drying out the wood. None of this could be seen on the surface. All this decaying was going on internally, and not only that, the ivy kept the rodents from being detected."

"Were you able to remove it?"

Benny smiled, knowing he had peaked Bryce's interest.

"Oh yeah, I removed the fence with the ivy still attached. But I had to do something my clients never considered."

"What's that?" Bryce wanted to know.

"I couldn't just remove the top vines and the branches. Oh no," Benny said, shaking his head. "To keep the ivy from returning, I had to dig deep and pull up the roots. I had to rent the proper equipment and study the underground plumbing to make sure I didn't damage any pipes. It took me a whole month to remove all those branches and I didn't make a dime; but to this day, the ivy has never returned and the lesson I learned changed my life forever."

Benny paused to allow the words, and hopefully the message, to sink in. Bryce rested his forehead against his thumbs, but didn't speak.

"Through that experience, the Lord showed me myself.

My life was the fence and my insecurity was the ivy. As a young man, I covered my insecurities by sleeping around with every woman that showed interest. Back then, I was starved for affirmation. I needed someone to tell me who I was and to accept me as a man. I tried filling the void with my wife, but that didn't last long. I loved her, but I hadn't dealt with the root of my insecurity, and because of that, I constantly cheated."

At the sound of Bryce's moan Benny placed his arm around Bryce's shoulder. "The Lord told me I had to expose the root cause in my life and dig it out just like I'd done with the ivy." Benny's voice quivered. "My ivy was planted when I was twelve years old. That's when my foster father raped me. I spent the next thirty years trying to prove I was a man. I convinced myself that sleeping around was the key to holding on to my 'maleness.' That warped way of thinking cost me a good wife and provided my daughters with a bad role model."

Noticing the tears rolling down Bryce's hands, he started to stop, but the still, small voice told him to keep on going. He squeezed Bryce tighter. "Son, my guess is your struggle is also related to sex. Am I right?" Bryce sniffled and nodded. "Pornography?" Benny pressed.

The sobs that poured from Bryce were answer enough. "Don't worry," Benny said holding him now with both arms, rocking back and forth. "We're going to pull up the ivy together."

"What is going on?" Denise mumbled, observing her husband and gardener from the kitchen window.

The intimate interaction reminded her of the father and son pictured in the article; the same article that was still tucked away in her briefcase. She'd forgotten for the second day in a row to discuss it with Bryce. Whatever Benny said reached Bryce's inner being, because her husband would never allow anyone to see him have an emotional breakdown of this magnitude.

"Lord, whatever it is You're doing, I thank you," she whispered.

Chapter 12

For the first time in weeks, the smile that creased Denise's face as she observed her husband step onto the platform was genuine. Last night, they didn't discuss what happened in the yard with Benny. Whatever transpired had a powerful effect on her husband. Of that, Denise was certain.

The sun had long hibernated when Bryce finally entered their bedroom last evening. Denise was studying her Sunday School lesson, something she did every Saturday evening so she could actively participate in class. She looked up from studying the lesson and straight into her husband's reddened eyes.

"Do you want to talk about it?" she asked when he hung his head.

"Maybe later; I'm exhausted." He then walked over to the bed, and after planting a kiss on her cheek, prepared to take a shower. Once in bed for the night and before reaching for the lamp switch, Bryce told her he loved her then fell asleep holding her.

She panicked this morning, awakening in an empty bed. Denise ran down the hall toward the study. Hearing the noise from inside, she stopped short of opening the door. Bryce was praying in a manner she hadn't heard in a very long time. The passion and fervency in which he sent up his petitions arrested Denise on the other side of the door. Before long, she was on her knees praying and crying. That's how Bryce found her.

"Next time join me inside," he invited, and at the same time, helped her to stand.

Denise accepted the offer with a smile, then laced her fingers with his and followed him to their bedroom where they quickly prepared for Sunday service.

Now seated in her reserved front row seat, Denise sniffed the back of her left hand, inhaling her husband's scent. He didn't say much, but he held her hand the entire drive to church. Driving down Interstate 580, Bryce raised her hand to his lips and affectionately seared it with a kiss. The kiss he gave her before exiting his Mercedes left Denise lightheaded to the point she leaned on him for support walking into the sanctuary.

Pastor Hightower, now seated in his chair, surveyed the congregation. The decorum was the same and so were the people; but for some reason, the atmosphere felt different. He felt different. For the first time in almost a year Bryce didn't feel the noose of his addiction dangling before him, ready to make him an open spectacle. Not wanting to set himself up for failure, Bryce acknowledged he wasn't totally delivered, but at least now he wasn't alone.

Who would have thought? Bryce pondered, looking over at Benny who was seated directly behind Lucinda.

Today, Bryce saw with his own eyes what attracted women to his brazen personality. Dressed in a suit and trimmed moustache, Bernard Johnson bore a striking resemblance to the late Ed Bradley, famed *60 Minutes* reporter. Bryce assumed the majority of the middle-aged women in the congregation thought the same. Observing their reactions, all Pastor Hightower could do was shake his head. Lucinda was the only mother not bothered by Benny's presence. Even Mother Gray gave Benny the thrice over before waving her hand in praise.

Bryce conceded; Benny was indeed sent to him by God. After praying until his mouth ran dry, God answered his request in the form of a pushy and nosey gardener. He still couldn't put into words what happened on that bench last night. What he did know was that his life would never be the same, and for the first time in years, deliverance was obtainable.

Following Pastor Hightower's admission to pornography addiction, Benny didn't judge him or preach a sermon. He didn't say anything; just assured Bryce he wasn't alone, then allowed the young preacher to release the pain that had kept him paralyzed for far too long. He cried like a baby and Benny held him as a father would console a son, praying and assuring him he had his back.

Bryce didn't ask, but Benny announced he would start visiting Word of Life since it was closer to home than the church where he held his membership.

"Besides, you could use the support," Benny added, walking Bryce to the back door. For once, Bryce didn't offer opposition. What would be the point?

Before turning to leave, Benny rested a hand on Bryce's shoulder. "It may not seem like much, but you made good progress today. Only a real man can admit his faults to another man. I'm proud of you." Benny left him standing there holding the patio door wide open.

Seated in his leather chair, Bryce attempted to massage the internal ache in his chest by rubbing his pectoral muscles. In God's own way, He was granting him the desires of his heart. Maybe one day he'd be confident enough to start the family Denise desired. Bryce shared the same aspiration, but was afraid he wouldn't make a good father. He used his job as a new pastor to persuade Denise to agree to wait five years before starting their family. Watching her now, dancing in the spirit, Pastor Hightower toyed with the idea of turning the service over to an associate minister and taking the first lady home. He was so caught up; he didn't see the usher approaching.

"Excuse me, Pastor." The usher tapped his shoulder, interrupting his mischievous thoughts. After getting the pastor's attention, the usher handed him a note.

"Thank you," Pastor Hightower received the note and after reading it, slipped it into the pocket of his cassock. He then nodded in Sister Anderson's direction.

At the appointed time, Pastor Hightower mounted the podium and delivered a powerful and thought provoking sermon about fulfilling destiny. Near the conclusion, he noticed Benny standing on his feet encouraging him. Pastor Hightower felt his 'help' come and preached for another twenty minutes.

"Baby, you look happy today," Mother Gray said, hugging Denise after service. "Keep on holding onto God. He knows how to work it out."

"Thank you, Mother," Denise verbally responded, although her attention was on Erin who was leaving without speaking to her. Erin seldom left Sunday service without speaking. In fact, she made a point of letting the congregation know she was the first lady's best friend.

"Keep praying for us," Denise said, directing her attention back to Mother Gray. Her eyes bucked at Mother Gray's next questions.

"Who is that man in the dark blue suit speaking with your mother and is he married?"

Denise laughed at Mother Gray's boldness. "He's our gardener, Bernard Johnson. I don't think he's married."

Looking in her mother's direction, the animated exchange between Lucinda and Benny alarmed her. "Excuse me." Denise rushed to get across the sanctuary before the two caused a scene.

"They let anybody in church these days," Lucinda said, turning her nose up at Benny when he greeted her after service.

"The only reason I'm speaking to you is because the pastor said to greet your neighbor with a holy kiss." Lucinda shook her head and prepared to speak, but Benny shushed her. "Don't worry; I'd rather drink a whole bottle of castor oil before I kiss you." Benny smiled.

Lucinda's face flushed hot with anger. "Why, I have never—"

"And you never will; at least not with me." Knowing he'd gotten the best of her, Benny heaped more coals to Lucinda's fire. "By the way, that's a beautiful suit you're wearing. Too bad I can't say the same about the person wearing it." He then turned to leave.

Lucinda closed her eyes and rapidly counted to ten; trying to keep from reaching for Benny's throat. "Demon seed, where do you think you're going?" she snarled when Benny started in Bryce's direction.

Benny calmly reached into his pocket. After removing a $20 bill from his wallet, he held it out to Lucinda. "Take this and go buy you some business."

"How dare you insult me in the house of God?" Lucinda managed through clenched teeth after snatching the money.

"Step outside and I'll do a better job."

Lucinda reached her breaking point.

"Mama; Mr. Benny." Denise stepped between them just as Lucinda drew back her Bible en route to the side of Benny's head. "Did you enjoy service?" she asked nervously.

Lucinda huffed and glared, but slowly lowered the Bible to her side.

"Oh yes," Benny exclaimed, ignoring Lucinda. "The Word of God is always good, even if the company isn't."

Lucinda still wanted to beat Benny with the Bible, but didn't want to draw anymore attention to herself. Mother Gray was already gawking at Benny like he was the last piece of fried chicken on a buffet table. Lucinda glared at him then stomped away.

Denise apologized for her mother's behavior.

"Mr. Benny, I'm sorry you and Mama don't get along."

"I'm not," Benny responded flatly, and after Denise accepted his extended arm, headed to greet his friend.

"Son, I didn't know you could preach like that!" Benny exclaimed, embracing Bryce. "I almost fell out under the power."

"Next time I'll preach harder; anything to see you slain in the Spirit."

Watching the two laughing and teasing one another, Denise doubted Bryce realized his arm was still around Benny. The father and son picture flashed before her once again. Tonight she would not forget to have a talk with Bryce about his dad.

"Benny, I would invite you to dinner, but I have an emergency meeting." Bryce sounded disappointed, but Denise was concerned. As a rule, Bryce didn't hold meetings on Sundays.

"Is everything all right?" she asked.

"I don't know. Sister Anderson sent an urgent message to me this morning. She wants to meet with us both." Bryce turned to Denise.

"I'll be in your office." Denise quickly dismissed herself.

Bryce didn't miss the trepidation on his wife's face, but

now wasn't the time to probe. He'd ask her about it later at home.

Inside the office, Denise prayed fervently the pending meeting would not end in disaster. The only reason Melanie Anderson would want to meet with both she and Bryce would be to divulge her husband's secret hobby; the very same hobby that ensnared Bryce. How would Bryce act in response to learning his Youth Minister shares his addiction? Would he require Melanie to be as tolerant as Denise, or would he play the morally self-righteous pastor role?

Denise cast her lot on the latter. The last twenty-four hours had been life-altering for Bryce, but not to the magnitude he'd be willing to admit his problem to a church member. If Melanie was seeking help from Pastor Hightower to correct Clay, she was in for a major disappointment. That didn't stop Denise from praying for a miracle. Before Denise could say "in your son, Jesus' name," Bryce entered the office followed by Melanie.

Pastor Hightower invited Melanie to sit in one of the black cushioned chairs in front of his desk. He then sat in his executive chair with his elbows on the desk. Denise stood beside him and made eye contact with Melanie, trying to send her a telepathic message not to tell Bryce about Clay, but it didn't work.

As always, Pastor Hightower opened the meeting with prayer. "Melanie, why isn't Clay joining us?" he asked afterwards.

Melanie fidgeted with her fingers then rubbed her thighs nervously before deciding to answer. "That's what I want to talk to you about."

Pastor Hightower nodded for her to continue.

Melanie hesitated again, this time looking to Denise for support. Denise's empathy for Melanie overruled her need to be politically correct. She left Bryce and stood behind Melanie for support. Melanie smiled her appreciation.

"Pastor, Clay and I are no longer living together."

Both the pastor and first lady gasped at that statement. "Melanie, what are you talking about? I saw you and Clay enter the sanctuary together this morning." Pastor asked.

"I know, Pastor. We entered the building together, but we arrived in separate cars." Melanie explained. "I moved out three days ago." She paused to allow that news to settle. "Clay feels, due to his position in the church, it's best if we keep our separation a secret."

"Melanie, what is going on?" Pastor asked, almost accusingly. "What brought this on? You haven't been married long enough to have a reason to leave."

Denise rested an arm on Melanie's shoulder. Bryce realized then that she knew more than he did about the situation.

Melanie closed her eyes and inhaled deeply before laying everything on the line. "Clay is an adulterer."

Pastor Hightower's jaw fell twice before he was able to formulate words. "Melanie, I don't believe you," he said flatly, causing Denise to flinch. "I know Clay, and he loves you. I remember your wedding; he vowed with his own words never to put another woman before you."

"He didn't put another woman before me," Melanie clarified. "Clay has an entire harem."

"What?"

"Clay is addicted to pornography," Melanie said plainly. "I left him because he wants me to watch movies with him to help get him in the mood."

From behind Melanie, Denise watched her husband's piety and authoritativeness slowly evaporate. Pastor Hightower slumped back in his chair, not knowing what to say to his parishioner. Denise gripped the back of Melanie's chair, bracing herself for what she knew Melanie would ask for next, but wouldn't be granted.

"Pastor, I need you to talk to Clay," Melanie petitioned. "Clay respects you and he'll listen to you. If you counsel him and explain that pornography is wrong, he'll believe you."

Bryce remained quiet.

"Clay talks about how much you've impacted his life all the time. He thinks more highly of you than he does his father. Please, Pastor, you have to talk to him. If you tell him it's wrong, he'll receive it."

Melanie's pleading brought tears to Denise's eyes. *Please Bryce . . . Please do not make her suffer like me.*

"I'm sorry Melanie, but what happens between a husband and wife in their bedroom is none of the church's business."

The manufactured answer didn't move Melanie at all. "It is the church's business if that person is up and ministering over the people of God every Sunday. It's not right to impart that filth and deception into innocent people."

The force from the truth of Melanie's words nearly made him double over in shame. How many people had he infected with sin? Denise turned her back so she wouldn't see him squirm.

"Operating as a leader in God's church requires integrity, honesty and at the least, a holy lifestyle. You can't tell me pornography is holy!" Melanie's voice escalated. "As his pastor and spiritual father, you need to address this now!"

Pastor Hightower sat there nodding, rubbing his hands together; his way of holding back the shame and guilt of his addiction. He honestly didn't know what to say to rebut Melanie. He learned a long time ago not to argue with the truth.

"Melanie, have you tried praying and fasting for Clay?" Denise bit her lip, hoping the suggestion didn't sound as hollow as she felt inside.

When Lucinda had given her that generic remedy, she felt deserted and abandoned. Basically, carrying the weight of her husband's deliverance on her shoulders; or worse, the reason for his addiction. If she had been praying harder, perhaps he wouldn't have the addiction. Maybe if she'd fasted three days per week instead of two, he would get delivered faster. Not one time was the responsibility placed on Bryce. She was doing the same thing to Melanie now.

Melanie was much braver than Denise. "I have prayed, fasted and laid out prostrate and nothing changes. Do you want to know why?" Melanie asked Denise, looking dead in her eyes. "Nothing changes because Clay doesn't want to change!"

Bryce cleared his throat, finally finding something to say. "Are you sure he doesn't want to change? It could be that he doesn't know how to change."

Denise prayed Melanie didn't detect the desperation in Bryce's voice.

"Well, participating in group sex won't help him figure it out!" Melanie replied.

"What?" Pastor and First Lady yelled simultaneously.

"That's what it is," Melanie reasoned. "He watches strangers have sex then wants me to join in with the big screen."

Silence filled the office as the pastor and first lady considered the analogy. Melanie was correct, but Pastor Hightower wasn't going to admit it.

"Melanie, I think that's an extreme way to view the situation. I agree with my wife, Clay has a problem and all we can do is pray for him." Not wanting to see Denise's reaction to him using her as a scapegoat, Bryce avoided looking in her direction. "In the meantime, you should return home."

"That's not all you can do! I know he'll listen to you. All you have to do is sit down and talk to him." Pastor Hightower remained quiet as Melanie continued to plead. "I love Clay, but I can't do what he's asking. I won't. And I will not go back home and live a lie just because of his position as Youth Minister."

Denise now was finding it difficult to stand upright. Every word from Melanie's mouth hit her in the pit of her stomach. At that moment, she envied Melanie for being strong enough and having the integrity to confront the issue. Unlike her, Melanie would not hide behind a title or a position in the church. She would not allow Clay to damage her self-esteem to the point of starving herself, while permitting him to satisfy his flesh. Melanie would not be placed in the position of runner up.

"Melanie," Pastor Hightower started after clearing his throat again, "I'll spend time in prayer on this for direction on what approach to take."

Melanie would not be pacified. "What do you need to pray for? You're the pastor. Your Youth Minister is addicted to pornography. As watchman on the wall, it's your job to counsel him, and if need be, remove him from leadership until he's delivered."

Bryce shifted in his chair and rubbed his forehead with his thumbs. He didn't have a clue as to what to say. Looking the other way wasn't the answer, neither was disciplining Clay for committing the same sin he practices.

The thick drops of perspiration trickling down Bryce's face worried Denise. Pastor Hightower looked as if he was on the verge of a heart attack.

"Melanie, I agree Clay's behavior should be addressed," Denise said, coming to her husband's rescue. "But because Clay is in leadership, we have to handle this properly. Pastor is correct; we should pray for guidance. We don't want to do anything to bring embarrassment to Clay or the ministry. I think it's a good idea if we begin praying right now and touch bases in a few days."

Melanie contemplated the compromise for a long time. What the first lady suggested made perfect sense. She didn't want Clay's name dragged through the mud. If his problem became public, parents might have a problem with him working with their children. Then where would that leave him?

"Alright, but I'm not moving back until he changes," she declared.

"That's fair," Pastor Hightower agreed, standing to his feet, preparing to pray before Melanie changed her mind.

The drive back to the subdivision was long and uneventful, bearing no resemblance to the morning's trip. Bryce didn't reach for her hand and Denise didn't offer it. She laced her fingers together and stared out of the window at familiar scenery that was now unfamiliar; blurred by the tears pooling her eyes.

Positioning his hands in the ten and two position on the steering wheel, Bryce concentrated on the road ahead. He didn't slow down when the odometer reached 80. The sooner he arrived home, the sooner he could hide.

Chapter 13

♪*What a difference a day makes . . . Just 24 little hours . . .* ♪

"Ain't that the truth," Denise grumbled, agreeing with the age old song echoing through the car radio.

The contrast between her life at that very moment and twenty-four hours ago could best be compared to a Shakespearian tragedy. The day held all the ingredients to become an instant classic: romance, suspense, drama, lies, betrayal and violence.

Once she and Bryce entered the confines of their home last evening, long gone were the kisses and touches he'd showered on her earlier that morning. So were the expressions loaded with desire; not one word of adoration expressed. After removing his suit, Bryce hibernated to his study all night, leaving Denise alone in their king-sized bed.

Staring up at their bedroom's ceiling, Denise tried to understand his deportment. Learning his Youth Minister is addicted to pornography was a serious blow to him, and if the information were to become public, it would damage the credibility of the church. But not any worse than the fallout that would occur if news got around that Pastor Hightower is also controlled by the same lust. Having finally fully grasped how his addiction hindered his ability to shepherd the flock God placed in his care rocked Bryce's world in a way her pestering couldn't. Bryce was at a crossroad, and as the old folks used to say, "It was time to pee or get off the pot."

Denise stretched and dozed off, praying for Melanie's strength and patience, Clay's deliverance and for Pastor Hightower to stop straddling the fence and completely submit to the will of God.

"You have to talk to her!" Bryce declared, storming into the bathroom this morning. Denise nearly choked on her toothbrush from the shock. After regrouping, she continued her morning ritual as if Bryce wasn't standing there huffing and puffing like a big bad wolf, ready to blow down the house.

"I mean it, Denise. You have to make her understand!"

Leisurely, Denise rinsed her mouth then slowly massaged the skin moisturizer into her brown skin.

"Denise!" Bryce yelled. "You have to make her understand!"

"Understand what?" Denise calmly asked after replacing the cap on the moisturizer.

"Talk to Melanie and convince her to reconcile with Clay and remain quiet!" Bryce yelled, throwing his hands in the air, frustrated by Denise's nonchalant behavior.

Negro please! Be for real. Denise thought, but voiced, "Why would I do that? I agree with her."

Bryce's mouth still hung open as Denise brushed past him in the doorway leading into their bedroom. "You agree with what? Exposing a minister before the church?"

"Yes I do, if it'll help him." Denise stepped into her walk-in closet before mumbling, "Maybe if I'd exposed you, you wouldn't still be playing with yourself."

"What did you say?" he snarled, snatching the skirt from her hands.

"You heard me!"

"Woman, how many times do I have to tell you; I am trying!" Bryce threw the skirt on the floor then turned to leave.

"Were you trying last night in your study?" Denise yelled after him. Bryce froze but didn't turn around. "When you didn't come to bed I went to your study to check on you. For some stupid reason I was concerned about your lying and phony behind. How do you think I felt watching my husband fulfill his own lustful needs while I lay in bed alone, praying? You said we would work through this together, but you hid yourself from me!"

Bryce's body cringed, but he didn't deny the accusation.

"I felt like an idiot for allowing you to manipulate me into feeding Melanie that crap about praying. Prayer ain't helping you!" she screamed. "Melanie is right; prayer only works when the person wants to change. I saw you; you like playing with yourself!"

"No I don't!"

"Who are you trying to convince? Yourself? I don't believe one word from your lying tongue. If you don't like it, you wouldn't sneak around and you would get counseling. The only way you'll stop is if I expose your sorry behind before the church!"

He faced her then, but Denise didn't melt under the heat of his anger. Bryce took a step, and before Denise could stop him, punched a hole in the closet wall.

"Bryce!"

Bryce transformed into a man barely recognizable. His temporal veins protruded and his jaws flexed involuntarily, causing his face to appear distorted. His fists flexed to the rhythm of his uncontrolled breathing. "What happens in this house stays in this house. If you can't handle that, leave! I don't need useless dead weight hanging around." He turned to leave the bedroom.

The ice-coated words first chilled Denise to her bones, and then infuriated her. Without thinking, she grabbed her umbrella from the corner of the closet and began beating Bryce on the back. "I hate you!" she screamed. "You sorry. . . . you can kiss . . . go to . . ."

Between blows, Bryce managed to maneuver the umbrella from her. Denise continued spitting profanities and commenced to punching him in the chest with her fists.

"Stop it!" he yelled after lifting both arms above her head and pinning her against the bedroom wall.

The sobs began as sniffles then escalated to loud gut-wrenching bawling as she slid down the wall. "Look at what you've turned me into. I don't act like this. You don't care about anyone but yourself!" she managed between cries.

He released her arms and backed out of the room, leaving her alone.

When Denise was finally dressed and composed enough to leave for work, she decided she wasn't going. She called her secretary and informed her she was taking a day off. Still dressed for work with purse strap on her shoulder, Denise started for the garage.

"The denomination's Annual Worker's Meeting is Friday in Los Angeles. I expect you to join me."

Bryce's voice was enough to make her pause, but not stop and assure him of her loyalty. Denise left without looking back. Thinking back now, she wished she'd hit him one more time—on the head.

Following an hour drive down Pacific Coast Highway most of which was spent repenting for the filthy communication that flowed freely from her lips earlier, Denise parked in the lot of a popular beach and watched the waves roll in and leave again. The scene paralleled the indecisiveness that scrambled her mind about her marriage. Part of her wanted to buy a surfboard and ride one of the waves so far out to sea that land was no longer visible.

Then there was the other part; the part that would always love Bryce. It was her heart instructing her to ride out the turbulence until a higher altitude could be reached. She couldn't do it. With Bryce navigating, they were destined for a crash landing and soon.

Without asking him, Denise knew Bryce was going to drag Melanie along for as long as possible, then give some lame line about letting the Lord deal with Clay. Pastor Hightower would willingly open the door for lawlessness in the church and damage Melanie in the process. The problem was Melanie wouldn't agree. She'd divorce Clay and eventually leave the church. Clay would place the blame on her and Pastor Hightower would sit back and say absolutely nothing while Melanie's name was dragged through the mud. All to keep his sins covered. The older saints used to have a saying: "What is done in the dark will come to the light."

"Too bad that doesn't apply to preachers," Denise grumbled, checking the time on her console.

It was eleven o'clock. How was she going to fill the rest of her day without gorging on fast food? The highway was lined with the restaurants that provided endless fat and calories. Her stomach growled and she remembered the leftover Jenny Craig meal bars inside her trunk. After retrieving a peanut granola bar and a bottle of water, she dialed Erin's cell phone. Denise needed a distraction. Erin's motorized mouth was perfect.

Bryce zipped his nylon jacket, then stepped onto the pavement; keeping his steps slow and measured. With a luxury vehicle at his disposal, Bryce didn't walk much. Normally, he drove everywhere. Other subdivision residents could be seen all hours of the day and night walking from the dry cleaners to the local bank. Not Bryce. He'd pull his Mercedes out just to drive two blocks to the neighborhood mailbox.

Taking in the early summer moderate weather, Bryce became fascinated by things he'd once considered insignificant. Like the trees that lined the streets and uniquely designed contemporary homes. Every lawn was nicely manicured with a reflection of its owner. Centering the Carter's lawn was a beautiful arrangement of multi-colored tulips in the shape of a "C". Multi-colored rose bushes lined the Roswell's walkway.

Bryce missed a step and tripped, passing the Green's yard. Most of it was covered with ivy, reminding him of Benny's story and the breakdown he had in his arms. The memory of that tender moment is what propelled Bryce into leaving his house in search of his pushy friend. Right now, he needed someone to talk to before the depression hovering over him engulfed and buried him.

He hadn't meant to fall last night; it just happened. He needed a way to numb the pain of knowing one of his members, whom he held influence over, was addicted to pornography and he couldn't address it. Bryce couldn't help him. He needed to escape the pain of knowing he was a coward and lacked integrity. He was too self-centered to put his parishioner's needs before his own. He wasn't fit to be called a man of God. He wasn't worthy of God's grace. His wife no longer respected him and soon she'd be gone.

The possibility of Denise leaving was never more real than this morning. In the four years Bryce had known her, profanity and violence was never her style. He hadn't meant to ask her to leave or insinuate her size was a problem, but the idea of being exposed scared him into self-preservation. The church was all he had; the only place where he was accepted and validated.

At church, people listened to him and respected his opinion. From the moment he pulls into the parking lot, someone was there attending to his needs. He could change the atmosphere of the service with one word. At church, there wasn't competition; Pastor Hightower was always the center of attention. He loved God and he loved God's people, but the reality was Bryce extracted more from the church than he gave.

Standing in front of Benny's two-story Mediterranean-style home, Bryce second guessed his decision to confide in Benny anymore than he already had, but figured, what was left? Benny was aware of his porn addiction and yet respected him. Just two days ago, Benny assured Bryce he wasn't suffering alone and proved it by showing up at church and supporting him without Bryce asking him to.

He continued up the brick walkway and conceded that Benny had the most immaculate yard in the subdivision. The colors and design fascinated him to the point Bryce stood there mesmerized. Benny must have noticed him standing on the brick walkway gazing. He opened the door before Bryce could collect his thoughts.

"Hey, son," Benny said after stepping onto the porch and began walking toward his friend

"Benny?" The body that the tank top and walking shorts revealed was better conditioned than Bryce's. For a sixty-something-year-old man, he was in excellent shape. Benny had more cuts and ripples than most men half his age.

"Didn't know I had all this going on, did you?" Benny teased. "Pray you look this good when you reach my age."

Bryce laughed at his friend, although he'd settle for being half as fit as Benny. "Please don't wear that to my church. The entire Mother Board would backslide."

After sharing another laugh, a peaceful silence settled between them.

"Your yard is magnificent," Bryce commented, breaking the stillness.

"Did you expect anything less?"

"I see you missed the Sunday School lesson on humility." Bryce grinned.

"Oh no, I was there, but I like the one about the truth setting you free better. I tell you the truth, my yard is the best and it's going to remain that way."

All Bryce could do was shake his head at his overconfident friend.

"Come on, I'll show you around the yard and explain what everything is cause I know you don't have a clue."

Bryce followed without arguing with the truth.

Benny started in the far corner nearest the street where an American Birch shade tree stood encircled by Kelsey Dogwood. Tea plants, accompanied by Spanish and French lavenders, outlined the perimeter. The lush green turf's center was marked by a two-foot-tall granite fountain. The patches directly in front of the house were overflowing with hydrangeas, Japanese spirea and periwinkle plants. A trellised sitting area with willow chairs and table completed what Benny called the Garden of Tranquility.

Bryce stood in the middle of the yard with his hands stuffed in his pockets. "Benny, you've outdone yourself."

"Have you had lunch yet?" Benny asked, ignoring the compliment.

"No."

"Come inside, I'll make you something," Benny offered.

Bryce waved his hands in protest. "You don't have to do that. I can eat when I get back home."

"What's that scripture about receiving a prophet's reward for giving a preacher a drink of water, some food, or common sense?" Benny chuckled up the stairs.

Bryce slowly followed, cautiously at first, but once he

stepped inside the oversized living room with vaulted ceilings, he lost his reserve. Benny's living room resembled a major retail electronics store. He had it all; a mounted plasma big screen, surround sound system with mounted wall speakers, two DVD/VCR combos, three six-feet tall CD towers completely filled with movies and music, and Benny's favorite, a Play Station 3.

"Don't just stand there, have a seat," Benny ordered on his way to the kitchen.

Bryce crept across the hardwood floor in awe; understanding why Benny suggested they watch games here instead of at his house. Benny's setup was better than the local sports bar. The two oversized double-stuffed recliners with a built in heated back massager tipped the scale. Bryce removed his jacket and prepared to sit, but the pictures on the mantel captured his attention.

Standing in front of the brick fireplace, he attempted to read the story the photos lined across revealed. There was an old crinkled photo of a kid wearing a football uniform with a football tucked under his arm. By the shape of the kid's head, Bryce guessed it was a younger picture of Benny. He didn't have to guess who the three women were in the portrait hanging above the fireplace. Benny's daughters were the spitting image of him. There were more pictures of his daughters' high school and college graduations; all posed with Benny, showing nearly all thirty-two of his teeth.

Bryce's eyes drifted back to the kid with the football. There was something familiar about the way he held his head tilted slightly forward when he smiled. The same pose could be seen in all the photos. Only momentarily did Bryce wonder why the pose was familiar.

"I see you've met my girls," Benny said from behind.

Bryce turned to find Benny smiling and holding the pose with a tray containing two turkey sandwiches and two apples with a pitcher of lemonade. He decided to knock Benny down a peg. "It's a good thing they don't look nothing like you."

Benny's laughter filled the room. "Son, it ain't good for you to be lying, considering you're a preacher and all." Bryce joined in with his laughter. "Sit down before lightning strikes you in the behind."

Bryce obeyed as always, but before biting into his sandwich asked about the pictures. "You mentioned you liked watching football, but I didn't know you played also."

"After my parents died, I played every sport I could to keep my mind going," Benny said before taking a bite from his sandwich.

Bryce noticed Benny had removed the crust from the bread just as he had. It was a habit Bryce picked up from his mother. "How old were you when your parents died?" Bryce asked after taking a swig of lemonade.

"Eight, and my sisters were six and two. My parents died in a house fire trying to save us. The day after my parents' double funeral, my sisters and I were separated. Back in those days relatives took the kid they wanted and left the rest. One sister was shipped to a great aunt somewhere in New York. I'm not quite sure what happened to my baby sister. I heard she ended up with a cousin somewhere in Tennessee or Virginia. Either way, I haven't seen or heard from my sisters in fifty-two years."

Noting the faraway look on his friend's face, Bryce ate the rest of his sandwich in silence.

"I became a ward of the court and ended up in a foster home." Benny resumed on his own accord. "My foster family never adopted me. After the rape, I was glad they hadn't. I would have hated to have to live with that man's name." Benny washed the sandwich down with the remaining lemonade. "But you didn't come here for a lesson on the history of Bernard Johnson, horticulturist extraordinaire. You're here because you're in trouble, now spill it," Benny said, then after biting into his apple, leaned back in his chair and started the massager.

"W-what makes you think I'm in trouble?" Bryce managed after choking on his lemonade.

Benny frowned then sighed heavily. "I thought you stopped playing games the other night on that bench." Bryce looked away remembering his vulnerability. "You're in a lot of trouble or else you wouldn't have come searching for me without your big car. My guess is you're about to lose everything: your wife, church and your soul. If any of those things are important to you, I suggest we stop playing and get to work."

"What?"

The news hit Erin with the force of a sledgehammer. Her head jerked back and forth and her breathing slowed. The full glass of iced tea slipped from her finger and shattered into pieces upon impact with the table.

"What did you just say?" Erin asked again, ignoring the cold liquid that ran across the table and down unto her skirt.

Denise was too concerned with cleaning up the mess her breaking story had caused to answer Erin's question. "Excuse me." She got the waiter's attention, and in the meantime, used napkins to soak up the liquid and covered the broken glass.

The busboy arrived and Denise leaned away from the table and allowed him to work. Aware that her friend's mind was filled with questions and would no doubt demand an explanation, Denise avoided making eye contact with her for as long as possible.

The second Denise verbalized the life-changing decision she'd made less than ninety minutes earlier, remorse filled her heart and settled in the pit of her stomach like a rock. It was one thing to talk through the available options within the confines of one's mind. There, everything made sense and the only debate came from the conscience, which could be ignored.

All afternoon, she'd argued in her head about what step to take. Her heart agonized over the possibilities of starting over versus remaining quiet and looking the other way. To be completely honest, Denise didn't know if she possessed the courage to live her life without Bryce. But two things were certain, she couldn't live without integrity and she couldn't manipulate Melanie into accepting Clay's behavior.

The busboy barely turned his back when Erin took off with record speed. "I know you didn't say what I thought you said. Repeat that last statement once more and this time, speak English!"

"You heard correctly," Denise leaned back against the booth. "I'm leaving Bryce."

Erin didn't understand what those words meant. "Leaving him where?"

"Wherever he wants to be," Denise said after a long sigh. "I'm divorcing him." She quickly tucked her head behind the menu, hoping the sadness she felt in her heart didn't show on her face.

Erin snatched the menu from her and tossed it to the side. "What are you talking about? You and Bryce are happy, always have been to the point I wanted to vomit, but that's beside the point. What happened?"

Denise scanned the table then the restaurant for a focal point; something or someone she could use to keep from facing her friend when she exposed herself as a fraud. She settled on the teenager sporting blue and green braids.

"Bryce and I haven't been truly happy in a long time."

"You have to explain this to me like I'm a two-year-old, because I watch you guys every Sunday—well the two Sundays a month that I attend. I've eaten meals in your home and spent the night. You have the perfect marriage. Your husband worships the ground you walk on. He honors you constantly and showers you with great gifts like that new Lexus parked outside." Erin pointed a finger and rolled her neck. "You're lying to me."

"I wish I was," Denise said, smirking. "Truth is, all that public display was a front to cover up the mess." Denise envisioned her mother swinging a belt at her for bad-mouthing her precious pastor. Lucinda warned her against sharing her husband's faults, but Lucinda wasn't there and Denise was tired of pretending.

"In the beginning, I believed his words and gestures were genuine, but turns out he's a selfish and manipulating perpetrator. The sad part is, after I learned the truth, I became an accessory to the crime. I helped him live a lie."

"What did he do?" Erin wanted to know. "Did he cheat?"

Denise was slow to answer. She was hurt, but not to the extent she'd expose her husband. After all, Bryce was Erin's pastor.

"Let's just say he hurt me."

"I can't believe it." Erin slumped back against the booth in disbelief. Just twenty-four hours earlier, she was jealous of Denise's marriage. Now Denise was telling her it was over. "Denise, I don't know what to say. I can't believe it. Are you sure about this? I mean, have you tried to work things out?"

Denise finally made eye contact with her friend. "I tried, but Bryce doesn't want to change, so I'm leaving."

"Wow." Erin's mouth continuously hung open. "Where are you going? What are you going to do? How are you going to survive?"

Denise dryly chuckled at those questions. "Have you forgotten I'm a hospital executive with a six-figure salary? I'll live just fine without Pastor Hightower's offering." She sipped water to swallow the lump that formed in her throat.

"Are you sure about this?" Erin asked once more. "This is not something to take lightly. You have only been married a little over three years. It's normal to have a rocky beginning."

Denise lingered before answering, mainly to gain control of her emotions. "I've been thinking about this for a while. At first, I prayed things would change, but they haven't and I'm tired of praying."

Erin gazed expressionless at Denise for a long time, unable to find the right words for her friend. What did she know? She'd never been married and hadn't enjoyed a relationship longer than six months. "I don't know what to say. I don't understand it, but if this is what you really want, I'll support you. You're welcome to crash at my place until you find a spot of your own," she offered.

"I knew I could count on you, girl." Denise reached for Erin's hand. "But I'll wait until I have my own place before I officially move out."

"Have you started looking?"

Denise wanted to ask how does one begin to plan how to dismantle one's life, but didn't. "No."

"I'm sorry marriage didn't work for you, but look at it this way; better you walk away now than waste years of your life with the wrong person."

"You've got a point there," Denise commented, remembering she thought the same thing for Melanie.

Chapter 14

Bryce exhaled deeply, closed his eyes, then hung his head so low it nearly touched his knees. He had told Benny every detail of the past twenty-four hours. He left nothing out. He expected Benny to yell or at least criticize him, but he didn't. Benny didn't bat an eye or seem surprised.

"Hold your head up, son," Benny ordered. "A man keeps his head up even when he blows it."

"But you don't understand how bad I've blown it." Bryce's head still hung.

"I understand better than you think," Benny retorted. "That's why you're here."

Benny maneuvered from the comfort of his chair and returned the dirty dishes to the kitchen. When he returned, he found Bryce still slumped over. "Son, I have two questions for you. Honest answers to these questions are the key to your deliverance."

That seemed too simple for Bryce, but he indulged the old man. "Shoot."

"Are you ready, because this is it in a nutshell?" Benny smiled.

Bryce nodded yes.

"Do you love yourself?"

"Huh?" Bryce frowned. "What kind of question is that?"

"One you need to answer."

"Of course I love myself," Bryce answered without reservation.

Benny smiled. "Next question. Who are you?"

"Now you're tripping," Bryce smirked. "You know who I am."

"The one hundred thousand dollar question is do *you* know who you are?" Benny corrected.

"I'm Bryce James Hightower."

Benny pressed. "Who is Bryce James Hightower?"

"I'm pastor of Word of Life Church." Bryce was growing impatient with what he considered foolish questions.

Benny leaned forward and slapped his hand on his knees. "Just as I thought." He was smiling although he knew his next statements were going to shake Bryce to the core. "You don't love yourself and you don't have any idea of who you are."

Bryce jumped to his feet and made pun of Benny's diagnosis. "Up until now, I thought you were smart."

"I'm smarter than you. Sit down and I'll prove it." Bryce continued standing. "Fine, suit yourself. Stand, but before it's over, you'll be on your knees."

"You think you know everything, don't you?" Bryce smirked, returning to the recliner. "This time you're wrong. I love myself and I love what I do. What I want to know is how do I keep Denise from leaving."

Benny leaned back in his recliner, slowly rubbing his thumb across his chin. When he bowed his head, Bryce perceived he was praying for the right words. When his head returned upright, Bryce discerned he wasn't going to like the words the Lord had given his friend. Benny's smile was gone and replaced by a hard penetrating gaze that dissolved Bryce's self-assurance shell.

"Son, I know you think you do, but you really don't love yourself. How can you when you don't know who you are. You don't know who to love?"

"Yes I do," Bryce insisted. "I'm a servant of God."

Benny slowly shook his head in disagreement. "No, son, you have it wrong. That's *what* you are not *who* you are. Pastoring and serving God is *what* you do, not who you are. You're like a lot of people in ministry; you use the church to define your identity." Benny paused to allow the words to sink in. "God is the one who defines identity, not positions in the church. You're using the church the same way you're using porn; to fill a void in your life."

Bryce slumped back in the recliner from the force of Benny's words, but didn't contradict him.

"I watched you closely on yesterday. From the second your foot touched the platform, you were a different person. Both your attitude and countenance changed. Gone was the man lacking confidence to stand on his own merit. When the church stood at your entrance, I literally saw you transform into the self-assured and proud man I know you're capable of being. But you're not there yet."

Benny ignored the tears welling in Bryce's eyes and continued. "You don't love yourself because if you did, you wouldn't continue to do the very things that are destroying you."

"I tried—" Bryce started, but Benny wouldn't allow excuses.

"You tried after you got caught, to pacify your wife, but it wasn't from the heart. You just sat here and told me you fell to temptation last night as a way to escape your problems, then demanded your wife's assistance with deception. Be honest with yourself; Pastor Hightower will do everything possible to hold onto his covenanted position because that is where he receives his validation. You need the accolades and praise as much as you need oxygen. I don't doubt you love your wife, but you'd let her walk out of your life before you come clean about your addiction."

"You make it sound as if I like being this way." Bryce pouted.

"I never said that," Benny clarified. "I know you don't like it, but you are so afraid you'll lose your church if you seek help, that you feed and nurture the addiction the same way a mother nurses a newborn."

"I did the same thing with sex. I used sex to validate me as a man. In school, I learned how to read and write and work with numbers. On the football field, I learned how to run patterns and dodge tackles. On the baseball diamond, I learned to time a fast ball and steal bases. In trade school, I learned my trade. All my life I was blessed with wonderful and caring instructors, but not one of them taught me what it means to be a man. Not one of them told me I didn't have to spread myself around to prove my manhood. None of my coaches told me being molested by a male didn't condemn me to a life of homosexuality. Since I didn't know, I put my energy into pleasing as many women as possible, and before I knew it, I was addicted to sex. So addicted, I lost my wife."

"I don't want to lose Denise," Bryce whimpered.

"I know; that's why I told you about the ivy. You need to find out the root cause, what's fueling the addiction. What voids are you using the pornography and the church to fill? What hurts are you covering up with pornography as the band-aid? What happened that caused you to need the church for affirmation?"

Bryce sat there shrugging his shoulders, not bothering to conceal the tears dripping from his chin.

"Did something traumatic happen in your childhood?" Benny pressed. "Were you violated?"

Bryce shook his head from side to side.

Benny sighed and allowed Bryce time to meditate on his words. He remembered the day he was forced to face reality. It's not easy for a grown man to accept that he's insecure and controlled by something that can't be seen. He'd give Bryce time; tomorrow he'd dig deeper.

While pulling into her driveway, Denise gave herself a pep talk. "You can do this . . . just a few more days." During the hour drive home she reasoned, trying to convince herself that leaving Bryce was in her best interest. She was so certain until Erin hugged her goodbye. There was sadness in her eyes that she'd never seen in eight years of friendship.

"I feel like mourning," Erin had said after asking once more if Denise was positive she wanted a divorce.

In the restaurant's parking lot, Denise emphatically screamed, "Yes," but now in the home she loved; the one Bryce purchased for her, Denise wasn't so sure.

"Why does love have to be so complicated," she mumbled entering the kitchen.

After this morning's beating, she didn't expect Bryce to be happy about seeing her, but she was a little disappointed when he didn't emerge to greet her. "He's probably in his study playing with himself." She checked there, but he wasn't there. He wasn't in the bedroom either. His car was there, but he wasn't. At first, she viewed her husband's absence as a reprieve, but after an hour, she began to worry. She didn't want to care, but she did.

It was Monday, the day Bryce used for resting. As a rule, he didn't hold office hours nor scheduled appointments on Mondays. Bryce barely got out of bed, let alone left without his car. On Mondays, emergencies were normally handled by the associate ministers.

Denise fished her cell phone from her purse. She'd turned it off on the highway almost eight hours ago. "Where is he?" she voiced after checking her voicemail. There weren't any calls from Bryce, but three calls from her mother wondering why she wasn't at work. After deleting her mother's messages, Denise checked every room in the house. Everything was in order, but no Bryce.

I'd better get used to this, she thought, sitting down at the kitchen table. *Bryce is a grown man; he can find his way home.* The thoughts were meant to squash the panic bubbling deep within, but it didn't work. She gave in to her anxiety and dialed his cell phone. Bryce and Benny walked though the door on the third ring.

For a brief moment, Denise was relieved to know all was well with her husband, at least physically. She wasn't going to let Bryce know she'd been worried for his safety.

"Hello, Mr. Benny." Denise hugged him then offered him something to drink without speaking to her husband.

"No thank you; we ate at my house."

Denise snapped her head around to Bryce. "When did you start making house visits on Mondays?"

"Since he started punching holes into walls," Benny answered holding up a metal can containing something that resembled paste and a spatula.

Denise continued staring at her husband with amazement. There was only one way for Benny to know Bryce punched a hole into the wall; Bryce had to have told him. It was totally out of character for her husband to present himself in a negative light.

"I'm going to show him how to fix the hole," Benny continued. "It won't take but a few minutes, then you can have your husband all to yourself." Benny smiled, but Denise rolled her eyes at Bryce and began sorting through mail as if they'd already left the room.

Bryce gazed at Denise's back; moving his lips and trying to find the right words to say. He needed to say something to make Denise understand how sorry he was for his behavior, but he couldn't find the words. He started to reach for her, but Benny tapped his shoulder and asked him for directions to the damaged wall.

"Give her some time," Benny instructed once they were in the bedroom. "She's too angry right now."

"She's going to leave; I can feel it."

"Maybe she will, maybe she won't. You still have to get yourself together regardless of if she's here or not. You have to do this one for yourself."

"I love her, Benny," Bryce said sadly. "I don't know how that's possible, since you've pointed out so eloquently that I don't love myself. That may be true, but I do love her."

"You do love her in your own way," Benny said examining the hole. "When you start loving yourself, you'll love her the way she needs to be loved."

Bryce nodded but didn't say any more. Benny had put enough on his mind for him to ponder the rest of his life. In the span of one afternoon, Benny ripped to shreds the delusions he'd manufactured about his life and who he was. He made Bryce face the reality he'd desperately tried to avoid. Yes, he was an insecure man who used his job as pastor to cover it up. It was true; he used pornography to suppress the inadequacies he carried as a man. Who or what represented the ivy in Bryce's own life, he didn't know; but he would find out, and soon.

Denise exhaled once Bryce rounded the corner. She felt the heat of his searing eyes burning a hole into her back. Without turning around, she was aware he wanted to say something, but as was his method of operation, he couldn't form words. It wouldn't have mattered anyway. There was nothing Bryce could say to her that would make her change her mind about leaving him. Unless he agreed to get counseling and talk to Clay, their marriage was over.

"Denise! Bryce!"

At the sound of her mother's frantic voice, Denise ran into the living room.

"Mama, what's wrong?" she asked, noticing the fear on Lucinda's face.

"I should be asking you that!" Lucinda replied, trying to catch her breath.

"Mother, what's the problem?" Bryce asked, joining them.

"You tell me. I have been calling the two of you all day on both the house phone and cell numbers to no avail." Lucinda turned to Denise. "When your secretary said you didn't show up for work, I began to worry."

Denise ignored the look Bryce shot her.

"I didn't know where y'all were so I drove over here and used the spare key to make sure nothing had happened to you." Lucinda took a deep, long breath then, after exhaling, continued. "Next time, please answer the phone, y'all know how I worry."

"That's because you ain't got no business of your own to mind," Benny said, coming from the hallway. "If you had some, you'd leave these kids alone."

Benny was behind Lucinda so he couldn't see her counting to ten and balling her fist.

"What happens between me and my family is none—" When Lucinda turned to face Benny, she lost her train of thought. He was still wearing the tank top and walking shorts, but carried his jacket in his hand. Lucinda stood there with her mouth wide open.

"Mama, I'm sorry." Denise jumped in before Lucinda embarrassed herself any further, but it was too late.

"About what?" Lucinda was rendered completely ignorant. "What are you sorry about, baby?" she asked, still staring at Benny.

Everyone but Lucinda laughed. Realizing she was the punch line of the joke, Lucinda snapped out of the trance. "Look here, you spawn of Satan; don't worry about what I do and go put some clothes on," she said, pointing a finger at Benny.

"I have clothes on, Jezebel. Why don't you stop lusting?"

"That's enough." Bryce jumped in before Lucinda hit Benny with her purse. "Mother, I'm sorry, I left my phone at home while I was at Benny's."

Lucinda snarled at Benny. "The more time he spends with you, Lucifer, the more irresponsible he becomes. You're a bad influence!"

"Mama, that's not fair. It's not Benny's fault Bryce left his phone any more than it's his fault I didn't answer mine. Mother, apologize to Benny," Denise insisted.

Lucinda threw her head so that her long salt and pepper hair flung and rested down her back. "Under no circumstances will I ever apologize to this old, dirty devil."

"Fine with me," Benny retorted. "I didn't expect it no way, Delilah."

"What is it with the two of you?" Bryce interrupted. "You're like oil and water."

"Pastor, you know what the Bible says, light and darkness don't have no fellowship," Lucinda responded.

"Mother, come with me." Denise grabbed Lucinda and ushered her into the kitchen before round two started.

When it was time for Lucinda to leave, Bryce walked her to the car. Benny took the opportunity to plead with Denise.

"I know it's hard right now, but please don't give up on him."

Denise gathered her dishes and placed them in the sink. "Benny, you don't understand. You don't know what I'm dealing with."

"Yes I do. He told me everything," Benny said, placing his arm around her shoulder.

"Everything?" she said, looking up at him.

"Everything," he assured her.

Denise didn't quite know what to make of that. She wasn't used to her husband sharing with anyone, and now he chose the gardener, of all people, to confide in.

"He has issues; but he loves you. Please don't give up on him just yet."

Denise wiped the tear that trickled down her cheek. "It's too late, Benny. I'm leaving him as soon as I find an apartment." She left Benny alone in the kitchen.

Chapter 15

From the doorway, Bryce watched Denise undress and prepare to shower. He didn't know if he should approach her or not. After much deliberation, he decided to take the chance.

"Niecy," he said softly from the doorway. "Can we talk?" She didn't answer and he assumed she hadn't heard him so he asked again.

"We don't have anything to talk about. You said it all this morning." She brushed past him into the master bathroom. She slammed the door so hard the print of a young child entering an outhouse, which hung on the wall, fell to the floor.

After this morning's attack, he knew better than to follow her into the bathroom.

Bryce crept over to the king-sized bed and studied his surroundings. Every thing in that room reminded him of Denise. Every piece of furniture was chosen by her. She decided on the Thomasville bedroom suit because her mother said it would last forever. The green, black and cream décor was her idea. "Green is a warm fertile color," she said when he suggested blue. Wanting to make her happy, Bryce quickly agreed.

Back then, he would have done anything to keep her happy and in love with him. Now, he wondered if he'd been driven by his insecurity. Had his fear of rejection clouded his decision making process? Did it prevent him from honestly expressing himself?

Before he could answer those questions, the bathroom door opened and Denise stepped out wearing flannel pajamas.

"I don't want to hear it," she said before he could speak.

"Just tell me where you were today."

"What difference does it make? In a few days my whereabouts will no longer be your concern." Denise pulled the comforter back and climbed into bed.

"I don't want you to leave."

"Of course you don't," she smirked. "You want me around for the trip this weekend. Sorry, my days of living a lie are over."

"Denise, please give me another chance." His voice broke. "I can't do this by myself."

Denise laughed hysterically out loud. "Bryce, you've proven you can do just about everything without me. I'll bet since we've been married, you've had twice the sex I've had." She laughed. "I hope it was good, because I'm checking out."

Desperation took over. "I'll get counseling," he vowed.

"For real?" Denise was being sarcastic.

"Yes."

"Good; then you'll be a better husband to your next wife." She smiled then removed a novel from her nightstand drawer. She'd completed reading two pages before Bryce stopped staring at her and left the bedroom. She didn't see him until the next morning.

He was sitting at the kitchen table when she left for work. He greeted her, but instead of returning the salutation, she said. "I'll be home late; I'll be looking at apartments this evening." She left without giving him a chance to object.

On the drive to work, Denise sang along with her favorite gospel artist on satellite radio. It was indeed a new season and a brand new day, and whatever was coming her way had to be fresher than what had been. Three months and twenty pounds later, she was a different person than the woman who packed a picnic basket and ended up with a bad case of porn.

Then, Denise thought she needed Bryce; that the world would crumble without her precious husband. Today was proof that life can and would go on without Bryce Hightower.

"It is too early for foolishness," she mumbled when her cell phone rang, assuming it was Bryce. "What?" she answered without checking the Caller ID.

"I see you're not a morning person," Erin retorted on the other end.

"I'm sorry, I thought you were Bryce," Denise explained while inserting her earpiece. "What's up?"

Erin paused before answering. "I guess by your disposition, you haven't changed your mind about remaining Mrs. Bryce Hightower."

"Nope, and after work I'm going apartment hunting."

"Really?" Erin said slowly.

"Don't be surprised, Erin, I told you last night and Bryce this morning. The only person left to tell is Mama. I think I'll mail her a letter," Denise laughed. She pulled into her parking space and turned off the engine.

"Is Bryce okay with this?"

Denise smirked. "As long as he keeps doing his dirt, he doesn't have a choice."

"Well girl, as long as you're happy." Erin was back to her

normal speed. "There are some vacant units in my building."

"Thanks, I'll look into it." They chatted until Denise entered the elevator and lost the wireless signal.

Seated behind her desk, Denise checked her e-mails and returned phone calls from the previous day. Fifty emails and fifteen calls later, she was finally able to take a breather.

"Remind me never to take a Monday off," she called out to her secretary who was actually in a good mood today.

"The next time you decide to take a day off, whatever day of the week, please tell your mother," Jennifer said, sticking her head inside. "She called here three times yesterday. On the second call, she insisted I check your office to make sure you hadn't arrived without my knowledge. On the last call, she had the audacity to tell me to check your calendar for any scheduled meetings I may have forgotten."

Denise apologized for her mother's behavior and offered to treat her to lunch as a consolation prize.

"As long as it's not one of those pre-packaged meals you love so much."

Denise retrieved a $20 bill from her purse and told her to keep the change. Alone again, Denise began her Internet search for her new residence. One of the benefits of living in the congested and expensive Bay Area was the plenteous availability of luxury apartments, townhouses and lofts, all within walking distance of major freeways and public transportation. Some complexes included restaurants, dry cleaners and grocery markets on the premises.

After an hour of searching, Denise narrowed her selection down to two townhouses and one apartment; all within walking distance of the office and miles from Bryce. After scheduling tours for later that evening, she increased the volume on the CD player in an effort to drown out the voice of warning in her head.

* * *

Placing his dirty dishes into the sink, Bryce spotted Benny working in the yard. He breathed a sigh of relief; now he didn't have to walk over to his house. That would only prolong the time and Bryce needed to talk now. Compiled on top of Denise's announcement, Melanie had called earlier and wanted to know if he'd finished praying about talking to Clay. It was difficult, but he managed to put her off for a couple more days, knowing he'd be away at the Annual Worker's Meeting when she called again.

Bryce dried his hands using a paper towel and exited the back door.

Benny toiled in the soil, but his mind wasn't on the yard. He could tend to a yard with his eyes closed . . . literally. Which was a good thing because most of the morning his eyes were closed as he labored in prayer for Bryce. His young protégé needed help—and fast.

In a short period of time, God had given him a genuine love for Bryce that was so strong, Benny doubted if he would love him any more if he were his own son. Benny couldn't understand how his heart just opened up to his neighbor, but he couldn't deny how much Bryce meant to him. He had always wanted a son, and now, in God's own way, He had given him one.

"Need some help?" Bryce approached from behind.

"From who?" Benny asked, trying to lighten his mood. Bryce's face was etched with stress. He looked like he hadn't slept in days.

Bryce studied Benny's face and recalled the last time he'd been this open and vulnerable with anyone. It was with his mother over eighteen years ago. After a disastrous first date, in which the young girl openly laughed at him for not being a good dancer or kisser, Bryce spent the night crying in his mother's arms. His father returned home from a sixteen hour shift at the port and upon seeing his teenaged son huddled against Mavis, labeled him a helpless mama's boy.

"You ain't worth nothing!" Thomas declared before storming into his bedroom.

"Son," Benny called for the second time. Bryce was so caught up in the memory, he didn't hear him initially.

"I didn't hear you."

"I know you have a lot on your mind, but I need you to focus for a while. I spoke with your wife last night." It wasn't necessary for Benny to finish the thought. He handed Bryce a spare pair of gloves and demonstrated how to lay the seeds into the soil then started on the next row. "What was your childhood like?" Benny asked.

"Funny you should ask. Since meeting you, I've thought more about my childhood than I have in the last seventeen years."

Benny continued down the row. "Were you close to your parents?"

"My mom and I were very close; we did everything together." Bryce worked, but at a much slower pace than Benny. "She was an only child, and after me, she couldn't have anymore. She was the best cook and I could talk to her about anything. I miss her like crazy." Bryce went on to share countless memories of his beloved mother, including how she accompanied him to the prom.

"What about your father?"

Bryce moved faster down the row. "My father was a longshoreman. He worked long hours so my mother could be a stay-at-home mom and I could attend private school."

Benny observed the way Bryce struggled with finding something good to say about his father. Bryce's arms flapped nervously and his eyes blinked rapidly. Benny had a feeling he was about to strike the ivy.

"Were you close to him?" Benny pressed on.

"No, not really."

"Why not?"

Bryce stopped moving and stood upright, searching for something, anything to distract him from recalling the painful memories of growing up in the house with a father, but yet not having the love of a father.

"I don't know. We just never seemed to connect. He was always busy working, I guess."

"What about when you were a teen?" Benny asked.

Bryce resumed working, but at a much slower pace. He moved so slowly, Benny took the seeds from him and finished his row and the remaining two rows. Bryce talked even slower, sharing the day his father came to his baseball game and how he struck out. Repeating his father's words on the night of the failed date brought tears to Bryce's eyes. He'd long forgotten the young girl's name, but his father's statement held permanent residence in his mind.

When he reeled his mind back to the present, Benny was smiling at him. Bryce's insecurity took over and he accused Benny of making fun of him.

"I'm glad you find this amusing," Bryce said with sarcasm.

Benny slapped him on the shoulder. "Son, I'm not making fun of you; I'm celebrating."

Bryce was confused. "Celebrating what?" he asked guardedly.

"Don't you see it?" Benny was so excited he leaped into the air.

"See what?"

"The ivy," Benny screamed and did a quick two-step dance. "We have just found the ivy. Now all we have to do is dig up the roots!"

"Here we go again," Denise moaned, stepping from her Lexus. She prayed this townhouse, unlike the one before it, lived up to the embellished advertised description.

The ad said it was 1600 square feet. What it didn't say was the square footage was divided among three levels; four if you included the garage. If the stairs hadn't turned her off, the bathroom located next to the kitchen would have.

The complex on Broadway Terrace held much promise. Already she liked the contemporary design and manicured grounds. For a split second, the yard Benny had worked so hard to groom flashed before her. She shook the thought away and made her way across the guest parking lot to the leasing office.

The manager greeted her and immediately Denise liked her personality. She liked the corner unit even more. It had everything she wanted; three bedrooms, one which she would use for a home office; two and a half baths and her favorite, a master suite with a fireplace and Jacuzzi sunken tub. *Just like home*, she thought.

"Ms. Hightower, I know you'll love it here. Our complex is usually quiet. Most of our residents are professional people who don't have the time or don't want the hassle of upkeeping a home."

"That explains the foreign luxury vehicles," Denise smiled and began filling out the application and consent to run a background and credit check. She'd just signed the signature line when a familiar voice greeted her.

"Denise?"

She looked over her shoulder and was pleasantly surprised to see Jonas standing in the manager's doorway.

"Jonas, how are you?" He walked over to her chair and the two shared a brief hug.

"I'm good and yourself?" Jonas followed Denise's eyes to the papers on the desk.

"I've been better," she answered with a half smile.

"You look good."

Jonas and the manager greeted each other by first names. That's when Denise realized Jonas was a resident and not a visitor.

"Do you live here?" she asked, to be certain.

He smiled. "Building three, corner unit."

"This is some coincidence. I'm considering building four, corner unit."

They chatted a while longer before Jonas apologized for interrupting and excused himself. Denise assumed he'd retired to his unit, but she was wrong. Jonas was waiting for her in the parking lot.

Jonas was direct and to the point. "Denise, would you like to tell me what's going on? Why are you moving here?"

"Why not here? It's a lovely place." Denise wasn't ready to share her personal business with Jonas.

"From what Erin told me, so is your home."

Denise took the opportunity and redirected the conversation. "I wasn't aware you and Erin were still seeing each other."

"We're not. She mentioned that to me once she found out where I live. I think it was her way of telling me she'd like a house similar to yours if we ever got married." As the words poured from his mouth, Jonas's face contorted as if he'd swallowed something bitter.

"You should give Erin a call; she's really an interesting woman," Denise suggested.

"You should stop avoiding my question." Jonas reeled her back in.

"What question?"

"Why are you moving here? Are you and your husband calling it quits?"

Denise forced a giggle. "Now, that's two questions." Jonas stood there gazing silently until she relented. "Yes, I am leaving my husband."

"Do you want to talk about it?" He didn't appear shocked or surprised. "I'm free this evening, I'm preparing stir fry chicken over rice. You're more than welcome to join me."

After she agreed to grace him with her company, Jonas started walking in the direction of his unit.

"Can you cook for real?"

"I didn't say cook; I said prepare. There is a difference." Jonas smiled.

It wasn't until she entered Jonas's townhouse did she realize she'd agreed to have dinner alone with him. Instinct told her to leave. Lucinda's teachings reminded her it wasn't good to be alone with a man while you're hurting over another one. Instinct and Lucinda didn't matter right now. She needed a distraction and Jonas was harmless.

He gave her a quick tour of the unit and proudly showed off photos of his boys.

She learned what he meant by prepare. Jonas's idea of stir fry came in a bag from the frozen food section and Minute Rice. Denise was hungry and wanted the company, so she didn't complain.

"Would you like some music?" Jonas asked.

"Sure."

Denise leaned her head against the couch and enjoyed the sounds of Najee while Jonas prepared the meal.

"So how have you really been?" Jonas asked from the kitchen.

Denise started to yell back, then decided to join him instead. "Jonas, why didn't you seem surprised when I mentioned the separation?"

"Because you didn't seem happy with him," Jonas answered, placing two plates on the counter.

"What do you mean?" Denise thought she had concealed the truth.

"For one thing, you didn't talk about him unless someone else mentioned him. And that day in the restaurant, your whole demeanor changed when he showed up. In a matter of seconds, you went from happy to melancholy." Jonas transferred the rice and stir-fry to the plates and handed Denise a fork.

"I didn't know it was that obvious."

"It is to a man who pays attention to women," Jonas explained. "Do you want to talk about it?"

Denise explained without sharing too many details that Bryce was not the man she thought he was, and it was best they part now before totally ruining one another's lives.

"How does he feel about it?"

"I don't know," Denise answered honestly. This morning she didn't give Bryce a chance to respond.

"Are you sure you want to give up being the first lady?" Jonas asked although he knew the answer. Denise wasn't the type to feed off of being the center of attention.

"Don't believe the hype. Being married to a pastor isn't all that it's cracked up to be," Denise smirked. "I'd rather be a regular church member at a church where nobody knows me."

"Sometimes I feel that way about being a doctor."

They enjoyed good dinner conversation. Jonas didn't press her about the separation or attempt to convince her to move into the complex. Mostly they talked about work and their shared taste in music and movies. Jonas popped in a Tyler Perry DVD and retired to the recliner, and Denise stretched on the couch.

At end of *Madea Goes to Jail*, they were both in tears. Jonas's were from the stage play, but Denise's were mingled with the regret she was beginning to feel. She hadn't officially left Bryce yet, and she missed him already.

"I'd better get going," she said casually, looking at her watch. "Thanks for dinner."

Jonas stood and walked her to the door. His silence told her he understood her sudden desire to leave.

"I know what it's like to have what you thought was going

to last forever die. If you ever want to talk, I'm here," he said before opening the door.

"Thank you, Jonas. You're a good friend." They hugged briefly once more and then she left. Before getting into her car, Denise looked back and saw Jonas watching from the window. She waved and he waved back.

Maybe I should rethink moving so close to him, she thought, shifting the gear shift into drive.

Denise entered the house prepared to battle with Bryce over why she was arriving home after midnight, but he didn't argue. He didn't say anything. He was sitting in the living room when she arrived. After a long hard gaze, he left her there and went into his study.

She went into the kitchen, and out of habit, opened the refrigerator. "Mama is always looking out for him," she mumbled at the food storage container with one of Bryce's favorite meals. She wondered why he didn't eat the roasted chicken, cabbage and macaroni & cheese. After tasting a pinch of macaroni & cheese and cabbage, she understood why. "Mama, you're slipping," she said of the bland food.

On the way to her bedroom, Denise stopped at Bryce's door. When she didn't hear anything, she grew angry, assuming he was at it again. What she didn't know was her husband was on the floor, crying quietly.

Chapter 16

"Mavis, it's not right how you smother that boy!" Thomas barked. "I know you're protective of him because he's your only child, but you're making him weak!"

"No, I'm not!" Mavis closed the bedroom door so Bryce wouldn't hear them arguing. "If anyone is making him weak, it's you!"

"Woman, what are you talking about?" Thomas fumed. "I take very good care of you and that boy. You haven't worked a day since we married, and that boy has the best of everything."

"That boy is your son!" Mavis yelled, which was out of character for her. "It's time you started acting like it. Stop insulting him and be a father to him!"

"I am the best father I can be, but he's too busy laying up next to you to notice." Thomas retrieved his pajamas from the bureau then slammed the drawer shut. "I take better care of that boy than my father ever did. I didn't know where my father lived until I was ten years old, and after that, I saw him twice a year. That boy knows exactly where I am at all times."

Mavis stepped closer to him and touched his arm. "Thomas, he doesn't know you. Yes, he knows you're his father, but he doesn't know you as a person." She sighed, exasperated. "Everything he does is to please you. You're his idol, but all he receives from you is rejection and criticism. You don't attend school events, and the only time you express interest in him is when disciplining him for not doing something you think he ought to know to do. How is he supposed to know anything, if you don't teach him?"

Thomas reached in the nightstand and pulled something out. "Mavis, I'm teaching him the best I can. You want me to be all tender and affectionate; that's not me. I came up the hard way and I made it. Bryce has more than I ever had. He has a father who cares enough to see to it that he doesn't starve and has a place to lay his head. That's more than I had. That alone should make him a better man than me. If that's not enough, that's too bad. That's all I can give."

Mavis started to follow him into the bathroom, but knew better. Talking about his absent father took Thomas to places she wasn't allowed.

Bryce awakened during the night, shaking and dripping with sweat. His eyes frantically surveyed his surroundings. The distant moon yielded the only light illuminating the dark coffin enclosing him. Hours had passed and he was still on the floor of his study, curled in the fetal position. The tears had long dried, but the sadness and longing remained with a vengeance, bringing with it a depression so deep he considered suicide as a remedy.

Bryce's recall of the argument he'd overheard between his parents so many years ago was salt to the wounds Benny opened hours earlier in the yard. It was two in the morning when his father returned from working a double shift. His mother assumed he was sleeping, but what Mavis didn't know was that Bryce couldn't fall asleep until his father was home. He worried for his safety.

Like a skillful arborist, Benny dug deep and hauled away not only the tree, but the roots as well. Out in the yard, Bryce found himself looking for something to use as a cover up. Under Benny's spiritual eye, Bryce felt naked as a newborn babe. Benny masterfully cut away the protective foreskin and exposed his very essence.

"Don't you see? Pornography is the symptom; not receiving love and validation from your father is the disease. That's where the insecurity stems from," Benny had explained. "You needed your father's approval, but what you got was criticism and rejection, so you thought something was wrong with you."

In the yard, Bryce argued that was not the case, but alone in his study preparing to masturbate as a way to escape the sting of Benny's words, Bryce conceded. Looking down at himself, the first time desire stirred in him flashed before his eyes. It was the day he went through his father's belongings.

Throughout his teenage years he wanted to talk to his father about the changes in his body; about the nocturnal emissions and why he lost his train of thought when his ninth grade English teacher entered the classroom. The only thing Thomas was concerned about was Bryce impregnating someone, not that Bryce was too young for sex. That was the one thing has father didn't criticize or belittle him about.

The day he discovered his father's porn, Bryce's distorted young mind told him it was all right for him to masturbate, that his father would for once be pleased with him. That that was what a man did. Seventeen years later, Bryce was still searching for that acceptance from the grave.

Having admitted that vaporized the pleasure from the act, and for the first time, Bryce saw pornography for what it really was: sick, satanic and the means by which he destroyed his marriage and deceived the church. Defeated, Bryce zipped his pants and fell to his knees, repenting from the pit of his soul. He didn't make any vain promises to God or make any vows. He didn't think he was capable of keeping them. He didn't know himself anymore.

Earlier, Bryce had wanted to talk to Denise about his discovery, but she wasn't around, and when she did return home, the look of disgust she bore crushed what little courage he had left. His marriage was over; soon, Denise would be gone. Bryce was still a man of God, but sitting alone on the floor in the darkness, Pastor Hightower wanted to commit suicide. He remembered the bottle of Vicodin the dentist gave him after removing his wisdom teeth. Slowly, Bryce rose from the floor and headed for the bathroom.

Benny, unable to shake the gloom he felt tugging at him, crawled out of bed and onto his knees. Still groggy, at first he couldn't think of what to pray for. A vision of Bryce flashed before him and Benny began to weep and cry, asking God to help him. "Please, God!" Benny cried from the pit of his belly. At the first sign of daylight, Benny dressed and jogged around the corner to check on Bryce.

Chapter 17

"How did the apartment hunting go?"

Denise stopped eating nonfat yogurt long enough to answer Erin. She was getting used to the daily phone calls from her friend. Since learning the truth about Denise's marriage, Erin called everyday to check on her, and instead of talking a mile a minute about herself, Erin listened. Her mother had been wrong. Erin wasn't jealous of her. "Great. You won't believe in whose complex I found a suitable townhouse."

"I don't have any idea, but I am concerned about you. I still can't believe you're actually going to leave Bryce."

"Is that the reason you've called me two days in a row?" Denise asked before tossing the plastic container into the recycle bin. "I usually place a distant third behind your court cases and shopping sprees."

Erin chuckled on the other end of the phone. "You know you're my girl. I just want to make sure you're doing the right thing. This is a major decision."

Denise wasn't sure she was. Lying alone in bed while her husband handled his business in the confines of his study, she was sure. But now, watching Bryce, in the yard with Benny, through the kitchen window, she wasn't so certain. Bryce looked wrecked; like he hadn't slept in days, and he was wearing the same clothes he had worn the day before. She was sure he hadn't brushed his teeth. He entered their bedroom once in the middle of the night. She felt and heard him standing over her, but pretended to be asleep. After a while, she heard him in the bathroom cabinet. He came back to the bed and whispered he was sorry, then left. The door to his study was closed when Denise passed by it this morning. Until now, she assumed Bryce was in there.

"So where are you moving and when?" Erin asked, breaking her concentration.

"I found the perfect townhouse in the same complex as Jonas's." Denise anticipated animosity toward Jonas from Erin for the way he rejected her, but Erin didn't offer any.

"That's great! I like that complex. When are you moving?"

"I'll know in a couple of days," Denise said with her eyes still glued to Bryce, who was now sitting on the bench with his shoulders slumped. "I'm going to start looking for furniture this evening."

"Why? Have you forgotten this is California; you get half of everything?" Erin reminded.

"Half of hell? No, thank you," Denise said firmly. "Bryce can have it all."

"Let me know if you need a good divorce lawyer. I can call in some favors for you."

"I'll keep that in mind," Denise said as the words 'divorce lawyer' registered in her mind. Those were two words she never expected to hear with her as the subject.

"Gotta go. I was just calling to check on you. I have to be in court in thirty minutes."

"Thanks," Denise said, but Erin had already disconnected.

Denise clipped her cell phone to her waist and resumed

observing her husband with the gardener. Her mother's assessment was accurate; Benny did more talking than gardening. Bryce obviously trusted and held him in high regard. Watching the two of them reminded her again of the photo still tucked away in her briefcase of the father and son that had overcame pornography addiction. They hadn't had a chance to discuss the information she had found, and now it was too late. Still, Denise couldn't help but ponder about Bryce's relationship with his father.

She wondered if it was as distorted as the one she had with her father. She thought Jeremiah Sanders was an angel without wings. He was her hero. That was then. Today, he was a liar and a cheat; a dirty old man. And she married a man just like him, but she was going to break the cycle. Unlike her mother, Denise was not going to share with anyone—real or not. She would end the generational curse.

Denise noticed Bryce and Benny heading for the back door. Denise grabbed her purse and briefcase and dashed out before Bryce's hand touched the knob.

Denise was in the middle of shutting down her computer when Jennifer knocked and asked if she could have a minute of her time. Denise was tempted to refuse, wanting to change and walk the Marina before stopping by Ethan Allen at Emery Bay.

"It's after five, what is it?" Denise hoped the irritation she felt wasn't evident.

"I've been working for you for over a year and you've invited me to your church on several occasions. I've always refused, but tonight I'd like to attend. I believe you have Bible Study tonight, I don't know the time."

Denise plastered on her church smile, although she felt God wasn't treating her fairly for giving her secretary an unction to attend Bible Study at her church, now that she was leaving Bryce. "It's from seven to eight. I'm sure you'll enjoy it, my husband is an awesome teacher." *Always the cheerleader.* Denise continued smiling. "Do you have the address?"

"Yes," Jennifer smiled. "I'll be there. She turned to leave, but stopped just short of the door. "Denise, I know I'm not an easy person to work with; thank you for being patient with me."

"I can't believe this," Denise mumbled after Jennifer closed the door. "Now that I've given up, she's ready to attend church." She continued complaining down the hall to the women's restroom. "I need to look for furniture . . . I don't have time to put on a show for Bryce's or Jennifer's sake . . . What about what I want?" Denise didn't finish protesting until she pulled into the parking lot of the Marina. "This is what I want," she mouthed, starting the trail.

She'd barely counted twenty steps when Jonas ran up beside her and slowed to her pace.

"What's gotten you all twisted up?" he asked, noticing her frown.

"Hi, Jonas." She attempted to adjust her attitude by offering him a smile. "I didn't expect to see you today."

"I decided at the last minute to run, and you're doing it again."

"Doing what?"

"Avoiding my questions," he answered, stepping in front of her path. She didn't have a choice but to stop walking and talk to him.

"I'm not in the best of moods. My day didn't end quite the way I had in mind."

Jonas placed a hand on her shoulder and she relaxed. "The day's not over; things can turn around."

"I doubt it." Denise retorted, thinking of spending an hour poised on the front row with an adhesive smile.

"Let's give it a try; have dinner with me," Jonas offered. "You won't have to endure my preparations. There's a Mexican restaurant in the north lot. They serve a great chicken Caesar salad that won't ruin your meal plan. We can walk."

Denise was prepared to automatically decline, then figured why not. She could be late for Bible Study. That's less time she'd have to spend looking at Bryce and she'd have a better chance of avoiding Melanie.

"Sure, I think I can squeeze in a quick dinner." Denise smiled mischievously. "Lead the way." Walking off the trail beside Jonas, Denise had a revelation. Bryce wasn't the only one who could have his cake and eat it too. Whereas, Bryce had pictures, she had a real-life specimen that she could touch, if she desired to.

Tucked in the corner booth, Jonas lived up to his word. Outrageous tales about his profession as a gynecologist, which kept her laughing. The most outrageous story was about a multiple personality patient who formally accused Jonas of marrying and impregnating her during the exam.

"She was so convincing, I almost believed her," he chuckled. "It's a good thing the medical assistant witnessed the exam. I could have lost my license."

"I'm glad you're able to laugh about it now," Denise said, wiping her eyes and inconspicuously checking her watch. Bible Study was starting, but Denise sat a while longer, listening to Jonas share his plans to travel to Africa as a volunteer for the Red Cross.

"That's awesome," she said, this time openly checking the time. "I've enjoyed myself, but I have to get going."

"I know," he said, placing bills on the table. "You've been checking your watch for the past twenty minutes."

"I was trying not to be obvious."

"I know that too." Jonas smiled then assisted her from the booth.

On the walk back to her car, Jonas casually held her hand. When Denise began to fidget, he released it.

"Thanks for turning my day around." She smiled, facing him once they reached her Lexus.

"You're welcome. Remember, I'm just a phone call away." Jonas's face inched closer to hers. Denise lowered her head and fished her keys from her fanny pack. Jonas used his thumb and forefinger to lift her head and quickly kissed her lips.

"You're a beautiful woman, Denise. Pastor Hightower doesn't know what he's giving up," Jonas said in voice Denise didn't recognize.

"Jonas . . . I . . . why. . . ."

Jonas grinned. "Don't worry; nothing will happen between us unless you want it to."

Standing in the parking lot, Denise didn't know what she wanted to happen. All she knew was she'd better get away from this gorgeous doctor before she asked him to kiss her again.

"Bye, Jonas." Denise slid into her vehicle and sped away.

Her thoughts were still scrambled when she pulled into her reserved parking space at Word of Life with only fifteen minutes of Bible Study left. She was too preoccupied with what happened with Jonas to notice Bryce's Mercedes was missing. It wasn't until she stepped into the sanctuary and saw Minister Jenkins standing at the podium did she realize Bryce wasn't there.

No sooner had she taken a seat in the back, Jennifer waved at her. Denise smiled and waved back. She needed to tell someone what happened with Jonas, but Erin wasn't there. Erin had never found a way to work Bible Study into her schedule.

Denise sat on the seat like a robot, not really listening. Out of habit, she nodded when Minister Jenkins made a good point and stood at offering time. It was the benediction that held her attention. That's when she learned her husband was feeling under the weather and resting up for his trip to the Annual Worker's Meeting, which was now only two days away.

Denise went through the ritual of greeting congregants, but neither her mind nor heart was in it. She couldn't help being concerned about Bryce. She couldn't recall one time he'd missed church because of illness. The image she had before ditching him this morning wasn't a good one. He looked sick. Now she wished she hadn't ignored his calls this afternoon and regretted frolicking with Jonas. "God, please let him be okay," she mumbled as Mother Gray approached her.

"Baby, don't you think you ought to get home and check on your husband?" Mother Gray suggested.

"She's right," Lucinda concurred from behind. "I left him a couple of hours ago and he didn't look too good." Denise never thought she'd see the day her mother agreed with anything Mother Gray had to say. But then again, Bryce was her beloved pastor.

"I'm on my way home now," Denise told both women.

"Well don't just stand here, get moving," Mother Gray ordered, and Denise obeyed.

"And next time, answer your phone. It doesn't make sense to have a cell phone if you're not going to answer it," Lucinda called after her. Denise just nodded. Her mother was right; avoidance was not the way to deal with her husband.

"Bryce," she called when she entered the house. Quietness answered her. Denise set her briefcase on the counter and threw her keys in the basket on the kitchen counter. Before going to look for Bryce, she noticed the stock pot sitting on the stove. She figured Lucinda had brought her sick pastor some of her famous chicken soup, when she visited earlier.

Bryce had every light in the house on. After finding his study empty, Denise made the dreaded trip to their bedroom, turning off lights as she went. She found him sitting up in their bed, writing in what looked like a journal. She'd never seen it before, but it appeared to be half full. They briefly made eye contact before Bryce continued writing.

"Are you all right?" she asked, stepping into their bedroom. "You didn't make it to Bible Study. Mama said you weren't feeling well."

"I tried to call and let you know I was staying in, but you didn't answer your phone."

Denise walked over to the bed with her head lowered. "Are you better now?" she asked, sitting on the bed.

"I'm getting there." He continued to write.

"Why were all the lights on?"

"I don't like the darkness." He continued to write.

Denise was becoming frustrated with his short and evasive answers. Maybe she should apologize for ignoring his calls. "Sorry, I should have answered the phone."

"No problem." He continued writing at a rapid pace. Denise assumed he was writing a sermon.

"Are you sure you're okay?" Denise placed the back of her hand against his forehead. "You look drained. I can bring you some soup."

Bryce stopped writing and covered her hand with his. While slowly removing her hand, his eyes pierced her from the top of her head down the side of her face and lingered at her lips. The gaze wasn't sensual or sexual. More like a microscopic examination. Denise wondered if he knew she had spent the evening with Jonas for the second night in a row and that he had kissed her.

"I'm fine," he finally answered, setting her hand on the bed. He resumed writing as if Denise wasn't there.

"Let me know if you need anything." Denise exited the room as quietly as she'd entered. While transferring the chicken soup into a plastic storage container, Denise didn't understand why she felt offended by Bryce's distance. Isn't distance what she wanted? It was, but something about this didn't feel right. Just like the soup didn't look right. Her mother's soup is never this watery. And where were the snow peas? Lucinda was the only person she knew who puts snow peas in chicken soup.

Chapter 18

Bryce placed the pen and journal inside his nightstand drawer seconds before Denise's alarm sounded. They'd slept in the same bed, but their spirits were as far apart as the Pacific and Atlantic oceans. Denise lay on the edge of the bed with her hands tucked beneath her. He sat up on the opposite end, writing. Aside from the silent tears he shed, Bryce wrote all night long.

It was a suggestion of Benny's. A way for Bryce to release the emotions he had buried deep down inside. So far, it was working. The more he wrote, the more he recalled and the more he hurt, but he worked through it. After the previous night's bout with depression, he had to work through it. He wouldn't survive another attack like that one. Benny might not be around to stand in the gap for him the next time. Benny said he'd been praying for him around the same time he couldn't get the bottle of Vicodin open. Now it was time for Bryce to pray for himself.

"Are you feeling better?" Denise asked upon turning and seeing him on his knees.

"Yes," he answered honestly. His spirit did feel lighter.

She yawned and stretched, then offered to fix him some breakfast.

"No thank you, but I would like to talk to you about where you have been the last two evenings."

Just that quick, Denise forgot she was exiting their pitiful marriage. Here she was, offering to cook breakfast as if they were a family. She sat up and looked him in the eyes. "Bryce, I meant what I said about leaving. I've found a townhouse near Broadway Terrace. If all goes well, I'll be moving in next week." She paused to let him digest the words.

"You don't have to do that, Denise."

"I can't live like this anymore. I've tried, but I can't. I no longer trust or respect you."

Bryce swallowed hard and sighed heavily before speaking. "That's not what I meant. I'm not asking you to stay with me. If dissolving our marriage will stop you from hurting, then I won't stand in your way. I don't want you to leave your home. I brought this home for you. I'll leave."

"What?" Denise shrieked at the same time her fists pounded the mattress. "Are you serious?"

"Yes," he said with a finality that instantly drew tears from Denise. "After the Annual Worker's Meeting, I'll begin looking for a place."

"It's really over," she whispered, after lowering her head and fiddling with the fringes on the pillow sham. "Do you still want me to accompany you to LA?" She managed after a prolonged silence.

Bryce laughed, not from humor, but to keep from crying. "What would be the point? Like you said, it's time to stop faking."

Denise pulled her legs up and rested her chin against her knees. "I guess this is the beginning of the end." she said just above a whisper.

“I love you, Niecy. I’ll never get over you. The best I can hope for is that one day I’ll forgive myself for hurting you. I am sorry.” He gently ran the back of his hand down her wet cheek. “There are so many things I should have shared with you; instead I hid myself from you. Maybe one day you’ll forgive me enough to stop hating me.” He went into the bathroom and returned with tissue, then handed it to her.

“I don’t hate you,” she answered after wiping her face. “I love you. I’ll always love you.” They sat in silence until Denise started laughing. “This is something; I love you and you love me, and yet we’re calling it quits. I guess Tina was right; what’s love got to do with it?”

“I’m going to miss your laugh,” he said once her laughter subsided.

Denise couldn’t decide what she would miss most about Bryce without shedding more tears. So she didn’t comment.

“I’ll get out of your way so you can get ready for work,” Bryce said, standing to his feet. “I can pray in the den.”

“What about your study?”

“It’s too dark right now.” *My life is too dark right now*, is what he wanted to say.

Seated in her office, Denise found it impossible to focus on her upcoming three-day weekend. When she purchased her airline tickets and booked the hotel suite a month ago, she was looking forward to the trip and shopping in the Garment District. Today, she didn’t care if she ever set foot on the chaotic discounted shopping strip again.

The understanding she and Bryce reached this morning should have brought her joy. Sitting at her desk rubbing her wedding band, joy wasn’t an emotion she felt. Quite the opposite, sadness enveloped her. The end of a marriage was like experiencing the death of a loved one. How does one go on after giving one’s heart and soul to an individual? How do I learn to love again? How do I trust again? Those questions were too much for Denise to answer alone; especially since she didn't desire to love anyone but Bryce.

Her cell phone vibrated; it was Erin with her daily call. "Hey." Her voice was laced with melancholy.

"What's wrong? Has Bryce gotten sicker?" The words rolled so fast from Erin's tongue, they ran together.

Denise didn't bother to ask her how she knew Bryce was sick. "No, but we talked this morning."

"Really," Erin slowed her pace. "What happened?"

"He agreed to the divorce."

"That's good news, isn't it?"

"Yeah." Denise paused before completing her statement. "He's also giving me the house. I don't need to move; he's moving out."

"What?" Erin shrieked so loud Denise pulled the phone from her ear. "Why would he do that?"

"He said he bought the house for me. He wants me to have it."

There was a long pause before Erin changed the subject. "Are you going to the Annual Worker's Meeting this weekend?"

"No, we decided it was time we stopped faking."

"Do you want to hang out this weekend?" Erin offered. "We can meet up with Jonas and catch a movie; no love stories, of course."

Denise had forgotten about the kiss. "Speaking of Jonas, you won't believe what happened last night?" she went on to tell Erin about the kiss. During the long silence that followed, Denise second-guessed her decision to share the information with her. They were never in a relationship, but was it possible Erin still harbored an attraction to Jonas? She was about to apologize for being insensitive when Erin began laughing.

"So that's why you weren't answering your phone, you were too busy kissing the good doctor," Erin teased.

"No I was not! It wasn't like that." Denise defended. "It was just a quick peck. I don't like Jonas like that and I doubt if he's really interested in me."

"Who are you trying to convince, me or yourself?"

"Neither. I'm a married woman."

"Not for long," Erin reminded.

Denise was glad Erin couldn't see through the phone. Her words brought instant tears. "I have to prepare for my eleven o'clock appointment. I'll call you later."

After disconnecting, Denise dialed her home number. She wanted to talk to Bryce, but he wasn't home. He didn't answer his cell either. "I had better get use to this," she said, pressing the red end call button.

"I did it," Bryce said sadly, when Benny opened the door before he had a chance to knock.

"Exactly what did you do?" Benny asked after closing the door behind Bryce.

"I wrote all night in that journal." Bryce paused. "And I told Denise if she wanted a divorce, I won't stop her. I'm moving out."

"I would ask how you feel, but I already know. You feel like someone has ripped your heart out and stomped it with steel toe boots then seared it with an iron press."

"That's close," Bryce admitted.

Benny slapped him on the back. "I wouldn't worry about it if I were you. That woman wants to divorce you about as much as I want to drink cod liver oil for breakfast. She loves you, but she's hurt. When you get better, she'll let you back in."

Bryce opened Benny's refrigerator and helped himself to a glass of apple juice. "You think you know everything, don't you?"

"No, son, I just believe your life will turn out a lot better than mine," Benny answered, taking a seat at the kitchen counter. "Now tell me about the journal."

Bryce returned home five hours later, feeling much better. The house was empty, but it wasn't nearly as lonely. The house was a little chilly inside, but that was due to the air conditioner he'd left running, not his demons. The early July heat was hitting the thermostat at eighty-five degrees outside, which made inside feel like a furnace.

Walking through the house, his emotions remained intact until he removed a suitcase from the closet and began packing for his trip the next morning. In a few days he'd be packing all his belongings, leaving the home he'd come to love because of Denise's presence.

Seated on his bed with his eyes closed, he inhaled deeply. If he concentrated hard enough, he could smell her scent in the air and feel her touch against his skin. He didn't have to imagine too much, Denise entered their bedroom in the middle of the fantasy.

"Sorry to interrupt," Denise said sarcastically.

Bryce silently scolded himself for the countless times he had fantasized about nameless women when fantasizing about his wife was much more fulfilling. "Would you believe me if I said I was thinking about you?"

"You'd have a better chance of convincing me to walk barefoot through the Florida Everglades."

"I was fantasizing about you."

"I don't care anymore." Denise thought she detected hurt in Bryce's eyes, but that was irrelevant. She pressed forward. "How are you going to explain our divorce to the church?" Bryce hunched his shoulders. He hadn't thought about it. "You're an advocate of marriage, how are you going to justify your failure?"

The last word made Bryce flinch. He'd been running from the fear of failure for years, and now with it was slapping him in the face. There wasn't any place to hide. He had to face it head on. He could hear Benny's voice. "*A man takes responsibility for his actions, even when he blows it.*"

"I haven't figured that out yet, but I won't assassinate you in the process. That's a promise."

"I hope that's the one promise you're able to live up to. However, I think it's a good idea for me to leave Word of Life. It would be too hard for me to sit under your leadership. I know too much."

He nodded his understanding, but didn't comment.

Her eyes roamed the room for a conversation piece. "I see you've started packing."

"Our flight—" he realized his error. "Sorry, my flight leaves at eight."

"Do you need a ride to the airport?" She wanted him to say yes. She needed just a little more time with him.

"No. I'll park in the long-term lot."

Disappointed and not exactly sure why, Denise stood to leave. "I'll let you get back to packing." She left before the tears she'd been keeping at bay, escaped.

"Niecy," he called after her. "Would you like to have dinner at Skates tonight?" He wanted to spend one more night loving her.

Denise smiled; he knew Skates was one of her favorite places. It was also romantic; he'd taken her there for their third anniversary. A part of her wanted to go. Memories of that night made the decision for her. "I'd love to, but that would only make for a more difficult ending."

Bryce waited until he heard the bedroom door close before giving in to his emotions.

Chapter 19

Denise arose from her knees for the third time on purpose. She'd called and asked Lucinda to stop by for lunch. Denise figured if she were going to tell her mother she's divorcing her beloved pastor, she was going to need the Father, Son and Holy Ghost to keep Lucinda from strangling her. So she prayed a prayer, soliciting help from the Godhead. Lucinda didn't believe in divorce outside of physical abuse, and after all the effort she put into training Denise to be a 'good' first lady, the news was not going to sit well with her. Truth be told, it wasn't sitting well with Denise.

It won't hurt always, Denise reasoned last night, lying with her back to Bryce. Her heart may heal, but Denise imagined the tongue lashing Lucinda Sanders would dish out would leave permanent scars.

She waved at Benny from the kitchen window just before he let himself in through the back door.

"Seven days; that's all I ask." Cool, calm and collective Benny, was near panic.

Denise was perplexed by her gardener's peculiar behavior. "Benny, what are you talking about?"

"God created the earth in seven days and one of those days He used for rest. The least you can do is wait seven days before ruining your life. Love is too hard to find to just toss it out the window like a broken toy. If that fancy car sitting in your garage breaks down, I bet you won't leave it in a junkyard."

"Huh?"

"If you would give my son seven days, he'll make you happy. I know it."

Exasperated, Denise finally understood Bryce's initial irritation with Benny's personality. He was nosey and pushy. "Mr. Benny, *Bryce and I* have come to an agreement concerning *our* marriage."

"What you've come to is a mess! He's already sorry, and soon you will be too. If you ask me, you're already regretting this foolishness. You know you love that man." Benny folded his arms across his chest and raised his chin, silently daring her to contradict him.

"Ugh!" She threw her hands up, "No wonder you and my mother can't get along; you're just alike." Denise stomped from the kitchen. "Let yourself out!" she yelled over her shoulder.

When she returned 15 minutes later, Benny was seated at her kitchen table, drinking coffee. Denise started to leave again, then remembered Benny was a visitor in her home, not the other way around.

"Darling, I know you don't appreciate me interfering, but I'm doing it out of love. Just in case you're too slow to notice, you kids are special to me. You give an old man something to do."

Denise replaced her frown with a smile. "Thank you, Benny. You're special to us also. Thank you for my yard that you refuse to allow me to pay for." She kissed his cheek just as the doorbell sounded. "That's Mama—"

Benny cut her off. "Say no more." He slipped out the back door before the second ring."

"Have mercy, Lord." Denise prayed one last time before inviting her mother in. After the customary hug, Denise ushered Lucinda into the kitchen and directed her to have a seat at the table.

"What time does your plane leave?" Lucinda asked after making herself comfortable.

Why did she have to ask that first? Denise wanted to ease into the subject. "I'm not going to LA," Denise said, reaching for two soup bowls from the cabinet.

"Is Bryce still sick?"

"He's fine." Denise placed the bowls on the placemats before speeding through her next statement. "He left for LA this morning." She then quickly turned and walked over to the stove and stirred the leftover chicken soup. From behind, she heard Lucinda breathing heavily and pictured her lips pursed.

"Denise Ann Sanders Hightower, why aren't you with your husband?"

"I'll tell you about that later." Denise stirred faster. "How have you been?"

"You will tell me now!" Lucinda banged her fist on the table.

Denise's hands shook as she spooned the soup into the bowls. "Mama, there's no easy way to tell you this, but Bryce and I have agreed to divorce." When Lucinda didn't readily respond Denise added, "He's moving out." She placed the bowls on the table and sat down.

Lucinda brought a spoonful of soup to her mouth and cooled it with her lips. "What is this mess?" she asked after tasting it.

Denise thought she was referring to her marriage. "Mama, I tried hard, but I can't be you." Instantly, the tears began and Denise didn't attempt to hide. "I can't share my husband."

"Baby, I've never wanted you to be me. I wanted you to

be better than me and have more than I had. I know you think I settled by staying with your daddy, maybe I did. But one thing that's concrete is I loved Jeremiah. I loved him the way God loves me; in spite of my faults." Denise let her spoon sink into her soup bowl. "Your father wasn't an evil man. He loved me. That was enough for me to keep holding on."

"It's not enough for me, Mama," Denise cried.

Lucinda reached across the table and touched her hand. "Baby, ask yourself this question; when Bryce walks out that door for good, will you stop loving him?"

"No," Denise admitted.

"Would you rather spend the rest of your life longing for the one you love, or would you rather love the one you love to life?"

"Mama," she whined.

"Love is too hard to find, to just throw it away."

For a brief moment, Denise wondered if her mother and Benny had talked, then surmised since Benny still had his two front teeth, that was not the case.

"Five years from now you'll kick yourself for preparing him to be a great husband to someone else."

"What?" Denise hadn't thought of it that way.

"That's what you're doing," Lucinda explained. "He'll learn from the mistakes he made with you and will treat the next wife like a queen. Then you'll be mad at yourself."

"Oh, Mama," Denise dropped her hands to her sides, exasperated. "I love that man so much."

"Then get on the plane and go to your man. Show up at his hotel room and do what I taught you to do."

"Mama!" It was incredulous to Denise that her mother could think of sex as the remedy to her dilemma.

"What? After service he's going to need some restoration."

For the first time in weeks the thought of 'restoring' her

husband warmed her. "You're right. I'm going to LA just as soon as I can change my ticket," she announced standing to her feet.

"Hallelujah!" Lucinda exclaimed. "Now if I can just get something to eat."

Denise was confused. "Eat your soup."

"I'm not eating this mess," Lucinda frowned. "That's what I was talking about earlier when you started talking that foolishness."

"Since when don't you eat your own cooking?"

"I didn't cook this watered down garbage."

Denise made fun of her mother. "Are you trying to tell me you're losing your short-term memory?"

"My memory is just fine, and so is my cooking."

Denise was no longer laughing. The soup didn't taste or look like Lucinda's and neither had the meal in the storage container a few days before.

"Mama, didn't you bring Bryce a roasted chicken dinner on Tuesday?"

"No, Tuesday, I had dinner with your aunt Melba."

Bewilderment covered Denise's face. "What about Wednesday? Didn't you stop here on your way to Bible Study and drop off this soup?"

"I did stop by, but I wouldn't have fed this to the dog, let alone my pastor."

Denise stood and paced the kitchen. "Where did this food come from? I know Bryce didn't cook it."

"Baby, go pack," Lucinda ordered. "You can figure out whose been feeding this slop for your husband on the plane."

Chapter 20

Bryce stepped into the elevator, and for the umpteenth time, Pastor Hightower was paid homage by a constituent of the Annual Worker's Meeting. During the opening reception and afternoon service, he didn't mind the formalities, but he'd hoped to bypass the ritual inside the elevator of the five-star hotel. There was a time, just a few days ago, when he thrived off the veneration, but today, he found it irritating and unnecessary. Protocol had its place, but inside the elevator wasn't one of them. The deeper Bryce dug into himself, the less pre-occupied he was with needing to feel important. The less he needed the church to validate him.

The elevator stopped on the fifth floor, and the newly appointed minister turned and once again said, "God bless you, Pastor Hightower."

"God bless you," Bryce said, "and much success in your ministry."

The broad smile displayed by the young man reminded Bryce of himself about eight years ago. Then, he was impressionable and believed he could use the church to accomplish nationwide name recognition. He had ambitions of being a renowned and reverenced preacher. He desired to travel across the country and outside the United States with his own personal staff and attendants. Today, the last thing he wanted was to be in the spotlight. If it weren't a requirement for the elders of the church, he would have skipped the conference altogether.

"Please don't stop." Bryce spoke to the elevator's control panel as if it were a person. He was tired. Sleeping on average of only three hours for the past four nights was taking its toll on him. The impending separation from Denise was weighing him down more, especially after fielding questions all afternoon about First Lady Hightower's absence.

It wouldn't have bothered him so much if a fourth of the elders hadn't arrived with different wives from the previous year. Divorce had become a commonality within the denomination. That offered little consolation for Bryce. When he married Denise, he had forever in mind.

Bryce exhaled loudly when the elevator opened to the tenth floor. He dragged slowly down the corridor to corner room 1024. After removing his jacket and tossing his tie across the chair back, Bryce rounded the corner and plopped face first onto the king-sized bed. He didn't bother to take off his shoes. Within minutes he was snoring.

Seated on the plane waiting for takeoff, Denise turned the cell phone over in her hand repeatedly; debating if she should call Bryce and tell him she was on her way. *I'm going to get my man*, she smiled. *I'm not giving his messed up behind to anyone.* She decided to surprise him. Good thing the flight was only an hour; she couldn't contain her excitement much longer than that.

At last, the flight attendants began the emergency evacuation instructions like synchronized swimmers. Denise listened absentmindedly; she considered the instructions frivolous because in the event of a plane crash, the fire would burn up the oxygen masks and the seat cushions/floatation devices.

Denise rubbed her phone; the anticipation of reuniting with her husband was overwhelming and Denise couldn't resist anymore. Right before turning off the cell phone, she sent him a text message: *cant wait 2CU.*

In past Annual Worker's Meeting, Pastor Hightower waited until after Praise & Worship had taken place to enter the service with the entourage of Who's Who in the denomination. The congregation would literally stop and stand with reverence that was customarily reserved for kings and presidents in honor of the church elders. Pastor Hightower, along with fellow clergymen, would walk a step slower than normal pace to prolong the veneration. Once on the platform, they'd sit, staring proudly over the congregation or instantly became preoccupied with the printed program.

This evening, Pastor Hightower wasn't a self-absorbed junkie needing a dose of artificial gratification. He inconspicuously entered the hotel's convention center and found a seat four rows from the back. He wasn't arrayed in his clergy collar or tie. Tonight, he was just another brother, and to his delight, no one recognized him.

When the pomp and circumstance began, from his layman's seat, Bryce realized what a spectacle he'd been making of himself and how he abused the respect of the people. *No more*, he vowed silently.

The choir delivered two foot-stomping selections that had Bryce on his feet and clapping his hands. Later, as the guest evangelist from a mega-church in North Carolina delivered the sermon, Bryce rocked back and forth in his seat with his arms wrapped around him. With the skill of a master orator, the preacher used the story of David to explain how God still loves and uses flawed men. He explained how God used David to turn a group of broken and down-trodden men into a mighty army.

"God knew you were flawed when He called you," the preacher fluctuated his voice and walked to the edge of the platform to emphasize his point. "But He called you anyway to bring you into a state of wholeness."

His location afforded Bryce the liberty to freely unleash his emotions. With raised hands, Bryce made a life-changing decision. He had come to a crossroad and now he knew with certainty which road to take.

Denise's hands shook with such anticipation she dropped the room key card twice before finally opening the door to room 1024. She'd requested a corner when she made the reservations because corner rooms were larger. Denise doubted if she was this giddy on her wedding night. Like on her wedding night, she was prepared for this night too.

Packed inside her travel bag was the new lingerie she'd picked up from Macy's on her way to the airport. At first, she packed Bryce's favorite camisole then changed her mind. If they were starting fresh, then new lingerie was in order. She also included Bryce's favorite fragrance and body warming massage oil, but not much else. She figured once she told Bryce she'd reconsidered the divorce, there wouldn't be any need for clothing. He might even skip service.

"Here's to new beginnings," she whispered stepping into the room. "Oh my!" Denise gasped at the sight before her. Bryce had prepared for her arrival.

Her heart warmed and her spirit soared; Bryce really cared. The scene reminded her of their wedding night; set aglow with scented candles. She paused and slowly inhaled the aroma. Cucumber Melon; her favorite. Kenny G's saxophone floated through the air.

She stepped into the separate sleeping quarters. She didn't

see Bryce, but through the closed bathroom door she could hear the ceiling fan. *He's getting ready for me*, she smiled. The king-sized bed covers had been turned back and fresh rose petals sprinkled the sheet. On the nightstand there was a bottle of chilled non-alcoholic champagne.

Pleased with the presentation, Denise began removing her clothing, starting with her blouse. She wanted to see Bryce's mouth drop when he stepped from the bathroom. She'd barely unbuttoned her blouse when Bryce entered the suite after the evening service, carrying his Bible and two bottles of water.

"Denise?" The plastic bottles slipped from his hands and rolled across the floor. "What are you doing here? Is something wrong?"

Denise thought he appeared a little too surprised to see her considering all the preparation and planning. She moved closer. "I see you got my message," she said after kissing him on lips that didn't readily respond.

"What message?"

She wrapped her arms around his neck. "Oh now you want to play innocent." She kissed him again. "It's lovely."

Bryce looked over her shoulder at the bed and candles then smiled. "Niecy, are you trying to tell me something?" His stomach fluttered at the possibility. "Have you changed your mind about us? I hope you wouldn't have gone through all this trouble if you hadn't."

Denise released him and stepped back and gazed at Bryce. Something wasn't right. He wasn't expecting her; he was under the impression she'd created this. The romantic scene before her wasn't created with her in mind.

"Bryce what's going on?" she asked, swallowing the lump that had suddenly formed in her throat.

Before he could answer, the bathroom door opened. Both Bryce and Denise turned and stared at the woman wearing black lace with long flowing black hair.

"Oh my God." Denise gripped the side of the dresser for support. Her legs suddenly grew weak, and heat, beginning at her feet, seared her entire body. Surprisingly, she kept her breathing under control. "You're sleeping with Erin," she managed while shaking her head at Bryce.

Bryce snapped out of the temporary trance Erin's exposed body reeled him into and denied the allegation. He then interrogated Erin. "What are you doing here in my room?"

Erin wasn't remorseful or embarrassed. She planted her fists on her tiny waist and stepped closer to him. "The same thing I've been doing all week; tending to your needs." She intentionally responded slowly.

Denise blinked rapidly as red dots clouded her vision. "Did you just say, you've been with him all week?"

"I'm sorry you had to find out this way, but if you don't want Bryce, I do," Erin said plainly.

Bryce began stuttering. "B-baby, there is nothing going on between us. I promise. All she did was bring me juice and food that I didn't eat. She said you asked her to—"

"Shut up, Bryce! I don't want to hear anymore of your lies!" Denise screamed and the tears dropped, heavy and hot. She turned and pointed at Erin. "You're supposed to be my friend!"

"I am your friend!" Erin shot back. "I only went after Bryce because you said you didn't want him anymore. Why should I let a good man go to waste?"

"It doesn't matter what I said! He's my husband and that makes him off limits. A friend would know that!"

She stepped closer to Denise. "When you said you were leaving, that made him fair game," Erin smirked. "I will always be your friend, but I'm tired of playing runner up to Ms. Perfect!"

The women continued as if Bryce wasn't in the room.

"My life is not perfect!" Denise threw her hands with balled fists angrily down her sides.

"Oh please, save the drama." Erin waved her hands in Denise's face. "You have everything. You come from the perfect little two-parent home. You were the perfect student in college. Without trying, you landed the perfect man. On your wedding night you were the perfect virgin. You live in the perfect house with the perfect job. You drive the perfect luxury vehicle. You attend the perfect church where everyone just loves you. If that's not a perfect life, I don't know what is." Erin smirked. "Your life is so perfect, it's sickening."

Lucinda's warning about Erin being jealous of her flooded Denise's mind. The blinders were lifted, and now she correctly interpreted Erin's sudden interest in her daily activities. The daily phone calls, weren't because Erin cared about her well-being. She wanted to make sure Denise wasn't home when she weaved her web to entice Bryce. Erin didn't mind her moving into Jonas's complex, because she'd planned on moving into Denise's house.

"I can't believe it; you're jealous of me?"

"I'm tired of walking in your shadow!" Erin screamed. "I'm prettier than you. I'm better educated. I'm thinner; but no one wants me. No one speaks highly of me. They only want Miss Holier Than Thou Denise; including Jonas!"

Bryce's head jerked upward at Erin's declaration. "What is she talking about?" His penetrating eyes rendered Denise speechless.

With a sadistic smile, Erin folded her arms across her chest, digging the knife deeper into her friend's back. "Go on First Lady; tell Pastor how you have been spending your evenings. Tell him where you were on Wednesday night while he was at home sick; the night I brought him soup and sat with him." Erin continued to prod. "Confess what you were so busy doing with Jonas that you couldn't answer your cell phone. Tell him you were planning on moving into Jonas's complex to be closer to him."

"Erin!" Denise snarled. "You know there's nothing going on with me and Jonas."

"I know you kissed him," Erin gloated.

"That's not true! He kissed me."

Like a skilled litigator, Erin pulled the distorted truth from Denise. Satisfied, Erin threw her head back and laughed out loud. "You're way too easy," she roared just as Bryce slammed the door to the suite.

"Erin, I could kill you!" Denise balled her fist and snarled. "How could you stand there and lie."

"How do you think I felt when Jonas dumped me for you?"

"He was never in a relationship with you!" Denise screamed. "And he's not interested in having one with me."

"Yeah right," Erin smirked. "He talked about you all the time. Denise is good with money . . . Denise is losing weight nicely . . . Denise is so easy to talk to . . . Denise Denise, Denise! I'm tired of living in your shadow."

Denise fell onto the bed and lay her head in her hands, crying now from the hurt and not anger. She'd lost her best friend and her husband. She didn't trust Bryce enough to believe he was an innocent victim in this fiasco. He deceived her before; what would stop him from doing it again? Besides, she saw how Erin's body captivated him. Her lean body probably reminded him of the many women he had his 'affairs' with."

"Erin, you are so wrong. My life is not perfect; never has been. I have problems and I hurt like the next person, if not more, because I have to hold it all inside." She gazed up at her former friend. "I trusted you. When my mother warned me not to, I trusted you because I thought you cared. But all you were doing was lying in wait for an opportunity to pounce on my husband. You have wanted Bryce all along." Denise came to the conclusion. "For weeks before our wedding day, you tried to talk me out of marrying Bryce. You said being a pastor's wife was too hard when all along you wanted to be the first lady."

Erin made no attempt to refute the conclusions.

"If you only knew the battles I've been fighting, trying to hold on to my sanity . . ." Denise didn't finish. She couldn't, the pain from the knife in her back intensified. "Erin, leave."

Erin smacked her lips and rolled her eyes at Denise. "Sorry, but you're not the one who invited me, so you can't ask me to leave. I'll leave only and when my new man asks me to."

The insinuation, true or not, drove Denise over the edge. Erin wanted to be her so badly, she probably introduced herself as Mrs. Hightower at the registration desk to gain access to the room. Denise's anger returned with a vengeance. After yanking Erin by the hair into a choke hold, Denise dragged her across the room then opened the door and threw her out into the hallway practically naked and barefoot. She turned from slamming the door and noticed Erin's room key on the countertop.

"Denise, are you crazy? I need my key . . . I don't have any clothes on . . ." Erin continued ranting and raving and banging on the door like a mad woman.

Denise blew out the candles before picking up the phone and pressing "0" then waited. "This is Mrs. Hightower, can you please call security? There's an indecent deranged woman beating on my door."

Throughout the night, Denise called Bryce's cell phone repeatedly without any success. Her calls went straight to voicemail, indicating he'd turned off his phone. She probably wouldn't have believed anything he had to say, but she needed him to explain to her why he'd been spending time with Erin without telling her. Why Erin was in her home when she wasn't. Why he was accepting meals from her. "I should have known that white macaroni and cheese came from her," Denise grumbled. Erin never could cook.

During their sophomore year in college, Erin tried her hand at barbequing to celebrate the end of the first semester. She succeeded in not only burning the meat beyond recognition, but also burning a hole in the bottom of a brand new Weber grill. For Thanksgiving that same year, Erin insisted on cooking the holiday meal for their dorm after several girls raved about Denise's cornbread dressing. Thankfully, the local supermarket was open for the holiday. After Erin ruined the meal, they ordered a pre-cooked dinner.

Cooking wasn't the only thing Erin competed with Denise in. Most semesters, Denise earned a high GPA along with carrying a full load. Maintaining good grades didn't come as easy for Erin. She'd have to work twice as hard to maintain a "C" average. Erin attributed Denise's success to her private school education and constantly made snide comments about Denise being a spoiled brat. Denise graduated Magna Cum Laude, but Erin graduated without any special honors.

On graduation day, Erin was too busy celebrating to take a photo with Denise. However, she found the time to take several with Denise's parents; particularly, her father.

Denise wondered why she hadn't seen all this before. Maybe she had, and just chose to hide under the umbrella of denial. Very seldom had Erin shown any real interest in Denise's well-being, and even less in her accomplishments.

Thinking back to when she landed the job with the hospital conglomerate, Denise couldn't recall one time where Erin congratulated her. But when Erin graduated law school and passed the Bar, Denise threw her a big bash. Erin spent the evening gloating, and socializing with everyone but Denise.

The painful reality of their one-sided relationship overwhelmed Denise so that she now lay sprawled across the bed, crying to the point of heaving. She cried herself into a fitful sleep and bolted up less than thirty minutes later, shaking. The voices and faces that tormented her dreams left her gasping for air.

The hotel room had become too small and too cold. Chills ran down her arms and she rocked back and forth as the veracity of life as she knew it pounded her head and heart, leaving her with a throbbing headache and heartache she doubted would ever heal. Everyone she loved had deceived her. Her father tricked her into believing he was an honorable man.

From a little girl, she wanted to marry a man just like her father and she did. She married a man who loved pornography more than her. The illusion Bryce created robbed her of her virtue. Erin used the delusion of friendship to seduce her unfaithful husband. Only hours earlier, her mother manipulated her into believing love was enough to cover the sins of infidelity, but it wasn't. It was all an illusion.

Everyone had willingly participated in making Denise believe what they wanted her to believe. They collectively tickled her ears with words to influence her into making the decisions that were self-serving; in *their* best interests not hers. Her father, Bryce, Erin and her mother weren't totally to blame. They didn't have to work too hard to steer her like a ranch hand steers cattle. Denise was an easy target; she trusted too easily and way too much, but not anymore.

She stood and reached for her bag. It was almost morning and Bryce hadn't returned. She resolved to the idea he was with Erin and she was fine with that. They could create whatever fantasy they so desired. Slamming the door behind her, Denise vowed from that moment on she was going to enjoy some illusions and fantasies of her own.

Chapter 21

Bryce slowly crept down the brick walkway to Benny's front door. It seemed every time he knocked on Benny's door he was hurting from invisible wounds. Perhaps one day he'd knock on Benny's door and they'd share a laugh and hangout like regular people, but today wasn't that day. Bryce needed to talk to bounce his problems off someone with much more wisdom than he had.

After learning his wife was spending time with another more handsome and stable man, Bryce spent the night tucked in a booth in the hotel's 24-hour restaurant, moping over Denise's betrayal. When he returned to the suite, both Erin and Denise were gone, and to his surprise, he was relieved. He packed and caught the next flight back. He didn't care if he ever saw Erin again.

Her shenanigans were unexpected. True, Erin was always chasing some man, but the idea she wanted him never occurred to Bryce. Erin had always been friendly, so he didn't think anything odd when she called two days in a row to check on him. When she showed up with food, she claimed Denise asked her to drop it off since she'd be out late. That, he did find odd. He was well aware of Erin's lack of culinary skills. But he didn't have any reason not to believe Erin. Thinking about it now, he realized he was a moron for believing her. During the past five days, Denise didn't care if Bryce lived or died, let alone ate.

As for Denise, the disappointment he felt in her couldn't be articulated with words. She belittled and berated him for cheating with pornography when she'd been spending time with a real and accessible person. A man she introduced him to and passed off as Erin's interest. He was good, but Denise deserved an award for the illusion she engineered.

He came close to hating himself for hurting her and destroying their marriage, shouldering the responsibility for its demise when Denise had a hand in the pot the entire time. He still didn't know why she'd showed up, but reasoned guilt had driven her to LA last night.

As always, Benny opened the door before Bryce could ring the bell. "What did you do?" Benny stepped aside and let Bryce pass.

"Why does it have to be me?"

"Because you're here looking like a sick puppy." Benny went into the kitchen, but Bryce turned into the living room. When Benny returned with two apple-shaped bottles of apple juice, Bryce had reclined the chair and was moaning as the heat soothed his tight back muscles.

"Thanks," Bryce said after taking a long swig.

"Come on, son, spill it." Benny placed his bottle on the end table and waited for the story. He sat quietly nodding as Bryce recapped Erin's failed attempt at seducing him and Denise's deception.

"I still don't understand why Denise flew to LA."

"I'm not worried about that," Benny grunted. "I'm trying to figure out how you didn't know that woman wanted you. Are you that out of touch with reality?"

"I guess I am. I didn't know my wife was stepping out on me either."

Benny's roaring laughter filled the living room, making Bryce uncomfortable. "What's so funny?"

"You," Benny declared unsympathetically. "Sitting here acting like the victim. If she was stepping out on you, which she isn't, it's your fault."

"What?" That wasn't what Bryce wanted to hear.

"Listen, son, I tell you a truth. The only time a man has to worry about his wife stepping out on him is when he's not doing his job."

Bryce turned his nose up at that theory. "Whatever, man." Taking a sip, the rest of Benny's statement resonated. "How can you be so sure she's not involved with Dr. Jonas Allen?"

"Oh, now you think I know what I'm talking about?" Benny pestered him. "Now you want my advice."

"Come on, man; you know I love that woman. Stop playing with my emotions."

"Let me put your mind at ease before you bust a head gasket." Benny chuckled. "I had a few words with her yesterday and so did her mother. She doesn't want a divorce; that's what she flew down to tell you."

"Don't play with me, man," Bryce warned, leaning forward in the chair.

If the smirk on Benny's face was any indication of his thoughts, Bryce figured he'd stop while he was ahead.

"Are you sure? Did she tell you that?"

"Have I ever steered you wrong?"

"No," Bryce said, slumping back and beating his head against the chair. "Man, on top of the porn, she thinks I'm having an affair with Erin."

"I wouldn't worry about that if I were you. Women have a way of sniffing out female schemes. She probably had doubts about that girl anyway."

"Then where is she?"

"My guess is somewhere trying to process the pain. It's

not easy losing someone you care about. Let her be; she'll return when she's ready. What you need to concentrate on is what you're going to do about that troubled couple at the church.

Denise sat up in the bed and pulled the covers over her chest. According to the clock on the nightstand, she'd spent the past eight hours in a foreign bed, but she wasn't alone. After crying for hours at LAX and the entire plane ride home, she needed someone to cherish her for a little while; just until the pain went away. She tried praying, but her spirit was too wounded to receive the soft soothing. She needed a physical touch. She needed to be held and cuddled, just for a little while. Just one illusion and then she'd deal with her shattered reality.

Denise turned her head and faced the closed bathroom door and smiled. The man singing in the shower had been everything she needed. He was kind and gentle and treated her with a sweetness she hadn't felt in a very long time. As long as she lived, she'd never forget how he cared for her during her time of weakness.

"Would you like for me to order something to eat?" Jonas asked stepping from the bathroom wearing a robe. "There's a deli on the corner."

Denise thought maybe she'd spent too much time at Jonas's townhouse already, but she hadn't eaten in over twenty-four hours. Avoiding reality a few more hours wouldn't hurt. "Sure," she smiled and thanked him.

"Any requests?" he called from his closet.

"Anything but tuna and pastrami."

He stood beside the bed sporting jeans and a t-shirt with the hospital logo. "Are you going to be okay by yourself?" His genuine concern warmed her.

"I'll be fine," she smiled. She watched him walk away with confidence.

Jonas was an attractive man inside and out. It was his inner beauty that nursed her wounds after she showed up at his door that morning. She must have looked a mess, because the second he saw her, Jonas had carried her trembling body inside and sat her on his couch.

"Denise, what's wrong? Did someone die?" he had asked her.

"Bryce . . . Erin . . ."

"What happened to them?"

It had taken Denise nearly a half hour to pour out the past twelve hours of her life, and once she did, Jonas had held her until the tremors subsided.

"I can't believe I was so stupid."

"You're not stupid; you were just a better friend to Erin than she was to you." Jonas continued holding her and stroking her back.

"You should have seen that room and that satisfied smirk on her face. If I hadn't shown up, I know they would have slept together. They probably already have."

"Did you ask your husband?"

Denise sniffled and blew her nose before continuing. "I didn't have to; he denied it, but I don't believe a word that liar says."

The name-calling caught Jonas off guard, "Denise, be careful; he's a man of God."

"He's a man, but he's not holy!" Denise smirked. "I could tell you some things that'll blow your wig back."

"I'm sure you have the inside track, but in this case, I'd place my chips on your husband."

Denise had pulled away from him, glaring. "Why?"

"From what I know of Erin, I wouldn't be surprised if she'd been planning this for a while. She was always comparing herself to you to her advantage. If I said anything good about you, she'd get mad, but she always spoke highly of her pastor—your husband."

Denise lowered her head back against his shirt and cried fresh tears. Everyone saw the signs but her. Jonas has only seen Erin a handful of times and he saw right through the mask. Why hadn't she?

"Jonas, this hurts too much," she'd said, standing to her feet and taking his hand into hers. "I want you to make the pain go away." She turned and started up the stairs.

Jonas willingly followed. Upon reaching the top of the staircase, Jonas took the lead, directing her to his bedroom. Standing face to face alongside his sleigh bed they stared at one another, silently debating what the next move should be.

Jonas reached out and gathered her hands. After bringing them to his mouth and warming them with his breath, Jonas kissed them softly. "We can't do this." He'd whispered the words, but his statement was firm.

"Why not? You kissed me the other day; I know you're attracted to me." Denise inched closer so that she could feel his warm breath against her face.

"I won't deny my attraction; you're a beautiful woman. I also remember telling you nothing will happen between us unless you wanted it to."

"I want this." She needed just one fantasy of her on her own terms, without strings.

Jonas had taken a half step backward to allow some space between them. "No, you don't. You really don't want to have sex with me. You're hurting and you're looking for a way to soothe your pain, and at the same time, get even with Bryce and Erin."

"What's wrong with that?" Denise asked, reaching for him.

He caught her hands. "What's wrong with that outside of you being a married woman, is the fact that I respect you too much to allow you to participate in something you'll regret later."

"I won't regret it. I promise," she pleaded. "I know what I want."

"Denise, although you plan on divorcing your husband, you love him. I saw it the other day after I kissed you, and even more so now." Denise looked away following that statement. "Why did you fly to Los Angeles in the first place?" Denise lowered her head in shame. "You were going to reconcile weren't you?"

Denise nodded her answer, then buried her face in her hands.

"That's exactly why I can't have sex with you. But if you need a shoulder to cry on, you have it."

"This is not fair!" she exclaimed, sinking onto the bed and pounding the mattress. "Why does he get to have all the fun?"

Jonas had sat beside her and allowed Denise to cry long and hard. When no tears remained, he removed her shoes. After laying her down, he covered her with his Down comforter and held her until she drifted off to sleep.

Thinking back now, Denise conceded that Jonas was right. Sleeping with him would have been a major mistake. Not that it counted for much in the day and age of causal sex, but they barely knew one another and she was a married woman. Jonas had a reputation of changing women as often as he changed examination gloves. What would happen to their professional relationship after she'd become another conquest? There were so many things to consider, and although she didn't want to admit it, Denise was concerned about hurting Bryce.

What if he were telling the truth? What if he was an innocent player in Erin's real life game of betrayal? If Bryce hadn't already broken her trust, those questions would have been easy to answer, but they weren't. The trust was gone. Denise still couldn't help but wonder what if . . .

She was seated on the living room couch, still wondering, when Jonas returned carrying a big white paper bag and a plastic bag from the local market. She followed him to the kitchen and sat anxiously at the table.

"I didn't know if you wanted diet soda or bottled water, so I grabbed them both," he said, unpacking the items.

Denise licked her lips, not caring one iota about diet soda or water. She was starved, and if Jonas didn't hurry she was going to sprinkle salt and pepper on him and take a chunk out of him.

"Would you like to eat in here or in the—"

"Here!" Denise cut him off then snatched the white twelve inch roll from him.

Jonas bent over with laughter watching Denise rip the deli paper to near shreds and then smile at the turkey sandwich just before devouring it.

"This is so good," she moaned. "But then again, I'm so hungry a jelly and mayonnaise sandwich would taste good right about now."

Before freeing his sandwich, Jonas handed her a bottle of water. "Drink some of this before you choke."

With one hand, Denise received the bottle and continued eating with the other. No words were spoken by her until less than half of the sandwich remained.

"Thought you'd come up for air?" he teased.

Denise made no attempt to justify her display of poor home training. So what Jonas witnessed her eating like a crazed animal? She didn't care. However, she didn't want him to hear the hideous burp she felt brewing.

"Excuse me." She got up and made it to the bathroom just in time.

"You look better," he commented when she returned smiling. "If I'd known you would be this happy, I would have fed you earlier."

Denise was laughing, but she was a long way from being happy. Her stomach was full, but her heart still ached. On top of that, she wasn't any closer to making a decision about her life than she was twelve hours ago.

"Thank you," she said, reaching across the table and placing her hand on Jonas's. "Thank you for not taking advantage of me. I didn't know you were so noble."

"I'm not," Jonas grunted. "Under almost any other circumstances, I would have taken you up on the offer, but you're a special person, Mrs. Denise Hightower."

Denise smiled and nodded her appreciation of his admiration.

"Besides," he grinned, "I want you on my side come next fiscal year."

Denise adjusted her position in the chair. "You called me Mrs. Hightower; you think I'm going to return to Bryce don't you?"

"What I think doesn't matter? What's important is what you feel in your heart."

Denise pouted. "Jonas, I don't know what I feel anymore."

"You're a Christian. I believe this is when you should pray for direction?"

Great! I'm so jacked up a non-believer is telling me to pray. "You're right, and eventually I'll have to return home. I can't hide out here forever." Denise sighed.

An hour later, she was still sighing; dragging through the garage door that led to her kitchen. The house was dark except for the flicker of light from the den. She knew Bryce was in there. Wanting to avoid him, Denise started toward the bedroom, but his voice made her stop dead in her tracks.

"You don't have to tell me where you've been, at least not tonight; unless you want to." Denise kept her back to him. "I'm just glad you made it home safely." She took a step. "I know I'm asking more of you than I deserve, but will you attend church with me tomorrow?"

Denise closed her eyes and squeezed them tightly and counted to one hundred by five's twice, trying to suppress her anger, but it didn't work. She turned around and began screaming. "Why would I go to church with you? I'm divorcing your sorry behind, remember? I don't care if the whole congregation learns how pathetic you are. You're not a man of God; you're a low down good-for-nothing dog! The only place I want to be seen with you is at your funeral!"

Bryce didn't offer a defense or justification to her tirade. He simply made his request again; this time moving closer and touching her shoulder. "There is nothing between Erin and me. Never has been and it never will be." He allowed both palms to rest on her shoulders. "Please think about it; I need to see you tomorrow."

Without warning, Denise slapped Bryce so hard her fingers ached from the sting. "You self-centered freak!"

Bryce remained dazed long after Denise slammed the bedroom door. "Benny, you had better know what you're talking about," Bryce mumbled, still massaging his cheek.

Chapter 22

The early morning sunrays awakened Denise prematurely from her fitful sleep. Her weary body would have settled for bad sleep over no sleep any day, but this Sunday morning, what she wanted was irrelevant. All night, she'd tossed and turned, regretting the words she'd harshly spoken to Bryce, not to mention hitting him, again.

Maybe if he hadn't sounded so sincere when he denied being a willing participant in Erin's scheme or when he said he needed her support today at church. But something was different about him on last night. In the past, his requests for her presence at church were more of a demand. Last night he was begging; something he never does. He was sincere and now she was angry at her heart for betraying her and believing him.

"Ugh!" Denise angrily threw the covers back and sat up on the side of the bed. "What am I supposed to do now?"

Denise proposed the question audibly, but didn't expect an answer. When the small voice answered back, "Talk to Me." Denise assumed it was Bryce and stomped into the bathroom looking for him. Not finding him there frustrated her more; she then stomped down the hall to his study only to find it void of not only him but in disarray.

Bryce had moved all the furniture and covered it in the middle of the room and removed the paintings. The walls had been washed and one side of the room covered with a fresh coat of paint.

"What is going on?" she mumbled, closing the door.

After checking every room in the house without locating Bryce, she returned to her bedroom and began making her bed. The clock on the nightstand read 7:30 A.M. Where was Bryce? Routinely, Bryce left for church at nine o'clock every Sunday.

"I don't care where he is as long as he's not in my face," she grumbled. "He's probably somewhere playing with himself anyway."

Denise continued venting until she threw the last decorative pillow in its place.

"Ouch!" she screamed when the metal object made contact with the bottom of her bare left foot. Denise had stepped on an ink pen Bryce, no doubt, had carelessly left on the floor. "Ugh!" She opened the top nightstand drawer and was about to discard the pen when she noticed the book she'd seen Bryce writing in the other night.

Assuming he'd been working on a hypocritical sermon, Denise opened the book to make mockery of her husband's *divine* revelations. What she discovered was much deeper than a Sunday morning sermon.

She flipped through the pages. Except for the last two pages, the journal was full with her husband's distinctive left-handed penmanship. Every page, both front and back sides, was covered with legible and illegible words. Sitting on the bed, Denise started at the beginning and began deciphering what appeared to be the musings of a madman. She soon learned those pages contained the heart of her husband; the part she didn't know.

The journal revealed the pain and rejection he suffered at the hand of his father. Bryce described in detail, feelings he had tried to forget; feelings of worthlessness and inadequacy. Statements like: My father didn't love me . . . I don't think my father liked me . . . My father hated me . . . Something must be wrong with me . . . were saturated throughout, along with dry running ink where Bryce's tears had fallen.

"Oh, Bryce," she whispered, turning page after page. Bryce bore all on those pages; exposing his soul naked as a newborn babe.

He expressed the hatred he felt toward his addiction and the way it controlled him. He'd become dependent on pornography because he felt insufficient without it, and in some strange way, he desired to be like his father; the man he'd idolized. Denise learned most times he prayed afterward and asked God to forgive him and how he became mad with God for not healing him.

He wrote about how he used the church to validate him and give him a false sense of self-esteem and worth. Bryce confessed he used his calling as pastor self-servingly. He'd taken his God-given gifts for granted and had failed to cultivate them. His agenda no longer included the will of God, just his desires. He came clean about his fear of fathering children and using his job to justify it.

Tears that had long pooled her eyes trickled down her cheek while reading about Bryce's attempt to take his life as she was lying there faking sleep; avoiding him like his father had.

"I've hurt the one good thing in my life so much; I now hate myself the same way my father hated me. Niecy has been the best wife; she's everything to me, but I have been nothing to her. I have given her nothing in return for the pure love she freely gives. . . . Tonight I finally put her needs before my self ambitions and agreed to divorce. Only God knows how I'll live without her . . ."

Denise used her t-shirt to wipe her face, and then turned more pages.

"I am no longer fit to lead God's people. How can I? I'm addicted to pornography. I'm afraid to confront sin and I can't live the words I preach. My wife doesn't respect me and neither will anyone else after she leaves."

Denise closed the book and wept for the husband she didn't know. She wept for the rejected child and the confused man and the misguided preacher. Slipping to her knees, Denise did something she hadn't done in seven days; she sincerely prayed for her husband and repented for her shortcomings.

"Benny, this has been the longest week of my life," Bryce declared, seated behind his desk in the church office. He'd come to the church early that morning to think. "I didn't know my life could change so much in so little time."

"Son, it doesn't take God a long time to work."

"It sure doesn't." Bryce sighed and rested his hands beneath his chin in prayer.

"I'll see you outside." Benny quietly exited without jesting or joking.

Bryce lifted his head to thank Benny for his help and support, but he was already gone. Leaning back in the black ergonomically correct chair he'd hand picked, Pastor Hightower surveyed his office. *Am I doing the right thing?* he wondered. It didn't take long for the still small voice to answer. Surrendering to the will of the Lord, Bryce bowed his head in prayer.

"Honey, can I talk to you for a minute?"

Honey? Denise's surprised appearance caught him off guard. After last night, the last place he expected to see his wife was at church and 'honey' was not a word he thought he would ever hear flow from her lips again in reference to him. They were alone in his office and there wasn't any need to pretend, so why the pleasantries?

"Can it wait until after service? I don't need any distractions this morning." That was true. All morning ungodly images were attempting to undo his resolve. One argument with Denise would send him over the edge.

Denise was disappointed, but nodded her head in agreement then turned to leave. Bryce waited until her hand was on the doorknob before saying, "You're beautiful in that suit. Thank you for coming."

Denise blessed him with a smile, but didn't verbally respond.

"Benny man, you better be right on this," Bryce vowed in the empty office. "That woman is too fine to let go of."

Pausing outside on the other side of the office door, Denise giggled with the joy normally associated with teenagers, then snickered with mischief. She was pleased with the response her meticulously chosen ensemble provoked from Bryce. Of course she was fine in the gold and cream suit with matching hat he'd purchased for her birthday. He loved that suit on her; that's why she'd worn it. It was also the reason he enjoyed watching her walk before commenting. To ensure Pastor Hightower wouldn't become distracted during his sermon, the first lady wore the gold pumps instead of the stilettos with straps that wrapped around her legs and stopped just below the knee.

"I can't wait to get you home," she whispered, turning into the sanctuary. Denise had taken five steps when Mother Gray accosted her.

"First Lady, you sure are looking good."

"Thank—"

"I see your gardener made it back," Mother Gray said before Denise could thank her for the compliment.

Denise followed Mother Gray's eyes, and sure enough,

there was Benny, sitting on the front row next to her chair. This Sunday, he was adorned in a black double-breasted suit with cream shirt and complementary tie. This Sunday, Lucinda had changed her unmarked stationary seat to the chair directly behind Denise's. On the second row end seat, Lucinda bowed her head in prayer. Denise imagined she was praying for strength not to lose her temper in God's house again and whack Benny on the back of the head.

Denise turned her attention back to Mother Gray who was staring at Denise with expectancy.

"Did you find out if he's married for sure?"

Denise couldn't resist; she'd learned a long time ago how to avoid being the 'go between.' Placing her arm around Mother Gray and nudging her forward, Denise said, "Let's go and ask him."

The first lady nudged and coaxed, but Mother Gray's feet were anchored to the floor as firmly as her soul was anchored in the Lord.

"I-I was just being curious," she stuttered. "I really don't need to know."

"Are you sure, Mother?" Denise questioned with the pretended innocence of a child.

Mother Gray's countenance had transformed from excitement to one of rebuke.

"I'm sure. Let me get somewhere and sit down before this old flesh gets me into trouble."

They shared a brief laugh before Denise continued on to her seat.

"Denise, Denise." She turned to see Melanie waving her down. Denise didn't have a clue as to what she would say to her. What answer could he give without telling a boldface lie?

"What's going on, Melanie?" Denise asked when Melanie reached her as if she hadn't been avoiding the young woman all week.

"I know I'm supposed to wait until after service, but can you give me a little hint?" Melanie looked worried.

Denise was in the dark. "Hint about what?"

"Clay and I. Pastor said he wants to see both of us in his office after service."

Denise was still in the dark, but to admit that would reveal the lack of communication she'd shared with her husband over the past seven days. "Don't worry about it; pray for the Lord's will to be done." *I hear you Lucinda Sanders.*

Denise presumed Melanie would take offense to the generic answer, but was pleasantly surprised when she hugged her tightly and said, "Thank you."

As Denise approached her seat, she began praying also. Not for Melanie and Clay, but for the Lord to keep her from hanging Erin from the chandelier by her hair. Erin was seated on the front row next to Benny.

The thought of seeing Erin today or any other day never crossed her mind. It was a good thing; Denise probably would have packed Vaseline and sneakers in her purse. What was she doing on the front row dressed in a rhinestone suit and hat? Immediately, wounds that were too new for protective scabs to have formed were ripped open, causing Denise to tremble.

Benny noticed her reaction and whispered something in Erin's ear. A second later, Erin moved down three seats. Benny reached for Denise's hand and guided her to the chair.

Once she was seated, Benny patted her hand indicating he was privy to the betrayal.

"Don't worry about her; she won't bother you."

"How do you know?"

"I told her if she didn't stay out of your way, I'd hold her down and let you beat her in the head with the heel of your shoe," Benny answered without cracking a smile. "Then I'll sic your mother on her."

The laughter that erupted from Denise prevented her

from crying and soothed her anxiety. "What am I going to do with you?"

"Nothing." Benny continued patting her hand.

"Stop all that talking in the house of God," Lucinda warned from behind.

Benny looked over his shoulder at his foe. "You're just mad because don't nobody want to talk to you."

Lucinda huffed. "I'll deal with you later," then added, "I want to get my breakthrough before I go to jail for assault and battery."

"Can you two senior citizens wait until after service to fight?" Denise scolded.

"Humph, I don't know who you're calling senior citizen," Lucinda balked. "I'm only fifty-six years young."

"And I'm sixty years strong," Benny cosigned.

Exasperated, Denise gave up. What was the use? They enjoyed acting like juveniles. She turned around and opened her Bible in search of scriptures to justify choking Erin. She didn't search long before devotion began.

While kneeling in her prayer posture, the first lady found herself repenting once again. The animosity she held for Erin, while justified, was not acceptable in the sight of God. As a follower of Jesus Christ, forgiveness and restoration were required. Having acknowledged that, Denise asked God to show her how to forgive her former friend and to lead Erin someplace, maybe Alaska, to seek help for her issues.

Pastor Hightower paused before opening his office door. This was his last chance to change his mind. He was at that invisible, yet very palpable fork in the road in his life where one step in either direction would determine the quality of not only his natural life, but his eternal existence as well. It was his choice to make; life or death was in his hands. Sure, he wouldn't die a natural death, but his spirit would crumble into ashes and he would be dead among the living.

"You can't go out like this . . . wait until you're stronger . . . it's not worth your dignity . . . what about your reputation . . . they won't understand . . . you'll lose everything . . . "

The voices pounded his head with such force, Bryce found it difficult to hold his head upright. "*God understands your heart; He doesn't expect perfection from you. He just wants you to try, that's all.*"

Abruptly, the multitude of voices ceased and only one remained. It was the voice he created and worshipped for years. It was the voice that had stroked pleasure in him; taking him to heights not matched by any human experience. The voice he'd given Dajia whispered," *Don't leave me, Bryce, I need you.*"

"Lord, heal me now!" Denise demanded, watching Erin dance in *a spirit* across the front of the church. Erin, who was rarely an active participant in Praise and Worship, hadn't sat down once since the first chord of the song the musician played on the organ. "Let me trip her, just once Lord, please."

Benny leaned in with the answer to her petition. "Stop letting the devil steal your praise. God will deal with her, but you had better make sure you stay straight."

Denise smirked at Benny. The more time she spent with her gardener the more she agreed with Bryce's early assessment of him. Benny was pushy and rough around the edges, but he told the truth. "Thank you," she replied after softening her facial expression.

Denise stood to her feet and closed her eyes, repenting, again. She then clapped and swayed to the beat of the song. "God, you mean more to me than anything and you're worthy in spite of everything." She was just starting to enjoy service when Pastor Hightower stepped onto the platform.

"What is going on?" First Lady, along with the rest of the congregation, was thrown off balance by his appearance.

Aside from the reddened eyes, Pastor Hightower wasn't

wearing his usual attire. Missing were the cassock, clergy collar and big medallion gold cross. Pastor Hightower, as if having an out of body experience, entered the sanctuary dressed in an opened-collar shirt, jeans and sneakers. The only thing remotely identifying him as the pastor was the Bible he clutched to his chest.

Instinctively, Denise started for him, but Benny restrained her. “Let him be,” he said, holding her arm.

“But—”

“You heard him,” Lucinda added, tapping her shoulder. Denise reluctantly sat back, but continued gazing at her husband inquisitively.

Pastor Hightower, still clutching his Bible, surveyed his congregation. They appeared to be just as nervous as he was, if not more. He’d known his attire would interrupt the Sunday morning routine, but the extent to which the church reacted was more than he expected.

The organ player changed keys prematurely, causing the Praise and Worship leader to forget the next verse of the song. The usher dropped the throw sheet she was carrying. The Mother Board, who held traditional beliefs about how a preacher should dress, was fanning at a rapid pace. Erin stopped dancing and sat down.

I can do this, Bryce coaxed himself.

He made eye contact with the first lady and instantly read the worry etched on her face. His eyes traveled down her left arm where Benny’s hand securely held her stationary. He traveled back to her face and offered her a smile. “I’m all right,” he mouthed. It warmed him to know she still desired to attend to his needs.

Realizing the congregation was observing her reaction to his demeanor, Denise pasted a smile on her face, then sat back as if it were a normal Sunday. Except this Sunday, there wasn't anything normal about her husband. Bryce never approached the pulpit to preach in casual clothing. He said it was holy ground and one should look holy standing before the podium.

"Lord, what is going on with my husband?" Denise silently prayed. She was worried, but panicked when Pastor Hightower walked to the podium in the middle of the combined choir's "A" selection. The choir director didn't know if she should keep directing or cut the song short until Pastor Hightower nodded for her to continue.

Denise locked eyes with Benny and asked point blank, "What's going on?"

"The wounded little boy you married is becoming a man."

When the choir finished with scattered applause, Pastor Hightower instructed the choir members, musicians and ministers to take a seat in the audience. He patiently waited the time it took for them to squeeze and fill in the gaps of the near full to capacity sanctuary, all the while, praying for courage.

Once the last person was seated, Pastor Hightower gripped the sides of the glass podium, closed his eye and inhaled deeply. Slowly exhaling, he opened his eyes then began without preliminaries.

"I know everyone of you is speculating about my attire and why I detoured from the printed program. Let me assure you, I have not lost my mind. Quite the contrary; I have found it." He continued over the "huhs" and "whats" that floated throughout the congregation.

"Before every one of you walked through those double doors this morning," he pointed toward the back of the church, "you dressed to present your best *church look*. You made sure your clothing coordinated with your shoes and hats. Men trimmed beards and, ladies, I won't guess at how much time you all spent styling hair." He paused momentarily for the men to voice agreement.

"Your everyday vocabulary instantly changed from a simple hello to the language of the church. You said things like, 'blessed and highly favored' and all that would be fine if that was who you really were, but it's not. What you present is not who you are. It's like a mirage in the Mojave Desert. We see what we desire but it's not actually there."

Pastor Hightower backed away from the podium. First, he rubbed his hands together, then used his thumbs to massage his head.

Denise attempted to send him a telepathic message: *What are you so afraid to say?*

Benny and Lucinda vocalized their support.

"Come on, son. There's nowhere to go but up," Benny pushed.

Lucinda, rising to her feet, added, "That's it, baby, free yourself."

Pastor Hightower, gleaning strength from his friend and mother-in-law, pressed forward. "I am not here to judge you. I understand, because that's what I have been doing for years."

Denise gasped. "Oh, my God," as did the congregation.

"I sold you the image I wanted you to buy. I pushed the illusion of godly and holy robe-wearing and cross-bearing Pastor Bryce Hightower." He paused. "I deceived you because that is not who I am. It's a delusion; the façade is not the real me. Today, forget the Pastor Hightower you honor every service and allow me to introduce you to Bryce Hightower, the man." He walked in front of the podium where the congregation could see him without obstruction. "This is the real me without the imagery and without the mask."

Murmurings and whispers he couldn't decipher filled the air.

Denise rocked back forth in her seat, both happy and fearful. Happy because her husband loved God enough not to continue in his sin, but fearful of the backlash the disclosure would bring. As if feeling her anxiety, Lucinda patted her shoulders.

"I, Bryce have many faults," he continued. "Selfishly, I used my calling as pastor to hide my insecurities and need for validation. I wasn't validated by my father as a child; therefore, as a selfish man, I used the church as a place to build my self-worth and to establish a platform for me to shine. I have been feeding off your reverence and respect, similar to how bees feed off sweet nectar. Seven days ago, I couldn't exist outside of the church because I didn't know who I was, but today I do, and I accept who and what I am." Bryce paused again long enough to draw support from Benny's nod and Lucinda, who was still standing with her hands on her daughter's shoulders.

Denise's head jerked to the left side of the sanctuary, when someone yelled, "He's about to come out the closet!"

Lucinda used her hands to slowly redirect her daughter's head toward the pulpit. "Let 'em talk. What do you care as long as he's delivered?"

"I am a man who loves God, and I love the church, but I have been addicted to pornography and masturbation for seventeen years."

Bryce ignored the bulging eyeballs and gaped mouths, even the outright derogatory comments couldn't sway him to abort his mission. "I have defiled my body; my home and this church. I devastated and contaminated my wife by manipulating her into tolerating my obsession. I was selfish to the point I justified my lust all the while, watching my wife's security and self-esteem plummet. The fantasy meant more to me than my wife's tears and pleas and respect. I refused therapy because I am a man of God and I figured all I had to do was pray and the urges would vanish. 'I can stop anytime

I want,' is what I repeatedly fed myself. The fact of the matter was that I couldn't stop, and no matter how hard I prayed, the lust didn't magically disappear. I had to come out of denial and deal with myself and come clean before God and the congregation to whom I misrepresented myself. I have already repented to God and I have received His forgiveness. Today, I want to openly repent to my wife."

He stepped from the platform and walked out until he stood beside Denise's chair. Kneeling before her, Bryce wiped her cheek with the back of his hand. "Baby, I am so sorry for everything. I humble myself before you today, a broken and battered man; however, the man you see today is greater than the man you married. Please forgive me."

Denise was too overwhelmed to speak and too concerned about the negative comments and murmurings aimed at her husband to freely express how much love and renewed respect she felt budding in her heart. "I do," she whispered, then bit her lip to stop the quivering.

Bryce returned to his place on the platform with his chin up and stretched his arms over the congregation.

"To every one of you; forgive me for not shepherding you the way God intended and for feeding you tainted food. Forgive me for using you to serve my ego and for not allowing God to use me to serve you. From this day forward, I vow to be a better man, a devoted husband, and if you will allow me to remain, the pastor God intended. I won't stand here and lie to you; I am addicted to pornography, but standing before you today and admitting it is the first step to my deliverance. Tomorrow, I will begin meeting with a Christian therapist, and from there, I'll take one day at a time until the chains are completely broken. I only ask that you uphold my family in prayer as I submit to the process."

Chaotic noise and chatter filled the sanctuary while Bryce remained at the podium and removed the cordless microphone. Bryce didn't know what to make of the response to his revelation. A portion of the membership was too shocked to express anything. Some members were crying, others murmuring among themselves. Then there was the group who wasn't shy about voicing their opinions and passing judgments. Several long time members walked out in disgust.

Would Word of Life cancel his contract or allow him to remain pastor and use his addiction to control him? Would the Elder's Council ostracize him? Outside of knowing God was pleased with his confession, Bryce didn't know much of anything else.

He'd just turned his back to the audience en route to the confines of his office when Bryce heard a male's voice from the side podium say, "I'm addicted too; I've tried to stop, but I just can't."

Bryce turned to face the man who'd served as a deacon long before he became pastor. He was the senior deacon, who had led devotions on a regular basis and whom Bryce considered a man of great wisdom. That same man stood before the congregation weeping openly. Before Bryce formed the right words to address the deacon, another man in the audience stood and bravely announced, "I've been involved in self-gratification since I was a teen." Two men in the balcony stood and more from the far side of the church. By the time Bryce re-clipped the cordless microphone to his shirt, more people were standing.

"Oh, God," Denise prayed after standing to her feet and skimming the sanctuary. "How can this be?" Bryce may have been the leader of the church, but he definitely was not alone in his addiction.

Pastor Hightower halted the continuous confessions by asking everyone who struggled with the sins he'd admitted to, and weren't ashamed, to join him at the altar for prayer. He made the plea once, and then lowered his head to the podium. When Pastor Hightower raised his head again, nearly one third of the church, women included, had found their way to the altar. Some stood covering their faces in shame and others fell to their knees. All were crying out to God for forgiveness.

It was that moment that Bryce comprehended the severity of his battle for deliverance. It wasn't about him, but about the souls standing and kneeling before him. Males and females of all ages; single and married individuals; laity as well as leadership laid sin and shame at the altar that day.

Humbled that God could still use him to deliver His people in this imperfect state, Bryce fell to his knees in reverence.

Denise stepped onto the platform beside her husband and embraced the awesome sight before her. She'd never experienced anything like it. The impromptu altar call yielded so many, people crowded into the aisles. Some lay prostrate on the floor while others curled in the fetal position. No one led the prayer, instead, each individual cried the words they needed God to hear and released the feelings they wanted God to heal.

Erin didn't approach the altar, but knelt at her seat. After pulling her long hair back several times, she lay with her face on the chair, soaking it with her tears.

Denise was distracted by someone tugging on her skirt. Without looking down, she knew Bryce was beckoning for her to join him; she did.

The portrait of the addicted pastor and the devoted first lady gave Melanie the momentum to find her husband and join him in prayer. The presence of God was so powerful that Benny and Lucinda joined hands and prayed over their children.

Long after the cries and praises ceased, husband and wife continued embracing one another while still on their knees.

"I'm so proud of you; I love you," Denise whispered repeatedly in his ear.

Bryce positioned his head so their eyes met and asked, "Enough to remain my wife?"

"Until the day I die," she answered softly, but firmly.

The celebratory kiss was meant to be short and light, but intensified by its own accord.

"Y'all better get out of here before y'all forget you're in the house of God," Lucinda warned, at the same time pulling them apart.

After assisting Denise on her feet, Pastor Hightower returned to the podium with the first lady. The unexpected noise began before he could collect his thoughts. One by one, congregants rose and applauded him. The standing ovation, given by the majority embarrassed the most stubborn spectators into standing and applauding.

Humbled once again, Pastor Hightower shed more tears. Denise squeezed him and whispered in his ear, "See what happens when you obey God."

An hour after the benediction, Pastor Hightower and First Lady remained on the platform, greeting parishioners.

On any given Sunday, most members rushed home to family dinners or to turn off the stock pot left cooking on the stove. This Sunday, it seemed everybody wanted to hug and encourage the pastor and first lady. Out of habit or perhaps spite, some sisters chose to speak to the pastor, but not the first lady on a regular basis. Today, everyone greeted and hugged Denise as well.

"Son, let me get my hug now." Benny wore the grin of a proud father. "Since you all done kissed and made up, I might not see you for awhile."

Denise analytically observed the strong and approving embrace Benny shared with her husband and understood, for the first time, Benny's role in Bryce's life. God sent a gardener to plant and nurture the seed of greatness in her husband that his biological father neglected. Benny was Bryce's God-given father.

"I'm so proud of you, son. I knew you could do it. You're an awesome man." Benny affirmed him the way only a father could. "I love you."

The smile that covered Bryce's face reminded Denise of J.J. from *Good Times.* It was a smile of peace, pride and complete happiness.

Remembering happiness, Denise thought, *I want to enjoy some happiness too.*

"Honey, are you ready to go?"

Bryce didn't miss the desire in his wife's eyes nor voice. He even caught the way she slightly lowered her eyelashes.

"I have to meet with the Andersons. Why don't you go ahead; I'll be home as soon as possible."

Following a brief kiss, and with each satisfied their message and intentions were successfully conveyed, Denise left and Pastor Hightower beckoned for the Andersons to join him in the back office.

"What a difference a day makes." Denise sang the words to the age old song for the second time in seven days, thinking the words should be changed to "what a difference a week makes." Just one week and God had blessed her and taught her the true power of forgiveness and reconciliation.

During the process, Denise also learned she wasn't as strong and unmovable as she professed. Like everyone else, she was subject to fall and she had. The drop would have been a lot worse had Jonas yielded to the rantings of her emotions. But just like He did for Bryce, God used someone to prevent her from destroying her life.

"Enough of that." Denise stopped singing and inserted her favorite Anita Baker CD into the sound system. "It's time for some happiness."

She inspected her surroundings once again before removing the robe and revealing the new lingerie. The setting was perfect; good music, candlelight, warm fragrance, chilled pear cider and a spread fit for a king arrayed in the master bedroom suite.

"Sweet Love . . ." Denise was singing the chorus when Bryce entered their bedroom.

"Wow," he gasped. "Incredible."

Denise assumed he was responding to the scenery, but he was taking in what little he could of the new lingerie.

"Thank you." She lowered her eyelashes, indicating she wanted a kiss. He obliged, but only for a brief second.

"I need a shower," he announced and trotted to the bathroom.

"A hot bubble bath would be better,'" she called after him. "I ran the water."

Bryce stopped abruptly in the bathroom doorway, faced her and extended the invitation. "Join me?"

"Maybe during intermission, but I'll keep you company."

Bryce was elated. The declination carried more promise than the bubble bath.

"I read your journal," Denise confessed once he was settled inside the tube. "I didn't mean to; I thought it was one of your sermons."

"I hope you're not mad at what you discovered."

"I'm not anymore," she admitted, "but I was disappointed I don't know the Bryce on those pages. You hid yourself from me; don't do that anymore. Trust me with your feelings. Please. If we're going to rebuild our marriage, you must trust me with your heart."

Bryce meditated on her words then decided to let her inside. Before releasing the drain, he shared his fear of fatherhood, fear of rejection and many other fears that had paralyzed him over the years.

Denise sat on the side of the tub, intensely listening as if meeting her husband for the first time. She then shared her father's addiction and how she blamed him for her having married a man with the same addiction.

"Let me help you with this," she said to Bryce after he'd stepped out of the tub. She removed the towel from his hands and dried his back.

"Denise, I need to ask you about something. It may sound—no, it is egotistical, but I have to know. Whatever the answer is, we can work through it."

Denise stopped drying and stepped in front of him. "What is it, honey?"

"Am I still the only man with whom you have shared your body?"

Denise had completely forgotten Erin's implications on that dreadful night in Los Angeles, but Bryce hadn't, and the allegations worried him.

Denise tipped her toes and kissed his lips before answering, "You're my one and only." Then after dropping the towel, asked her question seductively, "When are you going to make me happy?"

Bryce carried her to their bed and rendered all the happiness she could stand.

Chapter 23

Four months later

"Dinner will be ready in five minutes." Denise hung up the phone before Bryce could beg for more time. It was Thanksgiving Day. Bryce was over at Benny's watching the traditional Dallas Cowboys football game. He and Benny had become the best of friends, spending all of their free time together. Benny accompanied Bryce on ministry trips whenever Denise was unavailable or too tired to travel.

In the beginning, Denise was a little jealous of all the time Bryce spent at Benny's until she stopped in for a visit one day and saw his living room. Besides the male bonding going on, Bryce was in sports heaven and free to express himself without being asked to turn down the volume.

Mainly because of his confession before the church and the avalanche that followed, the church hired two therapists to meet weekly with those members needing help, Pastor Hightower included.

The sessions, conducted by Christian counselors, who'd

fought and won the battle against pornography addiction, opened Denise's eyes to the spiritual side of pornography addiction. In the sessions, she was finally able to understand how her mother was able to live all those years with her father, combating his addiction with prayer. Lucinda realized there was a spiritual void in his life that only God could fill, but Jeremiah tried to fill it with pornography. He died before allowing God to fill that void. Denise felt sorry for her mother, knowing she never experienced the contentment her daughter now enjoyed on a regular basis.

The love Denise now shared with Bryce often brought tears to her eyes. Bryce had cocooned into the husband she needed and expressed his love for her in ways she could receive.

Clay and Melanie still weren't living under the same roof, but they were attending the sessions together and Melanie expressed optimism for reconciliation.

Following redemption Sunday, Erin left Word of Life and her Public Defender's job and moved to Chicago. Denise received a letter from her two months ago, apologizing for destroying their friendship. Erin claimed to be saved *for real* this time. Denise prayed she was, but hadn't responded to her.

Jonas hadn't converted, but after witnessing the change in Denise's deportment, visited Word of Life on his own accord. He was so impressed with Pastor's Hightower's teaching that he had begun attending Wednesday night Bible Study on a regular basis. Bryce wasn't bothered by his presence because now he was fulfilling his role as a husband. Denise's glow was proof of that.

He didn't always get it right, but most times, Bryce was transparent; sharing his feelings and fears with her. He no longer hibernated in his study for hours at a time, but most importantly, he didn't justify or make excuses for his behavior. If he was tempted to fall back into his old ways, he told his wife, and together, they identified the root of the desire. If Denise wasn't available, he confided in Benny. Accountability was top priority. When depression knocked, he didn't answer, and in the process, Bryce learned he was much stronger than the enemy wanted him to believe.

Bryce still used the church, but for a different reason. He no longer needed the church to cover up his insecurities; instead, he used the pulpit to help heal others. He learned, almost too late that he could reach more people by being honest about his inadequacies than with the spurious lifestyle he worked so hard to portray. People needed someone they could relate to, not someone perfect without a spot or blemish. People needed honesty over idols.

"Let me get that for you," Lucinda said, taking the potholders from Denise.

She stood back watching her mother remove the peach cobbler from the oven. Denise didn't miss the smile creasing her mother's face. Lucinda was happy for her daughter.

"Mama, are you sure you can handle this?" Benny was joining them for Thanksgiving dinner and Denise knew that was cause for concern. "I'm in no position to referee today."

"Don't worry about me; I can handle myself," Lucinda said after replacing the potholders in the drawer.

"Are you sure, Mama? I don't want any problems; Benny's daughters are stopping by for dessert."

"I know." Before Denise could ask her mother how she knew about Benny's daughters, he and Bryce entered the kitchen, complaining about the score of the game.

"Hey, baby," Bryce said after kissing Denise on the lips. "Hey, baby," he said again, this time after raising Denise's apron and rubbing her extended belly. She was three months pregnant with their first child. Everyone was hoping for a boy, including Lucinda.

After greeting his mother-in-law, Bryce stood back and waited for the fireworks to begin.

"Happy Thanksgiving, Sister Sanders." Since joining Word of Life, Benny addressed Lucinda by her last name. Everyone knew he didn't like it by the way he gritted his teeth every time he said 'Sanders.'

"Happy Thanksgiving, Brother Johnson," Lucinda responded and went back to setting the table.

Bryce and Denise stood gaping at them with wide open mouths as Benny assisted Lucinda with the turkey and the trimmings.

"Did you remember the ice cream?" Lucinda asked Benny.

"I did, but you know your cobbler is so good, it really doesn't need ice cream," Benny replied.

"What is going on?" Denise whispered in Bryce's ear.

"Maybe they've called a truce for the holiday," he guessed. "Whatever it is, let's pray it continues."

Minutes later, the four of them sat around the dining room table holding hands with heads bowed.

"Dad, would you say grace?" That's how Bryce addressed Benny now. It seemed befitting since Benny insisted on referring to him as 'son' and Bryce was closer to him than he had been to his biological father.

Benny was more than happy to oblige. This was his first holiday with his new family and he prayed it wouldn't be the last.

"Heavenly Father, thank You for Your son, Jesus, and the love You have expressed toward us. Thank You for mending our family together and uniting us in Your love. May we always remain knitted together and grow in Your grace. Amen." He waited until the table echoed the Amen before adding, "And Lord, help Lucinda not to eat the whole pot of collards I made."

"Lord, help me not to take this turkey leg and beat Benny upside the head," Lucinda retorted. The bantering began, but it lacked its usual fire. Benny and Lucinda shared a quick laugh before diving into the feast.

"This reminds me of Thanksgiving years ago, before my parents died," Benny announced, making his second plate. "My mama used to cook meals just like this, except we'd add some chitlins, or as you city folk say, chitterlings."

"We'll have those for New Year's," Lucinda announced.

"I'll meet your daughters later, but tell me about your other family members." Denise said to Benny.

Bryce patted Denise's hand, trying to indicate that this was a painful subject for Benny, but it was too late.

"It's not much to tell," Benny said, shrugging his shoulders. "My parents died in a house fire when I was eight. My sisters and I were separated after that." Benny's discomfort was evident by the unsteadiness of his hand gripping the serving spoon.

"I miss them terribly, especially my baby sister Mavis Ann. I was close to Eunice too, but I took special care of Mavis Ann. Probably because she was the youngest and we shared the same birthday." Benny continued piling his plate, not noticing the grave look on Bryce's face.

"Honey, are you all right?" Denise asked when Bryce's fork clanged against the China plate.

Bryce didn't address her concern, but stared intensely at Benny. "My mother's name was Mavis Ann."

"I know—" Denise's voice trailed off upon realizing the coincidence.

"She once told me the cousin who raised her mentioned she had an older sister named Eunice, but didn't know how to find her. My mother never mentioned having an older brother."

Benny slowly set his plate down and clasped his hands together to stop the shaking.

The moment of silence that followed felt like an eternity as Benny and Bryce sat staring at one another but too afraid to ask the question that would explain their bond and love for each other. One answer would explain why Benny always seemed familiar to Bryce and why Benny had an overwhelming desire to nurture him.

"Ain't no use in us sitting here wondering," Lucinda broke the standoff. "Bryce, what is your mother's birthday?"

Benny swallowed hard then wiped the sweat that instantly beaded his forehead, waiting for Bryce to answer.

"April eighteenth." Bryce slowly replied.

"Oh my God," Denise gasped. Every year, on April eighteenth, Bryce visits his parents' double grave and places a rose on Mavis Ann Hightower's name.

"It could still be a coincidence," Bryce said, steadying his breath.

"Yeah, sure could," Benny quickly agreed, wiping more perspiration. He, like Bryce, was suppressing the joy bubbling in his belly for fear of disappointment. "Besides, little Mavis was born with a birthmark that looked like the state of Texas on the side of her face. What are the chances of that happening to two people?"

Without saying one word, Denise left the table. Bryce lowered his head and gave way to tears of joy. Benny held his emotions intact until he got the official word.

Lucinda prayed quietly for it to be so.

"Is this your sister?" Denise asked, returning with the framed photo of her mother-in-law from Bryce's study.

After receiving the picture from Denise, Benny let the levee break and wept like a baby. "I'd know Mavis Ann anywhere. She looks the same way as I remember my mother." He held the frame to his chest and released more tears. He raised his head to find Bryce, his nephew, standing over him. Watching the two embrace brought the onslaught of more tears, this time from mother and daughter.

"I can't believe it," Benny exclaimed beaming with pride.

"God sent me to Mavis Ann's little boy. I've got me a nephew . . . although I still prefer to call you son."

"That's fine with me, Dad," Bryce concurred with his arm still around his uncle's shoulder.

Benny's laughter stopped abruptly. "Wait a minute. You're my nephew; that means Denise is my niece." He turned to Lucinda, "Does that mean I can't marry you because you're my niece's mama?"

"Marry?" Bryce and Denise yelled simultaneously.

"Oh yeah, baby," Lucinda blushed. "I have been meaning to tell you about that. Benny and I have been kinda sort of dating for three months."

"What?" Nephew and daughter still didn't understand.

"Kinda sort of nothing!" Benny corrected. "We've been seeing each other everyday. When I'm not with you all, I'm with her. I proposed last week and she said yes. I've already told my girls and they can't wait to meet the woman who tamed me," Benny beamed.

"But the two of you hate each other," Bryce protested. "You argue all the time." He gestured toward Lucinda, "You called him the spawn of Satan."

With the wave of the hand, Lucinda dismissed her actions. "Pastor, you know how it is when you're trying to fight what the Lord has for you." She stood and wrapped her arms around Benny's waist. "I knew the first day I saw him in the yard with you, he was the one."

"And I knew that first Sunday I watched her switch away in that suit, I was going to get her."

Bryce's laughter erupted and filled the room. Denise joined in and so did the newly engaged couple.

"When is the big day?" Denise asked after congratulating her mother and future stepfather.

"As soon as we get the marriage license," Benny answered, turning to his nephew-pastor. "You think you can perform the ceremony next Wednesday? I'm not getting any younger and I won't be able to keep Lucinda's hands off *all* this too much longer."

Lucinda swatted her fiancé on the arm, "You devil."

"I'm your devil," he said just before gently kissing her lips.

Discussion Questions

1. In the beginning, Pastor Hightower's main focus was on how he "looked" in the eyes of people. In your opinion, has the church become more concerned with outer appearances to the point sin is overlooked?

2. Pastor Hightower refused to share his struggle with church leaders, for fear they would ostracize him. Do you feel the church provides a safe haven for leaders as well as laity to admit their faults and seek restoration?

3. Lucinda brushed off pornography as simply something that men do. She stated that sexual sin in church leadership was a common occurrence to be expected. Do you agree or disagree with her view? In your opinion, have Christians become desensitized to the effects of sexual sins?

4. Denise viewed pornography as adultery and a Biblical reason to divorce. Do you agree or disagree?

5. Pastor Hightower believed God allowed him to continue preaching in sin, because, as he put it, "his heart was right." Do you think Christians use what's in their hearts as an excuse to continue sinning?

6. Who was your favorite character(s)? Why?

7. Since her husband held a leadership position, Melanie felt it was Pastor Hightower's job to discipline Clay for

his pornography addiction. Do you agree or disagree with her view? Do you think today's church leaders turn a blind eye to sexual sins?

8. Has this story weakened or strengthened your stance on pornography addiction?

9. Pastor Hightower was surprised to learn that nearly one-third of his congregation struggled with masturbation or pornography. How should the church effectively address this problem?

10. At one point, Bryce thought prayer would cure his addiction. Lucinda believed the same for Jeremiah. At what point should Christians seek the assistance of a counselor or therapist in overcoming addictions?

11. What was your favorite scene in the story?

ABOUT THE AUTHOR

Wanda currently serves the public through her job at Alameda County Medical Center in Oakland, California, and by ministering to others in various capacities. She's an ordained elder and is in pursuit of a Bachelors degree in Biblical Studies. She resides in the San Francisco Bay Area with her husband of 19 years and two sons. Wanda enjoys hearing from readers. Email: wbcampbell@prodigy.net